A REQUEST TO DANCE

"May I have the honor, Miss Grimsby," Philip said as he held his hand out to her.

Isabella had been so intent upon removing Jamie from the ballroom that she hadn't seen his approach. She looked up into his brilliant blue eyes and felt her heart almost miss a beat at the warmth in them.

He was merely being kind, she told herself firmly. She hoped he did not notice that her hand trembled as she placed it in his large, warm one. The contact made her fingers tingle, just as it had the first time she danced with him during her first Season in London.

Jamie clapped his hands with glee.

Philip raised her to her feet and bowed over her hand. She curtsied to him.

"Pretty," Jamie said. "Dance now."

"I don't think he is going to go to bed until we obey, do you?" Philip whispered in that confidential voice that made her heart beat faster, no matter how much she told herself she dare not fall under his spell. . . .

Books by Kate Huntington

The Captain's Courtship

The Lieutenant's Lady

Lady Diana's Darlings

Mistletoe Mayhem

A Rogue for Christmas

The Merchant Prince

Town Bronze

His Lordship's Holiday Surprise

The General's Daughter

A Hero's Homecoming

Published by Zebra Books

A HERO'S HOMECOMING

KATE HUNTINGTON

ZEBRA BOOKS
KENSINGTON PUBLISHING CORP.
www.kensingtonbooks.com

ZEBRA BOOKS are published by

Kensington Publishing Corp.
850 Third Avenue
New York, NY 10022

All Kensington titles, imprints and distributed lines are available at special quantity discounts for bulk purchases for sales promotion, premiums, fund-raising, educational or institutional use.

Special book excerpts or customized printings can also be created to fit specific needs. For details, write or phone the office of the Kensington Special Sales Manager: Kensington Publishing Corp., 850 Third Avenue, New York, NY 10022. Attn. Special Sales Department. Phone: 1-800-221-2647.

Zebra and the Z logo Reg. U.S. Pat. & TM Off.

First Printing: November 2004
10 9 8 7 6 5 4 3 2 1

Printed in the United States of America

To good friends of almost fifteen years:
Jennifer Coleman,
Bernie and Norma Coleman,
Terri and Steve Pullara,
and Michaela and Jonathan.
It was a happy day when Jennifer's path
crossed with mine at Reader's Haven.

PROLOGUE

The Great London Road, 1812

Philip Lyonbridge's younger brother looked every inch the hero as he stood at parade rest before the fireplace of the private parlor of the inn. He was wearing his dress uniform, the one he had donned for his wedding to a young woman who should have been accepting the congratulations of all her friends at this moment, but instead would never be able to hold her head up in Society again because of Philip.

Adam never fidgeted. He never paced. Instead, his stance suggested that of a panther, ready to attack.

His brother. His rival. His nemesis.

Blast his eyes!

Philip had expected to be hundreds of miles away in Scotland by the time his brother found out what he had done, and by then Adam would have had to accept the runaway marriage as a fait accompli. He had not thought much on the matter beyond that, for he had been blinded by his desire for Isabella.

Isabella had begged him to save her from entering into a loveless marriage. Quite apart from Philip's lust for Isabella, he had been gratified to encounter *one* female who preferred him to his magnificent brother.

Heaven knew it seldom happened.

Philip might be the elder, but in the eyes of the world, Lord Revington's heir was merely a pale copy of the brave, the stalwart, the muscular and athletic Major Adam Lyonbridge. By the age of three, Adam had outstripped Philip in both size and girth. Thereafter, new acquaintances had routinely assumed that the bigger, stronger brother was the elder. In his heart of hearts, Philip had to admit that one of the attractions of going along with this elopement had been to embarrass his disgustingly superior brother.

Instead, though, here was Adam, looking like a hero about to chastise a recalcitrant recruit.

Philip was merely the contemptible cur who had disrupted the hero's wedding by ignominiously stealing his bride.

"And so it comes to this," Adam said contemptuously.

"Isabella is innocent. I alone am to blame," Philip said.

Adam's lip curled.

"Unless you bound her hand and foot, and bore her off against her will, she is no innocent. But you hardly need fear that I will retaliate against *her*. The vain, selfish little chit is beneath contempt after this day's work. I would not soil my hands on her."

"You will not speak of her in this way," Philip said, finding courage despite the deadly coldness in his brother's eye.

"I will speak of her in any way I choose, and *you* are hardly in any position to prevent me from doing so."

"Leave her out of this. I am at your disposal. Under the circumstances, I trust we can dispense with the convention of seconds."

Adam crossed his arms and gave him a wolfish smile.

"I could crush you with one fist."

"You could *try*," Philip said, but his heart wasn't in it. His brother was going to pound him to bloody pulp. And when Isabella emerged from the bedchamber to which Marian Randall, her half sister, had conducted her, she was going to know him for the paltry fellow he truly was. She had already watched Adam bloody Philip's nose after he caught up to them.

"Lord, what a figure I should cut," Adam said. He almost looked amused. "I outweigh you by at least three stone. It would be no contest."

"Even so," Philip said, gritting his teeth in defiance at his bigger, stronger brother. He could almost welcome the pain, for it would put an end to this wretched suspense. And, if Philip were very, very fortunate, perhaps he could pop a hit over Adam's guard and darken his daylights for him before Adam broke him in two.

It would be *some* consolation for his bloody nose.

Adam merely gave a snort of disgust.

"Do not flatter yourself. Like Isabella, you are beneath contempt. I would not soil my hands on you, either."

Philip positively hated the feeling of relief that surged through his body. He actually felt his knees go a little weak.

"You are wrong," Philip said, striving for a cool tone. He even managed to give his brother a smile of sheer bravado. "Oh, not about me. I am every bit as despicable as you think. You are wrong about Isabella."

"It is a bit too late to defend your lady fair," Adam scoffed. "You are a coward, Philip. You sought this means of disgracing me because you aren't brave enough to fight me man to man. You aren't brave enough to fight *anyone* man to man."

Philip knew exactly what his brother meant by that.

"Father refused to buy me a commission," Philip snarled, "and you bloody well know it."

"It makes for a convenient excuse . . . coward," Adam snarled right back. "You have that legacy from our mother's brother, quite apart from your allowance as heir. You could have purchased your own commission at any time these three years after our uncle stuck his spoon in the wall."

It was true. Absolutely true. Philip *could* have purchased a commission at any time and his father could have done nothing to prevent it, but he had been reluctant to go to war in his brother's shadow and invite the inevitable comparisons between them that were sure to be in his disfavor.

Instead, he squandered his allowance on horses and drink and supported the character of a sophisticated, fashionable fribble about town while he grew green with jealousy every time he read one of the newspaper accounts of Adam's bravery in action and watched his father's face glow with pride when acquaintances congratulated him on Adam's latest promotion on the field of battle.

"I think your cowardice makes you a prime match for the fair Isabella," Adam continued. "She could have broken our betrothal at any time by informing me that she wished to do so. All the girl had to say was no. *I* could not do so, for I was bound by our father's honor. No, Isabella did not merely wish to escape from the marriage. She wanted to humiliate me. And my own brother was her willing accomplice."

He made it sound so cold. So sordid.

Philip wanted to protest, to tell Adam that he had been powerless to resist Isabella's blandishments when she had begged him to save her from this marriage, but he could not, for he knew there was no acceptable excuse for what he had done.

He should have encouraged Isabella to tell Adam the truth and cry off from the wedding if she did not wish to go through with it, even if it was the very night before the ceremony. It would have been a seven-day wonder, but she could have emerged with her reputation intact, more or less.

Isabella had pledged her undying love for Philip with an eloquence no man could have resisted. She had *begged* him to take her to Scotland and marry her. But what if she merely had been suffering from bridal nerves, and he had taken advantage of her momentary confusion to steal her away because he *wanted* to believe that his brother's lovely fiancée might in truth prefer him to Adam?

What a joke! How *could* she?

She was desperate and confused, but as her childhood friend and future brother-in-law, he should have encouraged her to withdraw from the betrothal with some degree of honor instead of taking her off with him before she could change her mind.

Or, more to the point, he should have encouraged her to marry the better man by extolling his brother's superior qualities. It was what any man of honor would have done.

Philip could not marry her now, much as he wanted to. She would grow to despise him if he did. All the world would despise him—Isabella, his father, all the influential members of Parliament and the ornaments of Society who had gathered at St. James's Church for Isabella's wedding to the glorious war hero only to find that the bride had been ignominiously stolen away.

By him. The coward.

He squared his shoulders.

"Take Isabella back to London with you," he said to Adam. "You and Miss Randall between you can make up some tale. Make me the villain of the piece. Say I took her against her will. Say . . . I care not what you say as long as you minimize the damage to her reputation."

"Oh, I see. You are running away from the consequences of your actions," Adam said.

"No. I am running *toward* them," Philip said. "It is inadequate, I know, but tell Isabella I regret all this. Tell her . . . tell her I wish her well."

"See here! You are not going to put a period to your existence, are you? For if you are entertaining any such ridiculous notion—"

Incredibly, he sounded genuinely alarmed.

"Spare me your expressions of brotherly concern," Philip said wryly. "We both know I haven't the courage to put a bullet through my brain."

With that, he left the room to go in search of his carriage and his destiny.

"Where is he? What have you done with him?" Isabella Grimsby cried hysterically when she burst into the parlor to find Adam its sole occupant. Her clothing was disheveled. Her hair was hanging in damp wisps below her crushed bonnet.

She looked like a madwoman, and she did not care.

Isabella ran to Adam and pounded his chest with her fists. He caught her elbows to hold her away from him.

"Control yourself, Isabella," he said coldly. "I have done *nothing* to him."

"You lie," she cried, baring her teeth. "You have murdered him. I *know* it."

"Hardly! He has run away," he said bitterly. "And, might I add, I am not surprised. It follows a familiar pattern."

"Here, now, Isabella," Marian said, entering the room at that moment and rushing forward to catch Isabella's shoulders when she would have flown at Adam's eyes with her nails. She looked daggers at Adam, who merely raised a sardonic eyebrow at her. "Calm yourself."

"Run away," Isabella repeated dully. She sat down abruptly on a chair. "No. He could not have done such a thing to me."

"Oh, good lord," Adam said, rolling his eyes at Marian, who was now fussing over her half sister. "If she is going off in a swoon like some silly drama queen, I will wait for you in the carriage."

"Do not be an idiot," Marian snapped as she chafed Isabella's wrists.

Isabella pushed Marian's hands away.

She did not want to look at Marian. She did not want to look at *him*. They had ruined everything. And Philip—his desertion had been the worst betrayal of all.

"I am perfectly all right," she said, sticking out her chin.

She would not cry.

She *refused* to cry.

Her Philip, her savior, had abandoned her. She was beyond tears.

At that moment, Isabella's tender, hope-filled heart turned to stone and her limbs became steady.

She rose to her feet.

Marian made a motion to assist her, but Isabella waved her away.

She would have to face the disgrace alone. She might as well begin the way she meant to go on.

"I am ready to go home now," she said in a voice not her own.

CHAPTER 1

London, Summer, 1814

Captain Philip Lyonbridge had been surprised and disappointed to learn that Miss Isabella Grimsby—still unmarried, for he had made inquiries almost before his ship touched shore in England—was not in London with the rest of the world, celebrating the defeat of Napoleon at a succession of lavish entertainments.

He had somehow managed in the two years of hell since he had gone off to war to return to London a hero, and he found his triumphant homecoming decidedly flat without the worshipful welcome he had expected from the girl he so regretfully left behind.

Instead, he learned that Isabella was cooling her heels in Derbyshire, caring for her half sister Marian's child while Philip's brother, Adam, and his new wife, the aforementioned half sister, went on a peacekeeping assignment to Scotland with Adam's regiment.

Isabella? Missing the many fetes honoring the crowned heads of Europe in the wake of Napoleon's defeat in order to play nursemaid to another woman's child in the country? He could not imagine such a thing.

However, it was probably just as well. The first time he saw Isabella after their long separation, he did not want to be surrounded by a gaggle of silly chits making sheep's eyes at him in the middle of London. They had practically knocked him down in their zeal to be presented to the war hero whose name was on everyone's lips and who, thanks to Philip's father, had been the subject of a series of thrilling stories in the newspapers.

Philip's father, Lord Revington, had been busy puffing him off to Society's most eligible young ladies. Scores of them had met his carriage when he arrived in London to make his report to Whitehall. And they had been waiting—with their mothers—when he emerged from his meeting. Philip was the heir to a title and fortune, and therefore a valuable commodity on the marriage market. His recent celebrity as a war hero and spy who had infiltrated the French camp and provided his superiors with information that enabled them to win several crucial battles gave him an irresistible cachet, apparently.

It was no coincidence that many of these young ladies had fathers or grandfathers who were powerful members of Lord Liverpool's government. Above all things, his father wanted a distinguished political career for Philip so he could follow in his own footsteps as a powerful and influential member of the House of Lords. The first step to that, of course, was to marry well.

Philip, attired in his dress uniform for his meeting at Whitehall, gave his gleeful father a repressive look as he bowed to the fair flower now being introduced to him. He forgot her name a moment after his father pronounced it.

There was no room in his memory for any woman save Isabella.

Philip imagined her the way he did while he was at war, fighting for his life—or risking his life to spy for his country. When there was nothing to eat, when he knew that his life could end in a moment if his imposture was discovered, she would come to him.

In his imagination, he would interrupt Isabella as she was picking flowers in a formal rose garden. She would be wearing a lacy white dress with a pretty straw hat trimmed in pink ribbons to protect her delicate face and glossy dark curls from the sun. Dainty white lace gloves would cover her slim, graceful hands. And she would look up, smile, and hold her arms out wide.

For him.

Philip should not have let his brother intimidate him. He often wondered what would have happened if he had insisted upon marrying Isabella that fateful day instead of going blithely off to war to prove himself worthy of her.

Lord, what an idiot he had been! War was far from glorious, and he hardly deserved all the praise that was being piled on his head for his bravery.

He did what he had done to survive. He did it because if he hadn't, he might never see Isabella again. Now the war was over, and he was ready to resign his commission, marry Isabella, and forget the whole wretched experience.

But his father was not about to let him forget.

Resign his commission? Was he *mad?*

The Honorable Philip Lyonbridge, man about town, would hardly have the cachet of Captain Philip Lyonbridge, war hero. Resign his commission and his worth on the marriage market would plummet.

Philip's jaws hurt from smiling dutifully at all the little debutantes. Enough was enough.

"You cannot leave town as soon as you have arrived," Lord Revington snapped when Philip announced his intention of doing just that as the two of them were about to enter his lordship's carriage for the ride to Lord Revington's town house.

"I have reported my activities to Whitehall," Philip said. "As far as I am concerned, my duty here is over. I am for Derbyshire."

Lord Revington frowned thoughtfully.

"Very well, boy," he said as he patted Philip on the shoulder. "I understand. You need a period of rustication in the country. We will go there at once."

Philip's eyes narrowed as he looked at his father.

This was too easy.

It was unlike Lord Revington to revise his plans to accommodate anyone's wishes save his own.

No matter. Both his father's primary estate and his brother's small house, where Isabella was residing with his brother's stepson, were in Derbyshire, and that is where Philip most wished to be at the moment.

Poor Isabella. Stuck out in the country with a child for company. She must be bored silly.

Fortunately, Philip was about to come to the rescue.

"Miss Grimsby is not at home to visitors?" Philip repeated in disbelief to the housekeeper. "Are you certain? You *did* give her my card, did you not?"

"I am certain, sir. There is no mistake," the middle-aged woman said as she looked down at her hands.

At that moment, a small child scurried to the door.

"Jamie, come back here at once," a woman's voice rang out.

Philip smiled.

Isabella. He would know her voice anywhere.

Of the child, he had an impression merely of a thatch of dark hair and running legs. The boy was moving so fast he could not have gotten a clear look even if he had not been straining for a glimpse of Isabella beyond the gloom of the front door.

Suddenly she was there, and Philip found his throat so dry for a moment that he could not say a word. His eyes drank in the sight of her, even though she was frowning at him. The boy turned and buried his face in her skirt. She put her hand protectively on the back of his head.

"Take Jamie upstairs," Isabella said, tight-lipped, to the housekeeper.

"But Aunt Isabella—" the childish voice objected.

"*Now,* Jamie," Isabella said sternly. "It is time for your nap."

"I am not sleepy."

The housekeeper, after giving Philip an anxious look, grasped the boy by the hand and quickly spirited him away. Philip took the opportunity to sidle through the door and block Isabella's retreat from the doorway.

"What are you doing here, Philip?" Isabella asked. She crossed her arms over her chest and looked annoyed.

Hardly the welcome he had been imagining all this time.

"Are you not a little glad to see me, my dear?" he said with an ingratiating smile.

She raised one eyebrow.

"Are there not enough silly chits vying for your favor in London that you must come to Derbyshire in search of more?" she asked. "My congratulations. The newspapers are full of your conquests, Captain Lyonbridge."

Ah. So that was it. She had read the nonsense being printed in the newspapers about him and was jealous of his supposed attentions to the young ladies who had been eager to welcome the gallant hero home.

More confident now, he moved closer and attempted to take her in his arms.

"Come, Isabella, we can deal more comfortably together than this," he said softly.

She gave him a hard thump on the chest of his uniform and favored him with a look of injury when her hand scraped on one of the medals pinned there.

Philip suffered a moment of embarrassment at his vanity in wearing all of his decorations to pay a simple call in the country, but he had wanted to impress her with his magnificence.

Apparently, he had failed abysmally.

"I will thank you not to attempt to maul me in this undignified fashion," she said harshly.

"*Maul* you," he exclaimed. "Oh, do forgive me, Miss Grimsby. I had assumed you would be glad to see me."

"*Had* you?" she said with one uplifted eyebrow. "And why should you assume that? The last time I saw you, you were swearing eternal devotion. And then I learned you had run off to war to play at soldiering."

"You have changed," he said. "You were not used to be so hard."

She had changed in other ways, too.

Her dark curls were confined in a severe chignon that made her look more mature than the girl he remembered, and her muslin gown in a green print, though attractive, was obviously not the work of a modiste of the first stare. Her figure, instead of being almost boyishly slim, was now more womanly.

And had her jaw always been so stubborn?

But she was still beautiful, for all that. Her face was delicately flushed with color, and her dark eyes were bright with anger.

"How dare you saunter into this house as if you expect me to fall into your arms?" she demanded.

It was plain that he would have to grovel if he wanted her to forgive him.

Philip sighed. He very much wanted her to forgive him, so he started to kneel at her feet in the hope that it would make her laugh.

He could see her lips twitch, and he was encouraged to believe that this silliness might produce the desired result.

Farther back in the house, he heard the child's voice again.

With a gasp, Isabella froze, then drew back from Philip.

"You had better go," Isabella said huskily.

"I beg your pardon?" Philip said in disbelief.

It was the prerogative of the *caller* to take his leave and put an end to the visit, not the hostess. The Isabella of old *never* would have been guilty of such a breach of good manners.

"It is time for Jamie to take his nap, and he will not do so while there is a visitor in the house."

"I am good with children," he said, smiling. "Let's have the lad out, then."

"No," she said, sounding frightened. "You stay away from him."

Did she think he was going to *eat* the child?

"Very well, Miss Grimsby," Philip said, deeply hurt, as he sketched her an ironic little bow. "I will take my leave of you. Do forgive the intrusion."

"Fare you well, Captain Lyonbridge," she said, but she could not quite meet his eyes. "It would be best if you did not come here again."

"Be sure I will not, Miss Grimsby," he said coldly. "Good day."

So much for the hero's triumphant return, he thought as he mounted his horse and set out for his father's estate nearby.

So much for his vanity in thinking Isabella Grimsby had remained unmarried for his sake.

Leaving her to the care of his brother and her bossy half sister that day on the London road was the hardest thing Philip had ever done.

And now she hated him. Positively hated him.

The thought of Isabella waiting for him at home had been all that sustained him during those long days of fear and deprivation.

Now it seemed he had to forget the way she once melted in his arms, just as she, apparently, had forgotten that she once loved him.

CHAPTER 2

Philip had been right.

It *had* been too easy to escape from London and the tedious duty of doing the pretty at Almack's for the gratification of all the silly debutantes. When he returned from his humiliating experience at Isabella's hands, he found the housemaids in a flurry of cleaning and his father berating the cook and housekeeper about jellies and creams and bedchambers to be aired.

To his annoyance, Philip found that one of the overenthusiastic maids had, in fact, scented his own bedchamber with lavender, a fragrance of which he was not overfond. The stuff was even inside his wardrobe, which would make his uniforms and evening clothes smell of cloyingly sweet herbs.

No matter.

If his father intended to entertain his political cronies with one of his extravagant parties to puff Philip off as a budding young politician, he was doomed to disappointment.

Philip ordered his valet to pack his town clothes and sat back, impatiently drumming his fingers against a table, as the fellow took his time to fold each item with meticulous care and set it inside Philip's traveling case. After his war experiences, Philip was unused to being waited upon by a personal servant. He would have dispensed with the man altogether if he had not been waiting patiently in his father's house all this time for his young master's return from war. Indeed, the elderly Martin, who had been hired as Philip's first valet when he turned nineteen, would have accompanied him to war if Philip had permitted it.

"I will not need the half of those neckcloths," he said to the servant.

"You will, sir," Martin said calmly. "And, if you will permit me to say so, it would not be amiss for you to visit your tailor. Your figure is a bit more muscular now than it was when you left for war, and your coats are too snug over the shoulders."

"A fashionable gentleman has to be forced into his coat like a sausage in its casing," Philip reminded him. "Have you not told me so often enough?"

"The casing, with respect, sir, is losing the struggle," Martin said. "Your uniform coats fit well enough, but the evening coats you wore before you purchased your commission are abysmally inadequate."

Philip had to smile. If Martin had seen him in the rags he wore while he was masquerading as a Spanish peasant and ingratiating himself with members of the French army, he would have fainted dead away.

"Very well," he said resignedly. "To the tailor we shall go."

At that moment, Philip's father burst into the room.

"What is this, Philip?" he said, looking thunderous. "You cannot go off now. Our guests will begin arriving in two days."

"*Your* guests, Father," Philip said, "not mine. *I* did not invite anyone. I have had quite enough backslapping and handwringing from your political cronies to last me a lifetime. We are all agreed that I am a splendid fellow. Let us leave it at that."

"Political cronies? Did you think I have gone to all this trouble for a collection of old men? No wonder you were about to fly off to town." Lord Revington gave an abrupt laugh.

"Give me credit for providing my heir with better entertainment than that after he has risked his life in defending his country."

Philip's eyes narrowed at his father. He did not like his gloating expression.

"Just who is coming to this precious party of yours, then, Father?" he asked.

Lord Revington gave his son a smile of triumph.

"A round dozen of the prettiest, most eligible young ladies in Britain, my son, all gathered for your inspection. We will have a picnic, followed by a ball, and you will have various opportunities to spend time with each one—carefully chaperoned, of course, for there must not be a whisper of scandal attached to any lady who will someday bear our name. And we want to be fair. Each lady must have her opportunity to secure your affections."

Philip closed his eyes.

"You did not invite a gaggle of silly chits here," he said when he could trust himself to speak. "Please tell me you did not."

"Of course I did. How else can you expect to make a prudent choice?"

"So it is to be you and me and a round dozen, as you put it, of young ladies. And I am to inspect them like some Oriental potentate interviewing potential houris. I wonder that they would agree to such nonsense."

"Oh, they agreed," Lord Revington said. "The heir to my title, and a war hero besides, would be quite a conquest for any sensible girl. I am happy to say that the response to my invitations was most gratifying. I did not receive one refusal, even on such short notice. It is no mean compliment that so many are willing to abandon their plans to attend the peace celebrations to come into Derbyshire for the purpose of putting themselves forward as your bride."

"Pity they are to be disappointed," Philip said, standing up. The trick in dealing with his imperious father, he knew from long experience, was not to leave any room for negotiation. "Martin, that is the last garment. Put it in the case. We are leaving. Now."

"You cannot run off now. What will I tell all these women who have come all this way to meet you?"

"You should have thought of that before you invited them. Good day, sir."

Philip got all the way to the stable with his father in hot pursuit and Martin following at a more dignified pace when he stopped abruptly and turned to face his sire. Lord Revington nearly ran into him. He had to stop and struggle for breath, for he had been shouting at Philip at the top of his lungs since he left the house.

"These eager prospective brides," Philip said. "Is Miss Isabella Grimsby among them?"

"Miss Isabella Grimsby?" Lord Revington said in distaste. "Certainly not! You need a woman of the highest reputation and the most distinguished birth to be your bride, not the brainless little hussy who jilted your brother at the altar to run off with—"

"With me, Father," Philip said. "She ran off with me."

Lord Revington wrinkled his nose as if he smelled something sour.

"We will have no words on that account," he said. "A man cannot be blamed for taking liberties if they are extended to him by a woman who has no concept of loyalty to her fiancé."

"My brother consoled himself quickly enough with another."

Lord Revington scowled.

"That little tart," he said. "Old Grimsby's love child, whom he had the audacity to try to pass off as a respectable female. Well, breeding will tell. She was big with some man's brat before the cat could lick her ear. I had to agree to the match or lose my son, and I put that little humiliation, as well, at Miss Isabella Grimsby's door. If she had married Adam as she was supposed to, her half sister never could have got her hooks in him. Instead of cutting the connection, as any decent female would have done, she stayed by her bastard half sister's side throughout her confinement, and now she is at Adam's house, minding the boy in their absence. Become a virtual recluse, in fact. She has gone queer in her attic, if you ask me."

Philip smiled coldly as a diabolical plan occurred to him.

"I will stay for this precious party of yours on one condition," he said.

"Excellent!" Lord Revington said, looking relieved. "I knew you would see reason."

"I want you to send an invitation to Miss Isabella Grimsby. Or, better still, her mother. Lady Grimsby won't permit her to refuse it."

"Out of the question," Lord Revington said firmly.

"Invite her, or I will leave for London. Immediately."

Lord Revington threw his hands up in the air.

"Very well, then," he grumbled. "The military is the ruination of young men, if you ask me. It makes them headstrong."

"Better send the invitation to Lady Grimsby by special courier," Philip said.

Lord Revington looked sly for a moment.

"Of course," he said.

Oh, no you don't, old man, Philip thought.

"*I* will arrange for the courier," he said. "You need only provide the invitation. At once."

Lord Revington relieved his displeasure with a single huff of breath, turned on his heel, and stomped away to the house to do his son's bidding.

The sound of coach wheels brought the pair of eager housemaids to the window.

"A coach with your father's crest on the door, Miss Isabella," said the housekeeper after she had taken a look herself. There was little enough entertainment for the servants in such a quiet household, and the arrival of a visitor—any visitor—was cause for great excitement.

"It must be Mother," Isabella said with a little frown. She and her mother barely had been speaking by the time they last parted company. Lady Grimsby had been eager to marry her daughter off to some well-connected man or other, and Isabella had insisted upon coming at once to take over the running of her half sister's household and the rearing of her adorable Jamie when word was received that Major Adam Lyonbridge, her half sister's husband, had been posted to Scotland with his regiment and intended to take his bride with him.

Acrimonious words were exchanged, and Lady Grimsby had told Isabella that if she left Brighton for Derbyshire without her permission—which she had no intention of giving her—she washed her hands of the wretched, ungrateful girl.

"Mother," Isabella said guardedly with a little nod of greeting when Lady Grimsby flounced into the house after a day and a half on the road from London, looking as fresh as if she had just left the hands of her maid. Isabella disliked the big, predatory smile on her mother's face as she gathered Isabella into her scented embrace. "What brings you here?"

"The most wonderful thing, my dear," Lady Grimsby said excitedly. "We are going to a house party at Lord Revington's estate."

Isabella let out a mirthless laugh.

"Perhaps *you* are, Mother, although why you would want to is beyond my understanding after he made it abundantly clear that he suffered our presence throughout Adam and Marian's wedding with great reluctance. But I can hardly leave Jamie alone with the housekeeper and maids while I go traipsing off to some party."

"Yes, you can, my girl," Lady Grimsby said with a martial look in her eye. "Rumor has it that Philip Lyonbridge is going to pick his bride from among the flower of the *ton* at that party, and *you* are going to go there and be so charming that you will carry off the prize from beneath their noses."

Isabella felt her face flame with anger.

The *audacity* of the man! Who did he think he was? King Copetua making his selection from among the beggar maids?

"Absolutely not," Isabella said as she crossed her arms over her chest.

"You listen to *me,* missy. It kills me to watch my beautiful, once vivacious daughter dwindle into a peculiar old antidote."

"I am *not* a peculiar old antidote," Isabella snapped.

"Yes, you are. And it is all *his* fault. If he had not turned your head with his blandishments, *you* would be married to Adam Lyonbridge now instead of that little hussy. The very least he can do now that he's ruined your life is marry you."

"I would not marry Philip Lyonbridge if he were the last man on earth!"

"Oh, yes you will, Isabella, and you will be grateful for it! I know there is not a single lady invited to this party that you could not outshine with the merest crook of your finger. You have turned up your nose at every eligible gentleman I have been at such pains to introduce to you, with the result that there are no young men left for you to reject. And why? Because of your devotion to your precious Marian's little brat."

"Jamie is *not* a brat!" Isabella snapped. "He is a perfectly delightful little boy."

"He ruined my best hat at the wedding."

That again! Isabella rolled her eyes. She was never going to hear the end of Jamie's naughtiness in pulling apart the peacock feathers on her mother's hat while everyone at Marian's wedding was distracted by the bride's procession up the aisle of the church with Isabella as her bridesmaid.

"He merely ruined a few feathers, which were easy enough to replace. It was my maid's fault for not minding him closely enough during the ceremony. Jamie has a great deal of curiosity, for he is quite precocious for his age." Isabella could not stop the note of pride from sneaking into her voice.

"Precocious!" her mother scoffed. "A pretty name for sheer maliciousness."

"There is no maliciousness in Jamie. None at all!" declared Isabella.

"Be that as it may," Lady Grimsby said, "it is time you sought other company."

"I am not leaving Jamie here alone."

"Then he will go with us," Lady Grimsby said. "He is our host's stepgrandson, after all. I do not see why the boy could not stay at Lord Revington's estate instead of at Major Lyonbridge's just as easily. There was no need for you to come pelting into the country to run that little hussy's household."

"Leave Jamie to Lord Revington's tender mercies?" Isabella exclaimed. "Who could be so cruel?"

"Nonsense. He would not eat the boy."

"No, but he does not love him."

"Such sentimental twaddle. He would hire a competent nursemaid for the boy, just as your father and I did for you, and he would hardly see him apart from that."

Exactly my point, Isabella thought, but she bit her lips to keep from saying so. To ladies of her mother's birth and generation, the abandonment of their children to a staff of nursemaids and governesses was commonplace. Only vulgar, middle-class women carried out the homely tasks of childrearing themselves.

"We are wasting time, Isabella," Lady Grimsby said. "Go fetch your maid and, if you must, that child."

"You go too fast! I have not said I will come."

She might as well have saved her breath.

"Tell your maid not to bother packing any of your clothes except for your underpinnings. I have brought your clothes from London." She passed a critical eye over her daughter's figure. "You have not become fat. Good. I had feared you might once you got out from under my eye. One tends to eat too much in the country for lack of anything better to occupy one's mind, I've found."

At that moment, Jamie came running up to Isabella with his nurserymaid on his heels.

"Stop, Master James!" cried the breathless nurserymaid.

"Aunt Isabella," Jamie said as he rushed to tug on Isabella's skirts. She felt every muscle in her face relax into a smile as she caught his little hand in hers. "May I go for a ride on the pony, if I am very, very good?"

"*Must* he call you that?" Lady Grimsby said with a pained expression on her face.

"It is a perfectly appropriate title for the dear friend of a young child's mother," Isabella said as she smiled down at the little boy. When she looked up at her mother, her eyes dared her to make some further remark. They both knew that as the boy's mother's half sister, Isabella had every right to be addressed as aunt, although the truth of the child's paternity was not generally known.

"Oh, my lady," gasped the nurserymaid, red-faced with embarrassment at her young charge's boisterous entrance, as she sank into a curtsy before Lady Grimsby. "Master James," she hissed.

Jamie had been so intent upon his errand that he had rushed right past Isabella's mother without giving her a second look.

Now he turned the full force of his curious, bright blue eyes upon her. Isabella was amazed, as always, that her mother's haughty expression did not soften in any degree.

"Good afternoon, Lady Grimsby," Jamie said with a perfectly executed bow in her direction.

His enunciation was impeccable, which was quite marvelous for a child so young. But was Isabella's mother impressed? Hardly.

"Good afternoon, James," Lady Grimsby said in a tone of distaste. Then she gave the boy a speculative look. "A pony ride, is it? Would you not rather go for a ride in my carriage? It is quite a fine day, and I am certain your . . . aunt will have no objection if you ride on the box, next to the coachman."

"May I? Truly?" he cried with delight as he looked to Isabella for permission. Like many small boys, Jamie was mad for horses. He badly missed Marian's husband, Major Adam Lyonbridge, because that gentleman often indulged the boy by hoisting him up to ride before him in the saddle.

"Jamie—" began Isabella with a sharp look at her gloating mother. But that lady was still looking at Jamie with that predatory smile on her face.

"You and your Aunt Isabella have been invited to a party at your stepgrandfather's house, is that not delightful?" Lady Grimsby said, shameless in her single-minded determination to get her way.

Jamie smiled, and Isabella knew he was remembering with relish that other night he spent in Lord Revington's house. It had been Marian and Adam's wedding night, and by the time the boy had been indulged with too many cakes at the wedding reception and been permitted to clatter all over the house in his brand new shoes, Isabella, her maid, Lord Revington's housekeeper, and the nurserymaids had been exhausted in their heroic efforts to keep him out of mischief.

A viscount's major seat had so much potential for a boy of Jamie's imagination. Isabella could not help but shudder.

"Oh, Aunt Isabella!" the child cried, clapping his hands in glee. "Can we not go?"

"Jamie, I do not think it is a good idea—" she began.

"I'll be good," he said with a soulful look designed to melt a heart of stone.

Isabella did not believe this for a moment, but she gave a sigh of surrender.

"Very well," she said. "But you must stay upstairs and not bother any of Lord Revington's other guests."

"The boy will be as good as gold, will you not, my little man?" Lady Grimsby said as she patted Jamie on the head. When she turned to the nurserymaid, her smile had vanished. "Pack his things," she barked.

CHAPTER 3

Isabella's first glimpse of Captain Philip Lyonbridge when she entered his father's house gave her no satisfaction, for the dashing gentleman was surrounded by a bevy of pink-cheeked young ladies who looked as if they had been constructed of spring flowers and fresh cream in their light summer gowns and frivolous hats.

His dark hair had been brushed to a fine gloss, and he looked like the prince in one of her more insipid childhood fairy tales in his smart dress uniform. He stood at parade rest, flanked by an heiress on one side and the granddaughter of one of the most illustrious members of the House of Lords on the other, when the butler announced them. He raised one casual, interrogatory brow in her direction when she entered the room, and his fair companions' eyes gave a dismissive sweep of Isabella's yellow gown, now crumpled from young Jamie's small hands as he clung to her skirts and shyly hid his face in them, and the simple white straw hat she had trimmed herself with green and yellow ribbons.

Isabella's appearance was certainly acceptable. Her gown was hardly homemade, but the work of the most competent seamstress the county had to offer. In contrast to the London-made finery of her fair fellow guests, however, her attire was countrified and unsophisticated. And few young ladies attending a viscount's house party in pursuit of a husband boasted the novel fashion accessory of a child attached to her person.

"Good evening, Lady Grimsby. Miss Grimsby," Philip said with a regal inclination of his handsome head. "I trust you had a pleasant journey?"

"Quite," Isabella said, forbearing to mention that his brother's house was a mere ten miles away.

"You are acquainted with my other guests, I believe?"

"Certainly," she said, smiling impartially at all of the other ladies, of which there seemed to be a half dozen at least, for it was true. These fair, fragile flowers all were Isabella's own age or slightly younger, for all that she felt like an aging, lumbering cow in her country-made gown and her sensible shoes in the face of all their youthful prettiness. Their eyes shone with optimism and the thrill of the hunt as they vied for the fairy-tale prince's attention.

Heavens! Had *she* ever been that innocent?

But then, she must have. Because once she was taken in by his handsome face and polished manners herself.

"Miss Grimsby!" said the heiress with a self-satisfied smirk. "I never would have recognized you! You have . . . changed."

And not for the better, she may as well have said.

Not that Isabella cared in the least for the little cat's opinion, or for *his,* she told herself sternly.

"What a big boy," another of them said, referring to Jamie, just in case Philip had not noticed this little liability. No doubt she thought that calling attention to Jamie would embarrass a potential rival.

In this the young lady was mistaken, for Isabella could *never* think of her darling Jamie as a liability.

"Make your bow to the ladies, Jamie," Isabella said as her hand caressed the boy's dark hair.

The child bowed from the waist, every inch the perfect little gentleman, and some of the ladies made appreciative noises, for he really was a darling, Isabella thought proudly.

"Come, child," said Lady Grimsby, frowning. She had been uncharacteristically silent until now. "Wait with Betty."

She made an imperious gesture toward Isabella's maid, who was standing just inside the entrance to the room, blending into the wallpaper—as a good servant should.

"Are you Papa's brother?" Jamie said instead as he craned his head back to look into Philip's face.

"I am," he said, giving Jamie a curious look. Like most adults, he was surprised by the perfectly formed words that came from the mouth of such a young child. Isabella was fiercely proud of Jamie's precocity.

Philip smiled and would have bent to place his face at Jamie's level for further speech, but Lady Grimsby quickly snatched Jamie away by the elbow and practically flung him into Betty's waiting arms. If Isabella did not consider Jamie a liability, her mother certainly did, for all the world knew that Lord Revington had not approved of his second son's marriage to Marian Randall. Betty bent over the child and whispered into his ear to quiet his objections to this cavalier treatment.

"Captain Lyonbridge, we are quite fatigued after our journey," Lady Grimsby said. "If you will have your house-keeper show us to our rooms?"

"Certainly, my lady," he said with a nod of his head in the waiting housekeeper's direction. "If you please, Mrs. Peevey?"

That good woman dropped a curtsy before Lady Grimsby and led the way from the room.

"I told you, you should have worn a corset," Lady Grimsby snapped peevishly to Isabella under her breath.

Isabella was hardly fat. Her waist was as slender as it had ever been, but her figure had ripened to womanly curves in the years since Captain Lyonbridge left for war.

To her mother's critical eyes, Isabella knew, she might as well have put on five stone. Lady Grimsby believed that a young lady should be fashionably and boyishly slender—the better to show off the most inspired work of London's most expensive dressmakers and thus present herself at her best advantage—until she married well and could afford to let herself run to fat. Until then, it behooved her to subsist on biscuits and vinegar after the example of Lord Byron, if necessary, to achieve the all-important, hollow-eyed, gamin looks of Isabella's supposed rivals for Captain Lyonbridge's affections.

That Isabella refused to adopt such an unsavory diet was a bitter bone of contention between mother and daughter.

Isabella gave a long sigh. It was clear that she did not belong here, and wearing a corset would not have made the least difference.

She had nothing in common with the paragons of girlish prettiness vying for Philip's name and future title. Nothing!

Why on earth had she been invited?

But she knew the answer to that as soon as she and her mother had been announced and the young ladies hanging on Philip's every word gave her those polite, dismissive glances.

Philip had *wanted* her to feel clumsy and inadequate in his presence. He had *wanted* her to see him surrounded by the freshest flowers of English womanhood making fools of themselves over him in the setting of this stately mansion that would be the domain of his future wife.

She knew very well that his father hardly considered her a fit bride for the future viscount. She had *never* been considered that.

Philip had invited Isabella here in order to humiliate her.

She had thought him selfish and impulsive before, but only now did she understand his cruelty.

"Poor, poor Isabella," the blonde on Philip's right said in a pitying tone that belied the satisfaction in her eyes once Lady Grimsby and Isabella had left the room. "She used to be so pretty, but now she looks so . . . different. I did not know what to say when she was announced. I hardly recognized her."

"I know just what you mean," said the brunette on his left. "And that *gown.* I was quite embarrassed for her."

"Poor thing," said the blonde, with a glance at Philip to make sure he was listening. No doubt she wanted him to be impressed by her compassion for one less well favored than herself. "We must set the example, my dear, in being kind to the poor thing, for the others, of course, will follow our lead."

The brunette regarded the blonde with a disdainful look for her presumption in putting herself on an equal social footing with the granddaughter of the most illustrious member of the House of Lords. Who was *she,* after all, but some rich country squire's daughter?

But the young ladies were united, for now, in their zeal to make sure Captain Lyonbridge had not missed any of Miss Isabella Grimsby's manifold inadequacies. The brunette forced a wide smile to her lips.

"By all means," she said to her temporary ally and rival. "It is our Christian duty to be kind to the poor creature."

The blonde would be easy enough to vanquish in the end, for Captain Lyonbridge surely had the discrimination to see that *she* was the best of the lot. Her confidence had soared the moment she saw how Miss Isabella Grimsby, once the fairest of them all, had let herself go to seed. She needn't fear any competition from *her.*

Little cats, Philip thought tolerantly, well aware that they were seeking to discredit Isabella even further in his eyes.

Still, he had expected to enjoy Isabella's discomfiture in finding herself surrounded by London's most eligible females, all competing for his attention. Instead, he felt . . . in truth, he did not know *what* he felt now that he had seen her again.

He had still been angry with Isabella when he insisted that his father invite her to his private version of the marriage mart. In his wounded vanity, he had wanted her to see him for the dazzling catch that Society thought him. He wanted her to be *impressed* by him.

Foolish hope.

He had realized his mistake at once when she looked at

him with all the self-possession of a queen in those defiant dark eyes.

Impressed by *him?* Hardly. Instead, he was very much afraid that she despised him—as if there were any doubt of this after the way she received him when he called upon her.

When Lord Revington's housekeeper appeared in the doorway and caught his eye, he excused himself from the ladies.

"I do not like to disturb you when you are entertaining your guests, Captain Lyonbridge," she said, "but his lordship is unavailable and I thought it best to consult your wishes."

"Of course, Mrs. Peevey," he said, thinking it was just like his father to go off somewhere and leave him to the mercy of all these females. "What is it?"

"Shall I have Alphonse set dinner back an hour to permit Lady Grimsby and Miss Grimsby enough time to dress?"

"Yes, of course you must set dinner back," he said. "If the cook objects, have him speak to me about it."

"Yes, sir," she said, smiling with dour satisfaction. Philip was well aware that Mrs. Peevey and the chef had an adversarial relationship of long-standing, each believing that he or she was the true ruler of the household and jealous of the other's tireless efforts to become Lord Revington's most trusted deputy.

Lord Revington would not like waiting for his dinner, and that thought gave Philip some satisfaction. It was no more than he deserved for not being at hand to see to the matter himself.

"Naturally, we must wait for Miss Grimsby and her mother," the brunette said, deliberately eavesdropping, just as if she were already lady of the house and her opinion had been sought. "Perhaps we can entertain ourselves with a game of charades to pass the time."

Children's games, Philip thought as he looked from one pretty, unformed face to another. The blonde pouted, no doubt because she had not taken charge first. The brunette, already usurping the role of hostess, proceeded to divide the contestants into teams, taking care to appropriate Philip for her own.

One of the other girls clapped her dainty hands with glee at the prospect of the game. She was the daughter of a rich landowner whose acres marched perfectly with Lord Revington's and thus made an alliance with the viscount's heir eminently desirable.

Really, Philip felt like he had been dropped into the middle of a gaggle of geese.

Or goslings.

He tried, and failed, to imagine Isabella clapping her hands with glee at the prospect of playing at charades with these silly little girls.

For himself, Philip had spent much of the past year masquerading as a Spaniard behind enemy lines to save his skin. As games went, a bout of charades in his father's parlor was hardly capable of holding his interest.

Still, he forced a smile to his lips and graciously agreed to participate. It was hardly *their* fault that he lost his taste for their company as soon as Isabella was ushered into the room.

Philip found himself imitating his former carefree self in much the way he adopted his persona of Spanish servant during his spying days. Inside he played the cool observer as he made the ladies laugh with his jokes and played the role the bossy little brunette had assigned to him.

He vaguely remembered that once he had taken pleasure in such activities. In fact, from the way the ladies laughed and preened for him, it was apparent that he had succeeded in his imposture as a sophisticated gentleman with an infinite willingness to be pleased by parlor games.

With a feeling of disquiet, he realized that once he married one of these ladies—*if* his father managed to bully him into it—he would spend the rest of his life pretending to be entertained by vapid conversation and boring political maneuvering.

In other words, he had been mistaken when he thought

his days of playing a part were over once Napoleon was defeated.

They had only just begun, if his father had his way.

When his father told him about the ladies being invited to Derbyshire for his delectation, Philip should have followed his original desire and run away to London. Instead, he gave in to the unworthy impulse to punish both his father for putting him in such a ridiculous position and Isabella for treating him with disdain.

Now he was trapped for the duration of this silly party.

So much for vanity.

It consoled him, just a little, to know that Isabella was doomed to suffer along with him.

CHAPTER 4

Isabella froze when she saw the gown her mother had ordered Betty to lay out for her along with her chicken-skin fan and elbow-length gloves.

"No," she said, putting a hand to her throat. "I *cannot* wear that."

The gown in question was of cerulean blue with short, capped sleeves and a small bunch of artificial white roses at the high waistline.

"Why not?" her mother asked. "It is quite pretty, and, miraculously, it has not gone out of style like many of your other gowns. You wore it at the Castle Inn three years ago, and Philip Lyonbridge hardly took his eyes off you all evening."

"I remember," said Isabella. "I will not give him the satisfaction of having him believe I am wearing it tonight for sentimental reasons. It would be too embarrassing."

Lady Grimsby gave a sigh of impatience.

"Isabella! Every one of those girls will be dressed to the nines tonight at dinner. I could find only three presentable evening gowns in your wardrobe, and I will wager each of those girls has a new gown to wear for each of the five evenings that we will be here. You must seize every advantage you can, and this gown, which the man may remember fondly, may be the only one you have."

Isabella regarded the gown stonily. The young woman who had worn blue that night at the Castle Inn had been young and hopelessly in love with Philip Lyonbridge, the rakishly handsome and clever elder brother of her fiancé. It had been an innocent passion, which she had not known to be requited until that evening.

Oh, the happiness and despair! How she had trembled when their hands met in the progress of the minuet!

She had been such a silly little chit, Isabella thought wryly, writhing in the delicious torment of loving a man she could not have.

Moreover, she had been confident and graceful and more than a match for any of the girls in Lord Revington's drawing room this evening.

That girl, now, was a stranger. The contrast between that girl and Isabella, as she was now, would be too great. Isabella would feel like an impostor in her own gown.

"What else did you bring?" Isabella asked.

"I brought the pink gown you wore to Almack's during the Season, but, mark my words, one of those little cats will remember it and mention in Captain Lyonbridge's presence that it has been worn before, so you will not want to wear it the first evening. That and the blue are the only ones you own that have not gone out of style except for the yellow, which you wore to Major Lyonbridge's wedding. I brought that as well, but I think the blue—"

"The yellow, then," Isabella said abruptly, and turned away from her mother. "I doubt any of them has seen it."

Lady Grimsby put her hands on her hips.

"Honestly, Isabella! I do not know what has got into you. The day gown you wore today is yellow. You will hardly want to wear the same color this evening. That is no way to make an impression on Captain Lyonbridge."

"It does not matter what I wear," Isabella said with a creditable show of indifference.

"It does not matter what you wear?" Lady Grimsby exclaimed at such heresy. "Of course it matters! As for Captain Lyonbridge, you used to make such sheep's eyes at the fellow that you looked quite dotty."

"I *never!*" Isabella exclaimed, but she knew very well that she had.

"My girl, you are going to wear this blue gown, and you are going to dazzle the man tonight. You will wear the pink gown to the ball on Tuesday and perhaps on Friday. You will wear the yellow gown on Monday for the dinner party with the local gentry—a passel of countrified old bores, I have no doubt—and perhaps on Thursday. The blue again on Saturday, the final night of the party, when, if all goes well, you will be introduced to the company as Captain Lyonbridge's fiancée."

Isabella shook her head in disbelief.

"Mother, you are all about in your head if you think he is going to choose me as his bride."

"He invited you to the party, did he not? You will not convince me that his dreadful father did so."

Isabella bit her lip. She knew very well that Philip deliberately invited her here to punish her, but she could not tell her mother that without admitting that she had received him alone at his brother's house, and that she had sent him about his business without a civil word.

"Betty!" called Lady Grimsby sharply when she heard a shriek of laughter from the next room, where Isabella's maid and the nurserymaid were coaxing an excited Jamie into eating the dinner that had been sent up to the room for him.

"My lady?" Betty said breathlessly as she hastened into the room.

"Miss Isabella," Lady Grimsby said in a voice that would brook no argument, "will wear the blue gown. You will put it on her at once, and dress her hair in a Psyche knot with tendrils over one shoulder. And her sapphire set. I have brought it from town with my own jewelry. I will have my maid bring it to you when I am dressed."

"I cannot wear the sapphire set!" Isabella exclaimed. "It was a betrothal gift from his brother!"

"Nonsense. I daresay he will not remember it. It was not one of the Lyonbridge family heirlooms, but a modern set. He was not present when Major Lyonbridge gave it to you. I am going to my room to dress."

She fixed her large, predatory eyes on Betty.

"I shall return to accompany Miss Isabella to dinner. Do *not* disappoint me."

With that, she sailed majestically from the room, and Isabella gave a huff of annoyance.

"I will wear the yellow," Isabella told Betty.

"Please, miss. I daren't for my very life," Betty said tearfully. "You heard what she said." The maid touched the blue gown with reverent fingers. "Please, miss," she said again. "You have only the three gowns, and you will have to wear it eventually."

"Giving in to Mother's bullying only makes her more outrageous." Isabella knew *that* from sad experience.

"She cannot cut *you* off without a character," Betty pointed out. "And throw you out on the streets."

"True," said Isabella.

Betty was loyal and hardworking, and Isabella had no wish to risk losing her. Her wages were paid by Lady Grimsby's household, so Isabella's mother was well within her rights to discharge Betty if she chose to do so.

Isabella forced herself to smile at her maid.

"Very well," she said as she raised her arms to allow Betty to remove her day gown. "The blue, then."

Betty's anxious expression relaxed.

"Thank you, miss," she said, sounding relieved.

When Isabella was dressed, a gentle scratching sounded at the door. Betty opened it to admit Lady Grimsby's maid, who was holding a small velvet casket.

"Miss Isabella's sapphire set," the maid said as she gave the casket to Betty. Lady Grimsby's maid gave Isabella a cool inspection and finally favored her mistress's daughter with a cool nod. "You have done well," she said to Betty. "The mistress will be pleased." Betty acknowledged this praise with a relieved smile, and the older maid left the room.

"You are beautiful, Miss Isabella," said Betty with tears in her eyes when she stood back, in triumph, from her mistress.

Isabella stared into the glass, and saw a stranger—a vaguely familiar stranger, but a stranger just the same—staring back at her.

"Pretty Mama," said the voice of the person Isabella loved most in the world, and the serious look on the face of the girl in the mirror relaxed into a fond smile.

"Darling," she said, bending to accept a kiss on the cheek from Jamie. He turned his round, sweet face into her gloved hand and closed his eyes with the gusty sigh of someone who has come home from a long journey, and Isabella's heart turned over.

How she loved this child.

Jamie was not to call her Mama, but it was difficult for him to remember this. Isabella and Marian had lived together at the time he was born, and when he first learned to talk he called them both Mama. No wonder he had been confused. For appearances' sake, it was important that she break him of the habit, but Isabella could not bring herself to correct him now. He was so very sleepy and no doubt frightened at waking up from his too short postprandial nap in a strange house to find the unfamiliar room in semidarkness. Marian was far away in Scotland with her husband, and Isabella was the only one here who loved him.

"Where is Meggie?" Betty asked, referring to the nursemaid who was supposed to keep an eye on Jamie.

"She went to sleep," Jamie said with a pout. He gave Isabella a winsome smile. "Will you play with me?"

"I am sorry, sweet," she said regretfully. "I have to go to dinner now."

"Lazy girl," said Betty in disapproval.

It was a serious breach of her responsibilities for Meggie

to fall asleep and leave her charge to roam an unfamiliar house. No doubt she had expected Jamie to sleep through the night and saw no harm in dozing by his bed while he slept. Isabella would have to speak sharply to her about it, even though she knew that caring for such an active and clever child could be extremely fatiguing. That was why a healthy, energetic country girl had been chosen for the post.

At that moment an imperious knock sounded at the door.

"Lady Grimsby," said Betty, looking frightened. "Come, Master Jamie. *I* will play with you." She took the child's hand and started to hurry him from the room.

"But I want—" he said tearfully as he reached out his free hand for Isabella.

"Oh, Jamie," Isabella said regretfully. If she had her choice, she would infinitely prefer to stay with Jamie tonight.

Lady Grimsby opened the door and sailed in. Her disapproving eyes fixed on Jamie.

"What is *he* doing here?" she said, sniffing as if she detected an unpleasant smell. "Why is he not asleep?"

"I will take him, my lady," Betty said.

"But I want Mama!" Jamie said, still teary eyes.

"You are *not* to call her that. She is Miss Isabella to you," Lady Grimsby said.

"Do not scold him, Mother," Isabella said, rising in defense of her darling.

"I am *not* sleepy," Jamie protested as he knuckled his eyes with his free hand.

"Please, Master Jamie," Betty said as she tried to coax the boy from the room. She finally had to tow him with one hand as he dug his heels into the floor and began whimpering.

"He is so naughty because he is sleepy," Isabella said, before her mother could give voice to her annoyance. "He will go to bed now, and he will not make a peep for the rest of the night."

Lady Grimsby gave a huff of disapproval.

"You spoil that child, Isabella," she said. "You must teach him to obey you, or he will never learn his place."

Isabella gritted her teeth.

"His *place,* Mother, is as the stepson in a gentleman's house. His *place* is with me until Marian and Adam return from Scotland."

Lady Grimsby took a deep breath.

"You are not going to succeed in putting me out of countenance," she said. "This evening is too important." She ran a critical eye over her daughter and she gave a little nod of approval. "You look very well," she said. "I was right about the gown."

"Yes, Mother," Isabella said, accepting the change of subject with some relief. She picked up her fan and gloves.

"You are too pale," Lady Grimsby said.

She stepped forward and pinched both her daughter's cheeks to give her complexion a more becoming color. Isabella gave a sharp gasp of pain and surprise.

She absolutely *hated* it when her mother did that.

"That's better," Lady Grimsby said with smug satisfaction. "Come along, Isabella. We do not want to keep Captain Lyonbridge waiting for his dinner."

CHAPTER 5

Philip looked up from the face of a ravishing auburn-haired marquess's daughter and completely forgot what the girl had just said to him.

Isabella Grimsby, with slightly flushed cheeks and defiant eyes, had stepped just inside the doorway of the drawing room. Her mother, who had a proprietary hand on the girl's elbow, cast an appraising look over the gathered company.

This was the Isabella he conjured up in his dreams on a terror-filled night sleeping on the muddy ground in Spain with the acrid smell of spent gunpowder in his nostrils and the ominous whirring of predators' wings in his ears as they sought carrion on the ground all around his hiding place.

She was so beautiful. Still.

Every time he saw her he was newly amazed by how beautiful she was.

He recognized the gown at once, of course, from a certain magical night in Brighton. She often wore it when she came to him in his dreams.

How he missed her shy smiles, the sudden blooming of roses in her cheeks at that precise moment when she became aware of his presence in a room, the way her dark eyes grew soft and luminous with golden light when she looked up into his face.

But, although the dress was the same, there was no tenderness for him in her face now. Instead, there was a brittle smile that did not come anywhere near those remarkable eyes when she caught him looking at her.

The contrast between the girl he had adored despite the fact that she belonged to his brother and this . . . stranger was too painful. Philip deliberately turned his back on her to concentrate on what the marquess's daughter was saying to him.

When Lord Revington and the marquess's wife led the party into dinner, the marquess's daughter was on Philip's arm. Since there were no other gentlemen present, the less distinguished young ladies went into the dining room escorted by their mothers.

By luck or design—and if he knew his father, it *was* by design—Isabella and Lady Grimsby were placed far down the table from him so, mercifully, he would be tempted neither to stare at Isabella's lovely face like the veriest mooncalf throughout the meal nor have his dinner ruined by having to witness the sour looks that passed between his father and Lady Grimsby every time they found themselves in the same room.

"Captain Lyonbridge, I understand we are to go riding tomorrow morning," the marquess's daughter said brightly.

He forced himself to smile at her.

She was quite lovely, really, and she had a pert manner about her that he found most attractive. Her green eyes sparkled with anticipation, for she was well known to be a capital horsewoman.

Philip had been appalled when his father's secretary presented him with a schedule of appointments that had been arranged with each of the young ladies.

The first was tomorrow morning, to go riding with this girl. How else, his father had replied blandly when Philip stormed into his study and demanded to know what the deuce he meant by this nonsense, was he to get to know each girl well enough to make a decision?

"Indeed, Lady Anne," he said to the marquess's daughter. "I anticipate it with great pleasure."

It was a wonder his tongue did not turn black.

Isabella, he had noticed, was about halfway down the list with the other candidates his father considered the less desirable ones. They were to drink tea together just before the ladies would be expected to dress for the ball, which would naturally put her somewhat at a disadvantage because a mere half hour was allowed for the interview. Since Isabella already knew the much glorified war hero for a paltry fellow, it would be futile to attempt to support the character of charming, eligible party. He could be himself for a half hour. Thank heaven. They would no doubt have a blazing row, which would give him some stimulation in what promised to be several days of unmitigated boredom.

In his present mood, he positively looked forward to it.

"Do not forget we are to go sketching tomorrow afternoon," the blonde on his other side reminded him.

They would be virtually alone in a beautiful, romantic meadow filled with summer wildflowers, Philip knew, for the girl's parents greatly prided themselves on her talent for sketching.

They were very, very rich, and the position on the list assigned to her reflected this.

"I have not forgotten," he said, smiling at the blonde.

He thought the edges of his lips were going to crack from so much smiling. Fortunately, he had become accustomed to grinning all the time like an obsequious, simpleminded idiot in the presence of the French general and various enemy officers he had duped during the war, so the skill came second nature to him.

In many ways, this was no different.

Philip would not be expected to sketch during his assignation with the girl. Rather, he merely would be required to lean over the pretty blonde's shoulder so he could enjoy the sheen of her golden hair and the flowery scent with which she would no doubt anoint her person, hand her various pencils, charcoals, and brushes as she requested them, and exclaim upon the extraordinary beauty of her sketches. No doubt he would have every opportunity to gaze meaningfully into her pale blue eyes and even steal a kiss, if he had the least desire to do so.

Philip looked down the table and stifled an inward sigh of impatience.

He and his father and a few of the girls' fathers were the only gentlemen present, so the rest of his female guests were chatting with one another and stealing surreptitious glances at Philip, which was no doubt what his father wanted.

It put Philip in a dashed silly position, like some prize bull at a country fair surrounded by hopeful heifers.

His only consolation was that Isabella looked just as annoyed by the situation as he felt. For a moment, his eyes met hers and, incredibly, a brief, shy, involuntary smile of commiseration flitted at her lips. Her eyes danced with amusement, giving him a cruel glimpse of the innocent girl who had once loved him with all her heart.

Then, as if she had sensed his thought, she bit her lip and looked down at her plate.

There was a small flurry of activity at the doorway of the room as his father's butler remonstrated with a female servant. The butler turned and went to Isabella and her mother. Isabella's eyes went wide, and she excused herself from the table and fairly ran for the doorway.

Without realizing he had done so, Philip rose to his feet in concern. Recalling himself to his surroundings, he excused himself to his dinner companions and went around the table where Lady Grimsby sat with a scowl on her face.

"Is something wrong, Lady Grimsby?" he asked.

"Nothing at all," she said with an unconvincing smile on her face. The lady was furious, but she dared not show it here. "Just some trifling matter that should properly be the province of my servants. Such utter nonsense."

"Is there something I can do, or my **staff, perhaps?**" It was no trifling matter, he thought, if it sent Isabella away from the table in the middle of the fish course.

"No," she said. "I, for one, intend to finish this delicious dinner."

"I am glad to hear it," he said, taking her words for dismissal.

He went back to his place at table.

"I trust all is well," the marquess's daughter said.

"Perfectly well, Lady Anne," he said, smiling at her. He saw his father's scowl from the corner of his eye. It would not do, in that gentleman's opinion, no doubt, to ignore the most important young lady present. Lord Revington would dearly love to see a match between the two of them, Philip knew. "Now, where were we? I believe we were discussing an Irish hunter your father purchased for you at Tattersall's last year."

"Yes, indeed," she said, and Philip resigned himself to enduring a tedious description from the horse-mad lady of every bit of blood and bone in the marquess's stable.

Philip began to hope that the morning would bring a deluge of rain to postpone their rendezvous.

"I never was so embarrassed in my life," Lady Grimsby informed Isabella. In justice, she stopped to think. "Well, I *was* more embarrassed when you jilted Major Adam Lyonbridge at the altar, but that was the only time."

"Oh, Mother," said Isabella with a sigh as Jamie, who was seated on her lap, put his little arms around her and looked anxiously at Lady Grimsby as if she might tear him out of Isabella's arms.

"Such nonsense," Lady Grimsby said. "Why could you not have waited to come to the child until after the evening's activities were concluded? There is to be music in the parlor, and your singing voice is quite one of your most important assets. We could go there now."

"No. The nurserymaid said that Jamie was extremely upset because I had been gone so long," she said. "As a rule, I rarely leave him, and I know Marian did not. He is missing her very much just now, are you not, my precious?"

"Mama," said Jamie with a little sniff.

"You are spoiling the child," Lady Grimsby said. "His mother and stepfather will not thank you for that. And that silly girl should be discharged for her impertinence. Disturbing a lady at a dinner party merely because a pampered child chose to go into hysterics!"

"I will not permit you to discharge Meggie," Isabella said, "for I told her to notify me at once if Jamie needed me. You cannot do so, for Adam pays her wages, not you."

Lady Grimsby made a sound that could only be described as a growl, which caused Jamie to regard her with anxiety.

Isabella smiled at Jamie to reassure him and picked him up to swing him over her head as he erupted into giggles. She stood him on her knees so his face was above hers. He reached over and patted one of her long curls so it would bounce.

"Pretty Mama," he said.

"Jamie," Lady Grimsby snapped. "You are *not* to call her that!"

His lower lip quivered.

"Now see what you have done, Mother," Isabella complained. "There, there, love. Lady Grimsby did not mean to frighten you."

"Well, it presents a very *off* appearance, having the boy call you that," Lady Grimsby said. "And that gown will be fit for nothing but the rag bin if you will permit the boy to put his feet all over it."

"We do not care," Isabella said, smiling into Jamie's face, "do we, my darling?"

"Isabella!" Lady Grimsby snapped. "Do try to remember why we are here! You have seen those girls. Diamonds of the first water, every one of them. And from the very best families. You must exert yourself if you are going to carry off the prize."

"The prize," Isabella said with an unlovely snort. "Philip Lyonbridge."

"Isabella!" exclaimed Lady Grimsby, perfectly scandalized. "I never thought to hear *my* daughter make such a vulgar sound."

"I beg your pardon, Mother," Isabella said. "But you know that Captain Lyonbridge will hardly choose *me* from a field of such exquisite contestants. Why should he?"

"Why should he not? Your breeding is as good as that of any of these girls."

"Mother," Isabella said with a sigh.

"Well, if you ask me—and I am well aware you have not, so you can close your mouth and listen, missy—the *least* the man can do is marry you. You have not been the same since that ill-fated elopement. Your father should have *insisted* that the man marry you."

"What would you have had him do? Challenge Captain Lyonbridge to a duel?"

"It should not have come to that, if the so-called gentleman had any sense of honor whatsoever," Lady Grimsby said, tight-lipped.

"The truth is that he did not *want* to marry me, once he had the opportunity," Isabella said. Jamie, sensing the unpleasant tenor of the conversation, began sniffling, and Isabella hugged him to her. "Never mind, sweetheart," she said to him. "My Jamie is the only man I need, are you not, my precious?"

With that, the boy brightened and buried his face in her shoulder as she burbled and crooned nonsensical love words to him.

"*Must* you make those revolting sounds?" Lady Grimsby said.

"Yes, Mother," Isabella said without turning from Jamie, who had begun to giggle loudly enough to make Lady Grimsby wince. "I must."

CHAPTER 6

To Philip's disappointment, no deluge of rain thwarted his father's plan to throw him and Lady Anne together in a romantic tryst with nature. The rosy-fingered dawn of Homeric fancy lit the sky with pink and violet.

The sunlight shifting through the trees made a pretty pattern on the forest path as he and Lady Anne cantered along through the sturdy summer wildflowers.

Lady Anne, though, seemed impervious to this romantic setting as she displayed her excellence as an equestrienne, which was a blessing, because it was impossible for her to lecture him about horses or recount her triumphs at her many hunting parties when she set such a brisk pace.

He would have given much to have riders in his cavalry regiment as indefatigable as Lady Anne.

They had been all around the grounds and covered a good portion of the surrounding forest skirting the house before Lady Anne showed signs of slowing down.

Because he was becoming winded from the exertion of keeping up with her, Philip suggested they dismount for a time to admire the view of a pond through the trees from a clearing on a small, wooded hill near the house. It was a pretty place—a perfect spot, in fact, for a gentleman to steal a kiss from a willing young lady.

Lady Anne, it seemed, was entirely willing. She put back the veil of her fetching riding hat to reveal a complexion charmingly flushed from the exercise. The morning sunlight caught her auburn hair and turned it to pinkish gold.

"That was exhilarating," she said, smiling happily. "I do believe there is nothing more pleasant than a ride through the countryside in the early morning with a good piece of horseflesh between one's legs!"

Philip had to clamp his teeth down hard. She *could* not know how that sounded.

Or maybe she did.

She stepped closer to him and put her hands on his shoulders.

"There are not many men," she said huskily, "who can keep up with me. You are to be commended on your . . . stamina."

She turned her lovely face up to his and pursed her soft pink lips invitingly.

And Philip felt absolutely nothing.

Who would have thought that he would come to this, he who had earned a reputation for being quite a dab with the ladies during his carefree bachelorhood before he joined the army? The mere sight of a presentable female could heat his blood in those days.

And this one was practically throwing herself at him.

Oh, why not?

As a gentleman, he knew exactly where to draw the line before he became irreparably committed to the horse-mad Lady Anne.

More from curiosity and good manners than from any actual desire to sample Lady Anne's charms, Philip drew her into his arms.

Before he could kiss her, however, Isabella Grimsby and his brother's stepson came riding double at a plodding pace into the clearing on a gentle but sturdy horse from his father's stables. They were both laughing, but Isabella gasped and looked stricken at the sight of Lady Anne in Philip's embrace. In reaction, she sawed so roughly on the reins that the horse tossed its head and started to rear back.

Isabella cried out and clutched the boy to her, but she managed somehow to keep her seat. The boy let out a terrified shriek.

Philip ran quickly to catch the horse's bridle.

"Steady there, old girl," he crooned to it as it gentled under his hand.

"You should be more careful," Lady Anne said crossly to Isabella. "You could have ruined her mouth with such rough handling."

"I am sorry. I did not mean . . . do forgive the intrusion," Isabella said, sounding flustered. "I did not expect to encounter anyone."

"And *you,* young man," Lady Anne continued as she fixed her eyes on the boy, "should know better than to make loud noises around a horse that already has become unsettled due to inept handling."

The child's eyes grew wide as he stared at Lady Anne.

"Are you a witch?" he asked with bright-eyed interest.

"I beg your pardon?" snapped Lady Anne.

"Jamie!" exclaimed Isabella. She sounded horrified, as well she might.

"Aunt Isabella read me a story about a witch with red hair," the boy said. "She was mean and scolded everyone."

Isabella closed her eyes for a moment in utter mortification. Philip almost laughed at the expression on her face.

"I am so sorry, Lady Anne," Isabella said. "He has a very active imagination for such a young child."

"So I perceive," Lady Anne said with narrowed eyes. "Do go on with your ride. Do not let us keep you."

"Good day, then," said Isabella with a polite nod as she rode away. The boy twisted around to look curiously at Philip and Lady Anne, but Isabella pulled him into line in front of her to shield his view.

"Miss Grimsby is such an odd female," Lady Anne said, sounding nettled, "and that forward little boy. Some kind of connection of yours, is he not?"

"The boy? My younger brother's stepson," he said. "No blood relation of mine, as it turns out. Miss Grimsby is minding him while his mother and my brother are in Scotland."

"Very odd," Lady Anne said.

She put the veil back over her face and took her reins in her gloved hands. He moved to give her a hand up, and she sprang lightly and gracefully into the saddle.

"Shall we continue our ride?" she asked.

Apparently the romantic mood was quite spoiled for her, and Philip was ashamed of himself for being relieved by this. The sight of Isabella's consternation at seeing him with Lady Anne quite distracted him.

Isabella was not so indifferent to him, then, as she pretended to be.

Lady Anne insisted upon riding farther into the forest, but Philip did not flatter himself that it was from a desire to prolong her time with him. She hardly gave him a look.

"I rarely have a chance for a good gallop when I am away from my father's estate," she said sunnily when he helped her dismount in front of the stable some time later.

They walked past the stalls on their way to the house for Philip's next assignation, and in front of one of the stalls they saw Isabella and the boy feeding pieces of apple to the horse they had ridden that day.

"My horse," the child said to Isabella.

"No, love," she told him. "This horse belongs to Lord Revington."

The softness of her voice made Philip want to stop here and listen to it forever. There used to be just such a note of tenderness in her tone when she talked to *him*.

"Perhaps she is not so odd, after all," Lady Anne said to Philip after they had favored Isabella with polite nods and moved past them. "Obviously she likes horses, and the boy does, too."

"Just so," said Philip.

"But he did call me a witch," Lady Anne pointed out. "My dear parents have always believed it injurious to a child's brain to fill it too full of fairy stories, and we have seen what comes of it. You might drop a word in your brother's ear about that."

"Certainly, Lady Anne," Philip said, glad that their assignation had come to an end.

Philip had endured a hideously tedious two days, keeping his appointments with the young ladies his father had invited to try their luck with him. All were so flatteringly attentive that he might have become quite puffed up in his own esteem by their determined efforts to captivate him if he had not known very well that he had ceased to exist for them.

He was convinced that the ladies were not so eager to win him as they were to prove their mettle against the field of contestants and emerge victorious.

Every time he smiled at one of them, she looked from the corner of her eye to see which of her rivals happened to be watching.

As for his private appointments with each one, he was forced to listen to each girl recite an endless catalog of her own shallow accomplishments, rather as if she were being interviewed for a position in the household. When she was forced to abandon the subject of her watercolors, drawing, music lessons, foreign languages, and love for dancing, he was often forced to give an account of his adventures in the war in response to the girl's eager questions.

He could almost hear their mothers coaching them: *Men like to talk about themselves. Ask him about his adventures in the war.* For his part, however, Philip did not want to talk about the war. The world might perceive him as a dashing and heroic officer who risked his life to save Mother England from Napoleon and laughed in the face of danger, but inside he had felt only terrified and alone.

Not dashing and heroic at all, in fact.

The sooner he could sell his commission and resume civilian life, the better, and he would do so at the end of the summer, when the *ton* moved on to the continent for the Congress of Vienna, regardless of any objections his father might have. No doubt Lord Revington would consider the Congress a perfect opportunity for Philip to ingratiate himself with the world's most powerful men, but he had no desire to go there.

With the conclusion of this house party, Philip's obligation to his father would be discharged.

Today, however, his tedium was to be relieved by tea with Isabella Grimsby, and he could hardly wait.

She would hardly lower herself to reciting a list of her accomplishments to him, and he knew the last topic she wished to discuss was his heroic performance during the war.

So it was a bit of an anticlimax when he walked into a parlor beautifully set with refreshments to find no ravishing, dark-haired lady awaiting him.

Ah, well. Isabella had ever been fond of making an entrance. He seated himself comfortably and prepared to wait.

Ten minutes later, he was still waiting.

He did not know whether to be annoyed or amused.

Of course, it was lowering to his self-esteem to be left cooling his heels in the parlor with a pot of tepid tea for company when he had been accustomed to having eager young women fawn upon him for the past two days.

On the other hand, he had always admired Isabella's independence, although he would never make the grave error of telling her so. His brother, he knew, had dreaded marriage with Isabella because of her resemblance to her masterful mother in both looks and temperament, but these qualities were not enough to put Philip off the lady.

Lady Grimsby had been a famous beauty in her day, and Philip quite appreciated a high-spirited female.

With that thought, Isabella flounced into the room. She

was wearing a pretty green day gown and a scowl on her beautiful face. She looked thunderously angry, but he knew it was not with him, for he had not done anything to annoy her lately, so he sat back for a moment to savor the sight of Isabella's magnificent eyes alight with temper.

Good manners dictated that he stand, which he did, but before he could take up a station behind her chair to assist her, she sat down with a graceless huff of irritation. This was so unlike her usual polished manner that he laughed out loud.

"*If* you are quite through," she said, looking at him as if he were a clod stuck to her shoe.

"Quite," he said, unabashed. "Lord, that felt good. I have not laughed like that in weeks."

"Well, good for you," she said, still irritated. "Do not expect me to be charming company, Captain Lyonbridge, for I am quite out of temper. And you are being of no help at all."

"So I perceive," he said, smiling at her. "In what way may I assist you?"

"You may *assist* me by choosing one of these little ninnies as your bride so Mother will go back to London for the peace celebrations and permit Jamie and me to return to your brother's house."

Philip looked at her with half-lidded eyes and an unctuous smile on his face, just to further annoy her.

"But there are so many pretty girls from which to choose," he drawled. "Pity I can have only one."

"Coxcomb!" she snapped.

"There, there, Isabella," he said. "You have made it plain that you have no desire to make yourself conciliating to me as a prospective bride, so why can we not relax and enjoy one another's company as we were used to do?"

"Before you abandoned me at some horrid, stupid country inn with your horrid, stupid brother to go off and fight your horrid, stupid war, do you mean?" she said waspishly.

"Just so," he said.

She turned her head away from him.

"I will never feel that way about you again," she said softly.

"Isabella," he said remorsefully. He felt like the lowest beast in nature because of the brief expression of desolation that crossed her face. He could not tell her now that he had only done it to prove himself to her.

How foolish he had been.

He reached over the table and put his hand over hers because she suddenly looked so bereft, but she quickly snatched her hand away from him.

"Would it do any good to apologize?" he asked after an awkward moment.

"None at all," she said with a bright, false smile on her face. "Not after all this time. And then you came *strutting* up to my door—"

"I never strut," he said, feeling outraged.

"You do. You did." She made a little movement of agitation. "It does not matter, after all. We have a quarter of an hour left of this farce. Or shall I leave?"

"No! Please!" He started to rise in his eagerness to stop her.

"As you wish," she said. "I am of half a mind to linger beyond the appointed time just to annoy Mother, for she is concerned that I may not have time to embellish myself suitably for your inspection tonight."

"I am agreeable," he said. "Shall we go for a stroll on the grounds?"

"Good heavens, no! That will only give rise to expectations in her breast that I will vanquish my rivals and carry off the prize. There would be no *living* with her after that."

He winced.

"Very well, then, Miss Grimsby," he said, "will you have some tea?"

"Certainly," she said. "After my mother insisted that I change my gown three times, I may as well."

"Is she making your life miserable?" he asked.

"Yes. I suppose your father is making yours miserable as well. If we have anything in common, it is our familiarity with the crotchets of domineering parents."

"Too true," he said with a smile. "Will you ring for a fresh pot? This is quite tepid by this time."

"A rebuke, Captain Lyonbridge?" she said with one uplifted brow as she rang the tiny silver bell.

"Not at all," he said. "It is always a gentleman's chief pleasure to wait for a beautiful lady to make her entrance."

Her lips twitched with amusement, and Philip loathed himself for the pleasure it gave him. "A fresh pot, if you please," he said to the maid who answered the summons.

"And some of those delicious strawberry tarts we had last night for dinner, if you have any left," Isabella added.

"Yes, miss," the servant said.

"Gorging yourself while you are out of your mother's sight, Miss Grimsby?" he asked with an arch smile.

"How ungentlemanly of you, Captain Lyonbridge! I am quite shocked." But she was laughing. "She is afraid I am going to run to fat because I am not as slim as I was as a young girl. She scolded me for not bringing along a corset."

"A corset! How perfectly ridiculous," Philip said at once. He was quite certain that her mother would have an apoplexy if she knew Isabella had mentioned an item of such intimate apparel in a gentleman's presence. It told him quite plainly— as if he had any doubt—that Isabella did not consider him a desirable marriage prospect.

If anything, Isabella's figure was even more appealing to him than it had been when she was a young girl. Her breasts had ripened, and her hips were more womanly, but her waist was still so slim he had no doubt he could span it with his two hands. He could hardly say so now, however.

The hot tea and the tarts arrived, and Isabella poured for them both. She took a sip of the fragrant brew.

"Perfect," she said to the maid, who had waited to see if they wished anything more. The girl bobbed a curtsy and left.

Isabella took a bite from one of the tarts and closed her eyes to savor it. A beatific smile crossed her face.

"Heaven," she said, opening her eyes and smiling at Philip.

"Yes," he said, a little dazzled.

Isabella took one of the tarts and carefully placed it in a serviette. Philip raised one eyebrow.

"A little sustenance to get you through the ordeal ahead? There will be more at the ball, I venture to say." He took a bite out of the tart in front of him.

"These are for Jamie," she said with a sheepish smile as she added another tart to the serviette. "He loves sweets."

"I am rather fond of them myself," he said when he had swallowed the bite in his mouth. "You are not going to take them all, are you?"

"Certainly not. Here. Have the last one if you must be so greedy," she joked.

"We will share it, then," he said.

He took the last tart in his hand and held it to her lips. She flushed slightly and took a bite. Then with a twist of his wrist he turned the tart around and bit it from the same place as he looked deeply into her eyes.

She raised her eyebrows at him. "Playing off your tricks on me, Philip?" she asked. "You should know I am immune to them by now."

"Merely practicing, my dear Miss Grimsby," he said, matching her arch tone, "before I join the others."

She gave a burst of laughter and opened her mouth to reply.

He leaned forward eagerly. He had not enjoyed himself so much in a long time.

But whatever crushing retort she had for him died on her lips, for Isabella's maid came bursting into the parlor. The girl was so agitated, she did not wait for permission to speak.

"Miss Isabella, Master Jamie is gone!" she cried. "I cannot find him anywhere!"

With a little cry, Isabella sprang to her feet so quickly that her chair fell backward and onto the floor with a thud.

"Where did you see him last?" Philip asked.

"He was in his room, asleep. Miss Isabella, you must turn off that lazy nursemaid. She fell asleep again while she was supposed to be watching him."

"Turn her off? She will be lucky if I do not *kill* her," Isabella said between gritted teeth. She had tears in her eyes, and Philip could not bear it.

"I will organize the men to look for him," Philip said. "Do not worry. We will turn the house upside down if we must."

Isabella gave him a look brimful of gratitude. She started to make some reply, then bit her lip and ran from the room instead.

CHAPTER 7

Philip took command quickly and was about to deliver his orders to the last of the footmen when his father rushed into the parlor with a look of ferocity on his face that should have made Philip quail.

Instead, Philip merely gave his father a ferocious scowl and signaled for silence.

"You and I shall take the portrait gallery," Philip told the remaining footman. "I will take the north end; you will take the south. If you find the boy, give me a shout so I can get word to Miss Grimsby as quickly as possible."

"What do you think you are doing?" demanded Lord Revington. "We have guests arriving for the ball within the hour, and you are dispatching the servants all over the house to look for that wretched little boy."

After dealing with various members of the French Army, all of whom would have as soon butchered him as looked at him, Lord Revington's raving had no power to intimidate Philip.

"Then you had better hope that we find the boy quickly," he said. "Perhaps you would like to join in the search."

"Do not be absurd!" Lord Revington thundered.

"I thought not," Philip said wryly. He signaled the footman to follow him as he went at a half run toward the door.

"Come back here at once!" Lord Revington shouted.

"You must excuse me, sir," Philip said as he turned back to speak to his father. "*Anything* could happen to a small boy in this rabbit's warren of a place. Let us hope he has not found the room with the medieval weaponry in it."

"If he does, good riddance, I say!"

Philip's eyes narrowed dangerously.

"You do not mean that," he said softly.

Lord Revington threw one hand into the air in a gesture of annoyance.

"No, I suppose not," he said. "Very well, then. Get on with it. And find the brat quickly so we can be done with this business."

Philip gave his father a curt nod and took the stairs to the portrait gallery two at a time. As he passed each landing, he could hear the sounds of voices calling out the boy's name.

Isabella had wanted to join in the search, but he told her she must stay in her room in case the boy came back. If she stayed in one place, the searchers would be able to find her as quickly as possible once they found the boy.

She had agreed with his logic, but there were tears in her beautiful eyes when he left her. Hers, he knew, was the most difficult role, that of sitting in her room, waiting for news, when she would rather have been *doing* something.

Despite the fact that the summer sun had not quite set, the gallery was in shadows. To protect the valuable paintings housed there, the windows were covered in heavy draperies to keep out most of the damaging light.

Carefully Philip started searching every nook and cranny as he made his way through the gallery, looking in all the places he thought a small, curious child might hide.

To Philip's relief, he heard a soft whimper when he got almost to the end of the gallery.

"Jamie?" he said softly, for fear of alarming the boy.

He got down on his hands and knees, following the sound. He found the child curled up into a little ball, shaking with fear in the way of any small animal preparing for the worst.

"Jamie, lad," Philip said as he pulled the child into his arms. "There, there," he added soothingly as the boy buried his face in Philip's chest and burst into tears.

When the child spoke, it was with a raspy voice.

"I called and called," he said. "I want my Aunt Isabella."

"I know, I know," Philip said. "I am sorry, lad. You were too far away for us to hear you."

Philip raised his voice to call the footman searching at the other end of the gallery. "Go at once to Miss Grimsby and tell her the child is found. I will bring him to her in a moment."

The footman ran off at once to obey.

"Here, now, lad," Philip said as he took his handkerchief and cleaned the boy's tear- and dirt-smeared face. The maids, apparently, had not been doing a good job of dusting up here. "There. You look quite presentable now."

He picked the child up in his arms and felt a curious thrill in the general region of his heart when Jamie's small arms encircled his neck.

"I was afraid no one would find me," Jamie croaked.

Philip forbore to mention that the whole ordeal could have been avoided if Jamie had remained in his room with his nursemaid. It was not his place to scold his brother's stepson.

Jamie's head swiveled as they passed the portraits. He pointed to one of them.

"I want to look at the pretty pictures," he said.

Philip had to laugh at the resilience of youth.

"I will bring you back tomorrow to see them, I promise you," Philip said. "Now I must take you to your aunt."

But Isabella, it seemed, had not been content to await their arrival.

She met them on the stairway, breathless from the exertion of running up the stairs.

"Jamie!" she cried out as she opened her arms wide. Jamie leaped into them with a cry of relief, which almost caused Isabella to topple over. Philip grabbed her to prevent this, and somehow both Isabella and Jamie ended up in Philip's embrace as aunt and nephew indulged themselves in a fit of weeping.

"You are a bad, bad boy," Isabella cried brokenly.

"Sorry, sorry," the boy cried back.

At that moment, Isabella froze and looked up into Philip's face with an expression of consternation on her face. Philip had wondered when she was going to realize that she was in the arms of a man she disliked so intensely.

"Thank you," she said, surprising him. Her eyes were luminous with emotion. "I could not live if something happened to my sweet Jamie." Her lower lip trembled, and he thought she was going to burst into tears again.

"There, there, enough of this pathos," Philip said at last. "It is as dark as a dungeon up here." He spotted a servant with a candle poking his head interestedly into the room. "You, there! Come in and give us some light."

"Yes, Captain Lyonbridge," the man said as he lit some of the wall sconces. "Lord Revington sent me up here to tell you—"

"Yes, yes, I can well imagine what my father sent you to tell me, and you may consider his message delivered. There. That is better," he said, looking around at the now light-filled room. "You may go." The servant bowed and left. Philip grinned at Jamie. "You wanted to see the pretty pictures, lad. Here they are."

"That one!" said Jamie, pointing at one of the larger portraits.

"I see you already have quite the eye for the ladies," Philip said with one uplifted brow.

"We had better go. The ball *will* be starting soon," Isabella reminded him hastily.

"And ladies need time to dress for such things," Philip said. "I quite understand. The lad and I will look at the paintings, and I shall take him to his nursemaid when we are finished."

"No, I—"

"Jamie will be perfectly safe with me," Philip said. "Do you think I would let anything happen to my brother's stepson?"

"No, of course not," Isabella said. "I am most grateful—"

"Then be a good girl and run along so Jamie and I can look at the pretty paintings."

Isabella hesitated.

"I cannot bear to let him out of my sight just yet," she confessed with a shaky laugh.

Philip put his arm around her shoulders and gave them a brief squeeze.

"Here. He is too heavy for you," Philip said as he took Jamie from her arms. "See, lad, this portrait is of your stepfather's grandparents on his mother's side."

"Your papa," Isabella said when Jamie gave her an inquiring look.

"Papa!" Jamie said brightly. "When will Papa come home?"

"Not for some time yet, love," Isabella said.

"And this lady you so admired," Philip said, moving on to the portrait of the tall, dark late Lady Revington, "is Papa's mother, and mine, incidentally. I am said to resemble her, although Papa looks more like our father."

"Lord Revington," Jamie said, as if by rote.

"Yes," Philip said. "You are quite bright for your age, are you not?"

"I really should put Jamie to bed," Isabella said uncomfortably.

"One more. The best of the lot," Philip said, moving on to the next portrait. "You will like this one. Here, lad, is a portrait of Papa when he was an infant on our mother's lap. A handsome little urchin, is he not? And the boy standing next to his mother's knee is . . ." He broke off and looked closely at his own two-year-old painted face, then peered into Jamie's attentive little one.

Until now, Philip had not had a chance to look closely at the boy. Isabella had been at pains, he realized, to keep him from doing so.

Now he knew why.

The painted child and the living one could have been the same.

Philip gave a crack of laughter.

"Oh, by God! This is too rich," he said. "My little brother, it seems, is not the sterling character he would have us think. *He* is 'Papa' in truth."

"Papa!" Jamie said happily.

Isabella snatched Jamie from Philip's arms and gave him a look that could have curdled milk.

"You are being ridiculous," she snapped.

"Open your eyes," Philip said. "The proof is in the portrait. He could have been one of my mother's own sons, the resemblance to her family is so strong. So my brother anticipated his wedding vows. It happens all the time."

"Stop it," Isabella said. "You have no idea what you are saying."

"The sanctimonious prig, to lecture *me* on propriety, when he and your Miss Randall . . ." Philip did a rapid sum in his head and gave Jamie a speculative look. "Yes, the timing would be just about right."

"You are *disgusting,*" Isabella said, setting her jaw in that way that never failed to stir Philip's blood.

"Nonsense. Adam is only flesh and blood like any other man. No doubt he hid the truth from our father because he knew what the old man would have done—he would have had the boy handed over to some likely couple to rear as soon as the poor little bastard had drawn his first breath."

"How *dare* you speak of Jamie in such terms?" she asked furiously.

"I apologize," he said. "Poor little devil. It would have gone worse for the girl if her father were not a viscount. Of course, your father has had to dispose of several bastards himself, and so has had much practice doing so. The difference is, he had a penchant for females of a lower class, whose relatives were not likely to interfere."

"I beg your pardon," Isabella asked, sounding startled.

He looked her straight in the eye.

"I know who the boy's mother is, Isabella," he said softly.

Her face had gone dead white.

"Steady, my girl," Philip said in concern as he caught her arm. She flinched from his touch.

"I do not know what you mean," she said. Her eyes were wide with consternation.

"There is no use pretending. My father told me. My new sister-in-law is Lord Grimsby's love child."

"Oh," she said weakly. "That."

"Yes. That. Do not worry. I do not believe the truth is generally known. Father thought it only right I should know, since the girl is now a member of our family. If Father had known the girl was pregnant with Adam's child, he would have arranged with your father to marry her off to the first man who would have her and send both of them away with a suitable sum to ensure their silence on the matter of the boy's paternity. Who was to stop him from doing so while Adam was in the Peninsula?"

"How could anyone be so cruel?" she asked.

No doubt she thought it was incomprehensible that any man could send his own grandson away, never to see him again. But Philip knew very well that the old man was capable of such an act.

Lord Revington was a cold, calculating man to whom appearances were everything. Philip knew exactly how the old man thought. It was one thing for a young man of prominent family to sow his wild oats before he settled down to marriage and the serious business of begetting legitimate heirs, but in Lord Revington's view, it was quite another to have his by-blows cluttering up the countryside and causing potential embarrassment to his family. Bastard children were particularly troublesome to a man in public life. Lord Revington had hopes of brilliant careers in government for both his sons.

"I am glad it did not come to that," Philip said, smiling. "He's a likely lad, for all the mischief he has caused. I am not surprised you are so fond of him. No doubt my brother is as well. So all ends happily—with Mama, Papa, and little boy all together."

He tickled Jamie and smiled when the child giggled.

Such an innocent sound.

"You will not say anything about this to your father?" Isabella asked.

"Good lord, no!" Philip exclaimed, surprised that she would think him petty enough to do such a thing. "It is none of his business, or mine, for that matter. Adam would not thank me for meddling in his affairs. However, my father is no threat to the lad now that Adam has married the mother."

Jamie looked from one adult to another in confusion, but Philip patted the lad on the shoulder.

"There, my boy. You have seen the pictures, and your aunt and I must dress for the ball." He gave another crack of laughter. "Lord, how I shall roast Adam when I see him next!"

"*Men!*" Isabella said with a look of loathing, and flounced off with the boy perched on her hip as Philip grinned with amusement.

CHAPTER 8

By the time Martin had tricked Philip out in his most splendid regimental dress uniform, the receiving line had been disbanded. But any hope he had of making a quiet entrance was foiled when his father shouted in ringing tones, "To my son, Captain Philip Lyonbridge, the savior of Mother England!"

Good God, Philip thought as he stopped in mid stride just inside the doorway.

The old man made it sound as if he deliberately had set out to get himself captured by the enemy, plotted to escape, and disguised himself as a Spanish national to infiltrate the French army encampment in order to save Mother England.

What utter nonsense.

Philip had done what he did to save his own wretched skin. Mother England was a mere afterthought.

He half expected a snicker to sweep the room in response to this fatuous comment.

Instead, all the beautiful young ladies, his father's neighbors, and various distinguished members of Parliament who could be spared from the peace celebrations let out a cheer.

It probably appeared as if he deliberately had arrived late

so he could make an entrance. Who did they think he was? The Prince Regent?

Still, there was no turning back.

As he strode into the ballroom, the assembled guests raised crystal champagne glasses in their white-gloved hands and drank to his health while he forced himself to smile as if he were, indeed, a fine fellow.

They smiled back. And waited.

That is when it dawned upon Philip that they expected him to say a few words.

Unfortunately, nothing came into his brain that would not make him sound like a bloody coxcomb.

As the silence lengthened, he began to fear he might be destined to stand there, in the middle of the room, groping for words equal to the occasion, when a weight crashed into the back of his legs and threatened to topple him.

A collective gasp rose from his father's guests, and Lord Revington frowned thunderously as young Master Jamie attached himself to Philip's leg.

"Papa always gives me a horseback ride on his shoulders before I go to bed," the child told Philip.

Philip had to laugh. In truth, he was grateful to the lad, for he hardly could be expected to give some sort of graceful speech after this comic interruption.

He hoisted the child to one hip just as Isabella, wearing a frothy rose pink evening gown appropriate to the evening festivities, but with her hair half down her back as if she had been interrupted in the process of having it dressed, ran into the room and skidded to a stop next to him in her soft-soled dancing slippers. A nursemaid had followed her to the doorway, but stopped at the threshold as if prevented by an invisible barrier.

"Jamie! What have I told you about running away from your room!" Isabella said furiously. "Did you learn *nothing* from being lost? Off to bed with you at once, my little man! I am extremely displeased with you!"

The child's lower lip began to tremble.

"Here. None of that, lad," Philip said hastily as he handed Jamie into Isabella's waiting arms. "I will give you that horseback ride in the morning, I promise you."

Lady Grimsby appeared in the doorway with her hands on her hips.

No doubt Isabella and young Jamie were about to receive a rare bear-garden jaw.

But Lady Grimsby took stock of her company and turned her frown into a wide, insincere smile. She slipped into the room and greeted one of her acquaintances for all the world as if the young woman in rose pink and the boy in his crisp, white nightshirt were complete strangers to her.

"I want to watch the pretty ladies dance," the little boy said with an adorable pout on his face.

Incredibly, many of the pretty ladies emitted well-bred titters of delighted laughter.

Well, the lad did look sweet in his little nightshirt, Philip had to admit. He was rather charmed himself.

The little boy looked about him with a pleased, roguish smile at all the female attention, which caused more gentle chuckles to come from the guests.

"Oh, do let him stay, Miss Grimsby!" one of the ladies called.

"Yes! Where is the harm in letting him watch one dance?" asked another.

"A waltz! The prettiest dance of all!" said Lady Anne, who was not about to let an opportunity pass. She glided to Philip, all exquisite auburn loveliness in a gown of the most expensive white lace for all the world as if she were already a bride, and held up her arms to him, already in position for the waltz.

Philip had no choice but to take her gloved hand in his and position his other arm around her narrow waist. The orchestra struck up the tune and Philip led Lady Anne onto the dance floor as his father's guests applauded and emitted little cries of admiration for the pretty picture they made.

When he turned to face the woman and child, he saw young Jamie was clapping his small hands in delight and Isabella was crouched down next to him, whispering in his ear. The skirt of her gown was spread on the floor, which made it look as if her lovely face and shoulders were rising out of some sort of delicious pastry.

"Captain Lyonbridge," Lady Anne said huskily. "You are holding me so tightly that I can hardly breathe."

She was positively panting with excitement.

He immediately relaxed his grip on her. Since it would be ungentlemanly in the extreme of him to admit to Lady Anne that his sudden appearance of ardor had been for quite another woman entirely, he decided it would be the better part of valor to murmur an apology and keep his embrace at a polite distance for the duration of the waltz.

After a few moments, other couples began to join in the dance and he began to relax. In a few more moments it would be over, and he could excuse himself to speak to Isabella.

And get a glass of wine. Lord knew he needed one.

When he had escorted Lady Anne to her mother and done the pretty by her, he turned to approach Isabella, who seemed to be having an argument with her little nephew. She was whispering quite insistently to him, and he had a mulish look on his face.

"You must go to bed now, Jamie," he heard Isabella say as he drew near to them. "You promised you would do so if you could watch the pretty ladies dance."

"I want to see *you* dance now, Aunt Isabella," he said with a mulish look on his face. Until now, Philip had been convinced that the boy resembled his mother's side of the family. But frowning like that, with his eyebrows lowered, he looked exactly like a miniature version of Lord Revington.

Isabella gave a long sigh of exasperation.

"That is quite out of the—"

It was an opportunity too good to miss.

"May I have the honor, Miss Grimsby?" Philip held his hand out to her.

Isabella had been so intent upon removing Jamie from the ballroom that she hadn't seen his approach.

She looked up into his brilliant blue eyes and felt her heart almost miss a beat at the warmth in them.

He was merely being kind, she told herself firmly. She hoped he did not notice that her hand trembled as she placed it in his large, warm one. The contact made her fingers tingle, just as it had the first time she danced with him during her first Season in London.

Jamie clapped his hands with glee.

Philip raised her to her feet and bowed over her hand. She curtsied to him.

"Pretty," Jamie said. "Dance now."

Isabella colored with embarrassment, for everyone was staring at them. She wished Betty had been able to finish arranging her hair. She must look like a hoyden.

"I do not think he is going to go to bed until we obey, do you?" Philip whispered in that confidential voice that made her heart beat faster, no matter how much she told herself she did not dare to fall under his spell.

"Possibly not," she said with a creditable assumption of coolness. "Let us get on with it, then."

Mercifully, it was not a waltz but a country dance that the orchestra struck up. Philip escorted her to a circle. Was it a mere coincidence that Lady Anne was a member of it? The redhead fluttered her eyelashes prettily at Philip, and he favored the marquess's daughter with a smile and a nod of his head.

Nettled, Isabella would have left the circle if she could. There was nothing more irritating than partnering a man who spent the duration of the dance flirting with another woman.

She and Philip had bowed to one another and joined hands when a little commotion at the doorway distracted her.

To her amazement, Major Adam Lyonbridge came striding into the room with a face stormy as a thundercloud. His brown hair was streaked with gold, which told Isabella that the imposing mountain of a man had spent most of his assignment in Scotland out-of-doors. She could hear every woman in the room give a gasp of rapture at the sight of him, for Adam Lyonbridge was quite impressive when he was tricked out in full scarlet regalia.

"What is the meaning of this ridiculous farce!" Adam shouted as he approached his father.

"Adam!" Lord Revington cried out as he practically ran to his younger son. "I did not know you were to return from Scotland. You are well? Nothing is wrong, I hope."

"Yes, there is or I would not be here, but we will go into all that presently," Adam said ungraciously, although he did shake hands with his father. "Where is he?"

Lord Revington's brow furrowed in question, but Adam looked around and found his victim without his help.

"*There* you are," he barked as he approached Philip, paying no attention whatsoever to the fact that Philip was dancing at the time. He caught Philip's coat front and yanked him out of the circle. "I will have a word with you, sir! *Now!*"

Philip had since followed the pattern of the dance that compelled the gentlemen to move to the next lady in sequence, so he had joined hands as a prelude to twirling with her. Lady Anne, his current partner, gave a squeak of distress as her partner was so abruptly taken from her.

"In the library," Adam said, jerking his head toward the door.

He no doubt would have frog-marched his brother out of the room if Jamie hadn't spotted him and come running.

"Papa! Papa!" the child shouted out gleefully. He held out his small arms as he ran, and Adam gave Philip a little push away as he bent to pick up the child. Philip looked on in amazement as his brother's ferocious face was transformed into a softness he had never seen before.

"Jamie, my boy," Adam said softly as the small arms closed around his neck.

"I have missed you, Papa!" he said, kissing Adam on the cheek and craning his small neck around to look toward the door. "Where is Mama?"

"Here I am, love!" Mrs. Marian Lyonbridge called as she was shown into the room by the butler. She, like Adam, was in evening dress, and Philip had to admire the splendid impression she made in emerald green silk with her auburn hair dressed in short, stylish ringlets that resembled a halo about her head. The last time he had seen her, she had been wearing girlish muslins and her hair had been long. It was obvious from the healthy glow of her complexion that marriage agreed with her.

She tried to pluck the child from Adam's arms, but the boy managed to hold them together in an affectionate grouping of three by looping one arm around each adult's neck.

"We have missed you so much," Mrs. Lyonbridge said. Her voice was choked with tears. "You have grown so much, darling. Where is Auntie Isabella?"

"Here, Marian," Isabella said as she stepped from her partner's arms and joined them.

"Good heavens! What on earth happened to your hair?" Marian exclaimed.

"Never mind that. Come with me. We will put Jamie to bed and I will tell you everything," Isabella said as she took her half sister's arm and attempted to guide her from the room. "I am so glad to see you!"

There was a brief struggle as Jamie attempted to retain his hold on both Adam and Marian, but Marian won, mainly because Isabella had joined her efforts with her half sister's side.

Jamie tried tears, but finding that they did not work their magic for once, he twisted around in Mrs. Lyonbridge's arms and reached his hands toward Adam.

"I will join you in a moment, son," Adam promised the child, whose face lit up immediately. Docile now, Jamie laid his small head against Mrs. Lyonbridge's bosom and sucked his thumb. "Lady Anne," Adam added as he recognized the marquess's daughter. He kissed her hand. "I am delighted to see you in such beauty. As always," he said.

Then he grasped Philip's arm and towed him from the room.

"Since when did you become such a dab with the ladies?" Philip could not help asking as Adam strode so quickly across the polished floor that he practically had to run to keep from having his arm dragged from his socket. If Adam had set out to make him feel like an imbecile, he could not have made a better job of it. The gudgeon had such long, long legs, blast his eyes!

"You forget that I endured several entertainments just as ridiculous as this when we thought you dead and my father sought to marry his heir, as he then thought me, to one of the fair flowers even now gracing the ballroom," Adam said through gritted teeth. "I was never so happy in my life as I was the day I learned you were alive."

"Your expression of affection quite unmans me," Philip said dryly.

"Why did you not put a stop to this nonsense at once?"

"Why did *you* not?" Philip countered.

"I did," Adam growled. "I married Marian."

At that point, he yanked open the library door and thrust Philip inside. Philip had to perform some intricate footwork to remain upright. Even when he wasn't angry, Adam often didn't know his own strength.

Somehow, though, Philip thought that Adam would have been delighted to watch him sprawl in an ungainly heap on the floor.

He was not about to give him the satisfaction.

He drew himself to his full height—such as it was in the presence of his much taller and more muscular mountain of a brother—and brushed fastidiously at his coat as if it had been smirched, because he knew it would annoy Adam.

"Well, it was the least you could do after you got her with child," Philip said.

Adam drew back with a dumbfounded look on his face.

"After I—what *are* you talking about?" he asked.

"Jamie, of course," Philip said. "Your Miss Randall's little bundle of joy. Do not bother to deny it. No one could mistake him for anyone but a child of our mother's blood."

"That is because, you bloody idiot, he's *your* son, not mine!" Adam shouted.

CHAPTER 9

Adam rolled his eyes and gave a sigh of long-suffering when Philip stared at him for a moment in speechless indignation, but finally managed to say, "I beg your pardon? You think *I* impregnated your wife—"

"Do try not to be more of an idiot than the Almighty made you," Adam said. "*No one* impregnated Marian. Isabella is the boy's mother, of course."

At that, Philip's face turned chalk white.

"Isabella," he said faintly. "That means I . . . yes. I quite see."

Adam felt all the anger leave him. He looked at his own hand to see it had been clenched in a fist preparatory to planting his brother a facer for refusing to make an honest woman of his wife's half sister.

But it seemed as if Isabella was not the only one who had been wronged. Philip looked as if someone had hit him in the stomach.

"She did not tell you, did she?" Adam asked ruefully.

The only sound that emitted from Philip's lips was a frustrated sputter as he shook his head.

"Here, sit down, old man," Adam said in a tone of commiseration as he eased his brother into a chair. "Lord, if this isn't just like her. Isabella was always a flighty piece, but I thought she would have the intelligence to tell you the truth when she found out the father of her child was alive."

"My God," Philip said. "I am a father."

"There, there. Do not take it so hard," Adam said as he tried not to enjoy the look of pure imbecility on Philip's face. His elder brother had a positive gift for making Adam feel like a blockhead. Now Philip was the one caught at a disadvantage. "Young Jamie is really the most engaging little fellow."

"I am going to strangle her," Philip said matter-of-factly.

Thank heaven he no longer had that lost look about him.

Adam smiled, glad that his brother was feeling better once the first shock was over, and moved to the decanters on a shelf to pour Philip a generous glass of his father's strongest and most costly spirits.

"I am afraid I cannot permit you to do so. Marian would never let me hear the end of it," Adam said as he handed his brother the glass. Philip gratefully took it with both hands and lifted it to his lips. "But you *are* going to marry her."

Liquor spurted all over Philip's coat front.

"Blast it, man! What a waste of fine liquor!" Adam remonstrated.

Philip put the glass on his father's desk and buried his face in his hands, as well he might.

"I am as sorry as I can be for you," Adam said, not unsympathetically, "but I am afraid there is no help for it. You are going to have to marry Isabella Grimsby, and may the Lord have mercy on your soul."

Philip's face was grim when he raised it from his hands.

"What have I done?" he asked plaintively. "I left her behind to deal with *this* while I went off to join into the army. And now she hates me."

"Regardless, honor demands that you marry her."

"Yes, I understand. What if she will not have me?" Philip asked.

"Not have you?" Adam repeated in disbelief. "Good God, man. Not even Isabella would be so foolish. You are not only the father of her child, but you are the heir to our father's title. Not one of those overembellished little chits in our father's ballroom would hesitate to snap you up. She will be no different, mark my words."

After all, Adam thought wryly to himself, his handsome, sophisticated brother had always been every little debutante's dream come true. And that was *before* he came back from the war a hero.

Adam felt a lump grow in his throat, and he realized that all his old resentment of his brother was gone. He was inexpressibly moved to be in the same room with Philip. They had not been together since the day Philip had visited him in the Peninsula where he had been stationed with his regiment and vowed to bring honor to his name. Adam had laughed in his face and told his heretofore pampered and hedonistic brother that he would not last three days on campaign.

Then Philip had been reported missing in action, and Adam belatedly realized that, in a peculiar way, he had loved his irritatingly well-favored brother.

A thousand times since that day, Adam had regretted not clasping his brother's hand and wishing him well.

Incredibly, a kind fate had given him the opportunity to make amends for his spitefulness. And so far he had threatened Philip, mocked him, and nearly planted him a facer.

He felt heat rise to his cheeks. His vision blurred with sudden tears. He was going to feel like a bloody fool, but it had to be said.

"Um, Philip?"

Still seated, Philip looked up at him with those dark blue eyes of his, the ones all the ladies swooned over, but for once there was no mockery in them.

"I, um, never thought to see you alive again," Adam persisted doggedly. A hint of incredulous humor lit Philip's eyes, but he managed to keep a straight face. "I, ah, I just wanted to say that when I learned the news of your death was deliberately put about by the war office to cover your activities as a spy, and you were still alive, I was . . . glad."

"Glad," Philip repeated skeptically. "I am touched beyond measure by this effusive expression of goodwill."

Adam scowled at him. Phillip wasn't going to make this easy for him.

"All right. I was damned near ecstatic, if you must know the truth," he admitted.

He had wanted to bawl like a baby, but he wasn't about to tell Philip *that*.

He wished the floor would open up and swallow him.

Then, amazingly, Philip's expression softened and he smiled at Adam.

"Thank you," Philip said as he held out his hand to his brother and Adam clasped it. "I am rather glad to be alive."

Incredibly, a touch of pink crept into Philip's face.

"I suppose it would be fair to admit," he said with a rueful look in his eyes, "that when I learned you had survived the war, I, too, was glad."

Before the brothers could embarrass themselves further, the door to the room crashed open and bounced against the wall before it came to rest ajar.

Adam's maudlin mood dissipated as he grinned at the auburn-haired whirlwind who rushed into the room. When she was angry, his wife did not know her own strength.

God, how he loved her!

Marian, whose other hand grasped the elbow of a protesting and clearly embarrassed Isabella, thrust her half sister into the room before her. Isabella was still wearing the rose pink evening gown, but her hair was even more of a tangle than it had been earlier. She looked as if she had been raking her hands through it. Adam, who had known the formerly elegant Isabella from her cradle, regarded her curiously, for it was one of the few times since Isabella had been a drooling infant that he had seen her look less than exquisite.

"She did not even tell him, Adam," Marian said as she

gave her half sister a look of great disapproval. "Did you ever hear such nonsense? I hope you did not hit him yet."

"No," Adam said. "Fortunately, I discovered as much for myself before it came to that."

Isabella's passionate dark eyes blazed into Philip's with defiance.

Philip knew that what he did now would change his life, Isabella's, and their child's forever.

He must not bungle this as he had all else.

Philip rose from the chair and approached Isabella as she watched him with a wary expression on her face. He put his hands on her shoulders. She turned away so her beautiful face was hidden from him by the dark curtain of her hair.

"Out," he said, conscious of Marian's and Adam's eyes upon them, as a strand of that silky, bewitchingly disheveled hair brushed the top of one of his hands. The sweet rose scent that he always associated with her teased his nostrils.

When he did not hear the sound of retreating footsteps, he barked, "Now!" in a tone of voice that would not be denied, but he did not turn his gaze away from Isabella. When he heard the door close softly, he let out the breath he had not known he was holding.

Isabella flinched slightly when he gently touched her cheek. Her skin was so perfect. He had never forgotten the softness of it.

"Don't," she whispered. "Please. I cannot bear it."

Dear God. What had he done?

"Isabella," he said softly. "I am so sorry, my dear. For everything."

"Marian and Adam took it into their heads that we must marry," she said, turning away from him in agitation. "But you need not be bothered by either of us. No one else knows you are Jamie's father except Marian, Adam, and now you. No one else needs to know."

"What are you talking about? He is my son. Do you think I will permit my brother and his wife to rear *my* child?"

"I have seen the way great men treat the fruits of their little indiscretions . . . and their mothers," Isabella said harshly. "Do you think I want a fate like that for Jamie? My own father's bastard children populated half the countryside during my childhood, being reared in some likely trade by persons who were paid well to keep them from causing my family embarrassment. Marian's mother was forced to marry an army surgeon and go on campaign with him to give her child a name. I have no illusions that you will not be the same, once the novelty of Jamie's existence has worn off for you."

"Isabella—"

"No! You would be willing enough to play at being a father to Jamie until you had legitimate heirs. *Then* you would send him away, after he has learned to love you. Better to let Marian and Adam have him, and for him to be left in my care while they are serving with the regiment. I cannot be his acknowledged mother, but I can have some of the rearing of him for now, at least." She forced back a sob.

He realized it must be torture for her to play the part of a doting aunt to her own son.

Their son.

"He is *mine*," he said firmly. "It is for me to say who will have the rearing of him."

Her eyes were huge with fear.

"You would not take him away from me," she said. "Your father is capable of such cruelty. But surely *you*—"

"Certainly not," he said. "I agree that his place is with you, even if the world thinks Marian is his mother at present. And as the mother of my son, your place is with me."

"You do not *want* to marry me," she said.

"Are you so sure?" he said as he put his hands on her shoulders again. "We dealt together well enough once."

"I am not the girl you knew," she said with a little catch in her voice. "I look at those young, pretty girls in the ballroom, and even though I am of an age with them, I feel so much older. I have changed too much."

"Any one of those little ninnyhammers would bore me

senseless within a fortnight. I am not the foolish man who deserted you," he said solemnly. "I have changed, too. Jamie is ours. I will acknowledge him publicly. At once."

"No, you must not," she said. "Jamie is going to be so confused. He has been told over and over again that Marian is his mama, not me. He is accustomed to thinking of Adam as his father. We would have to tell my father the truth. And Mother."

She gulped with dismay, as well she might. When Lady Grimsby found out that he had impregnated her daughter, Philip realized, she was going to come after him with a club.

"What I do not understand is why it was necessary for Adam and his wife to return from Scotland merely to bring to my attention the small matter of a son I wasn't aware I had fathered," he said. "After all, they could not be bothered to delay their departure until I came home."

He would not admit it to Adam for the world, but he had been disappointed to learn that he had not waited to welcome him back to England and civilization.

"Oh, *that* is not why they left Scotland," Isabella said. "Father was injured in a mishap on the hunting field there, and he was sent home to London to recuperate. Marian bundled Father into a coach for home and Adam, of course, obtained leave to accompany them. When they arrived at Father's London house, Marian settled him into his bedchamber, gave strict instructions for his care to the housekeeper, and, not wishing to inconvenience the household further, Adam and Marian went to your father's town house to spend the night. There they learned from the servants about your father's house party here, and the fact that you and your father apparently were in the process of choosing a young lady of high birth to be your wife from a field of a dozen debutantes."

"So they rushed into Derbyshire to make certain I would not commit myself to one of them," he said ruefully.

Isabella bit her lip. "Yes."

"Perfectly understandable," Philip said. "What I fail to understand, Isabella, is why you did not tell me about Jamie yourself."

"I thought you were dead!" she cried. "I was afraid! What else could I do but hide the pregnancy? Marian protected my reputation by pretending that *she* had given birth to Jamie. As the daughter of an army surgeon—or so the world believed—with no ambition to be accepted by the *ton*, she insisted that she had no reputation to lose. Mother's friends had found some rich, doddering old invalid for her in Bath for her to marry, and Marian was desperate to avoid the match. When she and Adam married, they vowed to rear Jamie as their own. It seemed the perfect solution, although I cried for days when I had to leave him in Derbyshire with them and return to London with Mother."

"This makes no sense," he said, frowning. "Why did you not go to my father when you learned you were pregnant with my child? He would have provided for both of you for my sake."

Isabella planted her hands on her hips and gave him a look that suggested he was the dimmest creature in nature.

"Are you insane? He would have taken him away from me and hidden him with some likely couple so I would never have seen him again! Did you not tell me yourself that would have been Jamie's fate if your father learned one of his sons had fathered a child on the wrong side of the blanket?"

"But I am alive. You could have told *me* as soon as I returned from the continent. I would have married you at once."

"Is that what you think I want? A hole-and-corner marriage to a man who does not want or respect me?"

"My poor girl," he said softly. "How can you ever forgive me? I had no right—"

"It gave me Jamie," she said earnestly. "Having Jamie is worth anything." Her voice broke. "I love him so much. I would have done *anything* to keep him safe from your father."

She looked frightened again.

"When he learns the truth, he will try to persuade you to send Jamie away," she said.

Philip took both her hands in his. They were cold as ice, and he warmed them between his palms.

"He will do *nothing*, I promise you."

"You made a promise to me once before," she said in a small, hurt voice.

"I know," he said. "But I shall keep this one. Believe it."

He would have drawn her into his arms, but the door crashed open again and Philip rolled his eyes when his father stalked into the room with Adam right behind him.

"Is this true?" Lord Revington demanded. "Did you get that wretched girl with child?"

"Yes," Philip said, "and I will do right by her."

"Over my dead body!" roared Lord Revington.

"If need be," Philip murmured.

"I will arrange for the boy to be taken—"

"You will arrange for *nothing*, Father. Do you hear me?" Philip shouted right over Adam's outraged bellow. "Isabella and I will marry, and that is an end to the matter."

He looked at Isabella, whose head was bowed. Her hands were trembling.

Poor girl. As a proposal of marriage, his declaration left much to be desired.

"I had hoped at least *one* of my sons would make a good marriage," Lord Revington grumbled. "Under the circumstances, I think a small, quiet ceremony, perhaps here, in the house, as quickly as possible might be—"

"No," said Philip. "Absolutely not."

Isabella looked up at that.

"My bride is going to be married at St. Paul's during the Season. If her father will not stand the nonsense, I will."

"That would hardly be appropriate," Lord Revington said, frowning.

Philip took Isabella's hands in his. "Not for *my* wife a hole-and-corner marriage," he said with a crooked smile. "I will leave the world in no doubt that I respect my wife and the mother of my child above all women."

Isabella's lips parted, but she said nothing.

Lord Revington threw his hands up in exasperation.

"And what am I going to tell all those young ladies in the ballroom?"

"Excellent point," Philip said. He tucked Isabella's hand in his. "Come, my dear. Let us go at once to the ballroom and make the announcement that you have consented to make me the happiest of men."

But when they moved to the doorway, they found the way barred by a determined Lady Grimsby and Marian, who shrugged her shoulders when Isabella gave her a questioning look. Obviously Lady Grimsby had been told the truth, because she was looking daggers at Philip.

"So, you are going to marry my daughter, are you, young man?" she said angrily. "And high time!"

"We are going to make the announcement now," Philip said as he unflinchingly met her gaze. "Do you care to join us?"

Lady Grimsby attached her fingers to Isabella's wrist.

"You are going *nowhere,* my girl, until Betty does something with the rat's nest you have made of your hair!" she exclaimed. She cast her eye over the assembled gentlemen. "You," she told them, "will wait."

Then she gave a dismissive sniff in Marian's direction, for she had always heartily disliked her husband's love child, and marched Isabella out of the room.

"Bad blood in that family. I always thought so," Lord Revington growled. "I hope you know what you are doing, boy."

"I do," Philip said firmly.

CHAPTER 10

When Philip walked into the ballroom some time later, all the young ladies turned toward him with smiles of expectation on their pretty faces. To his left, well to the back of the room, Isabella waited for her cue. Now her hair was dressed in an elegant chignon, which emphasized her beautiful eyes and exquisitely sculptured cheekbones. Her face was expressionless.

At her side, her mother whispered instructions in her ear, but Isabella plainly was not listening. Instead, she stared at Philip.

Expecting him to make this right.

He straightened his shoulders, and a hush fell over the group as he stepped up to the platform where the orchestra played. His father already had raised his arms to signal for attention. One dour look from Lord Revington sent the musicians scurrying off.

"It is my pleasure," Lord Revington said solemnly, "to announce the betrothal of my son, Philip, to a young woman who is one of your fellow guests. Her father, General Lord Grimsby, is not here to do the honors, so, in his place, I will present to you the future Mrs. Philip Lyonbridge, Miss Isabella Grimsby."

Philip extended his hand toward Isabella and she approached him, unsmiling, but with all the grace and self-possession of a queen going to her coronation—or her execution—as the guests made exclamations of surprise and, after a startled moment, broke into scattered applause.

He took her hand and drew her close beside him as those guests who had recovered their composure approached the couple to offer their congratulations.

The marquess, who stood soothing his daughter, a crestfallen Lady Anne, shot Philip a look that should have felled him on the spot. The marchioness gave a hiss of displeasure and stalked out of the room.

Impatiently, Lord Revington signaled the musicians to return. They had been skulking at the edge of the ballroom, not quite certain what to do with themselves.

They struck up a waltz. Because it was clearly expected, Philip put his arm around Isabella's waist and guided her into the dance.

"I used to dream of this moment," she said softly. "The flowers. The music. Your arms around me. It would have meant so much once. Now I feel nothing."

"Isabella," he said reproachfully.

She looked up into his eyes.

"I want you to know the truth. There have already been too many lies between us. I might, in time, learn to respect you. That is the most that you can expect of this marriage. If that will not be enough for you, we must end this now."

"It will be enough," he said.

Another lie. It was a wonder his tongue did not turn black in his mouth.

He once had possessed the whole of Isabella's earnest young heart. Her face had once lit from within at the very sight of him. She had been too innocent to hide her love, and the sweet agony of wanting her while she was betrothed to his brother nearly drove him mad.

God help him, he wanted her to love him like that again.

To say this now, he knew, would be fatal.

She would never believe him, for he had betrayed her when she needed him most.

He could hear the derisive whispers all about him. The young women who had competed so fiercely for his attention were united, now, in their jealousy of the woman who had captured the prize. He knew that they were criticizing her gown, her manner, her circumstance of having come to the contest saddled with a child of dubious origins. They would be quick to spread ugly rumors about her if they detected the slightest irregularity about their betrothal.

"My desire was to protect you from the censure of Society, but I seem to have caused the opposite effect," he said ruefully.

"It does not matter," she said. Her chin was lifted in defiance, and her face was like exquisitely sculpted marble for all the emotion it showed. "I am no stranger to mean-spirited gossip."

It occurred to Philip that he had never heard Isabella say an unkind word about anyone, for all her air of fashionably blasé sophistication. This made her unique among any young lady of his acquaintance. He knew that any young woman in the ballroom would have been quick to rid herself of an unwanted child conceived out of wedlock so she could resume her social life and make a good marriage among the *ton*.

Thank heaven it was the brave and compassionate Isabella who had given birth to his child. Otherwise, he might never have had the opportunity to know him.

"Philip, the music has stopped," Isabella whispered.

He blinked and realized the music, indeed, had stopped, and he still held her waist in a possessive grasp. Finger by finger, he forced himself to release her. Every eye in the room was upon him.

Philip pulled himself together, smiled for the sake of his audience, and offered his arm. Isabella accepted it, and he escorted her to her mother in silence. Lady Grimsby favored him with a smile so fierce he had to force himself not to retreat a step.

Lady Grimsby, it was plain, was delighted to emerge victorious from among all the matchmaking mothers who had been determined to procure Philip's status and future title for their daughters. He did not make the error of attributing her seeming pleasure in the match to any fondness for Philip himself.

He knew her kind.

She would marry Isabella off to a performing bear if it had a suitable pedigree and was in line to inherit a fortune or title, especially now that she perceived her own daughter as damaged goods. At least he could spare Isabella *that*.

"I will leave for London in the morning, my lady," he told his future mother-in-law, "to do myself the honor of calling on Lord Grimsby."

She gave a little nod of compliance.

"Naughty, impetuous boy," she said for the benefit of all the cocked ears surrounding them. She gave him a little pat on the shoulder with her closed fan for emphasis. "You should have called on my husband *before* you and your father made the announcement."

Philip was too accustomed to such games to let this one catch him off guard.

He gallantly raised Isabella's hand to his lips and kissed it.

"I would apologize, my lady, if I could do so with any conviction whatsoever. Your daughter is such a delight to me that I could not bear to wait a moment longer before proclaiming our happiness to all our dear friends."

Isabella gave him a look of utter incredulity.

"Very well, Philip," Lady Grimsby said. "I would consider it a great favor if you would escort Isabella and me to London with you." She gave her daughter a look that defied her to argue. "It is time we returned home."

"I suppose you are right," Isabella said. "I will order Betty to pack Jamie's clothes tonight along with mine, and—"

Lady Grimsby fixed her with a forbidding glare.

"Surely you do not expect me to listen to his chattering all the way to London!"

"But . . . you would not expect me to leave him behind," Isabella said, shocked.

"He can very well stay at Major Lyonbridge's house with his staff. Or here with Lord Revington's. I care not which."

"The boy goes with us," Philip said quietly but firmly.

"I beg your pardon," Lady Grimsby said, transferring The Look to him.

But Philip was too accustomed to dealing with his own difficult parent to be cowed by her.

"My brother and his wife are returning to London, as well, and we will travel together," he said. "Their purpose in coming to Derbyshire has been accomplished, and once Marian is assured of Lord Grimsby's comfort and eventual recovery, she will return with Adam to Scotland. Naturally, Isabella will keep the child with her."

"Surely there is *someone* in your brother's household who can take charge of this boy while we are in London. There are all the wedding plans to make, and London is no place for a—"

"The boy goes with us," Philip said again.

Lady Grimsby compressed her lips.

"As you wish," she said sourly.

"Philip," his father called from behind him. "Come here, boy. There is someone here whom you must meet."

Philip glanced behind him to see Lord Revington standing with one of the more tedious members of the House of Lords, no doubt someone whose patronage he wished to procure for his son. Apparently the old man had not given up his ambition to set Philip on the road to a brilliant political career.

He sighed, but there really was no help for it.

"Until tomorrow," he said to Isabella.

"Thank you," she whispered. She gave him a shy little smile, and he forced himself to walk away to keep from making a complete fool of himself.

Isabella watched him go and sighed.

"You have much explaining to do, young woman," Lady Grimsby said under her breath.

"Not here, Mother," she said, looking about uncomfortably.

Adam and Marian had slipped into the room while the announcement of Philip and Isabella's engagement was being made.

Incredibly, Adam solicitously settled his wife with some of the other ladies and approached Isabella with a smile on his face that could almost be described as friendly.

"May I have this dance, Isabella?" He lowered his voice. "We are to be brother and sister twice over, it seems."

Lady Grimsby looked as if she might protest, but the forceful Major Lyonbridge swept Isabella away without a backward glance.

"Bless you, Adam," Isabella said in relief. "How did you know I was in dire need of rescue?"

"I know the sign of an impending bear-garden jaw when I see one, even if I cannot hear it," he said with a lopsided grin. "As for blessing *me,* you had better direct your gratitude toward Marian, for she is the one who insisted that I dance with you. For my part, I would have stood back and watched Lady Grimsby have at it. The lady has terrified me since I was a child."

Isabella had to laugh.

"*That* puts me in my place. My thanks to both of you, then."

"This business of your marriage is going to be exceedingly awkward," he said, sobering. "You know, I quite liked the idea of being Jamie's father."

"As long as you were stationed four hundred miles away from him," she said dryly.

"He is very . . . active. A good boy, but a handful," he admitted. "Marian and I would like to take him with us to our house tonight."

"Is that necessary?" she asked. "He should be fast asleep

by now, and if you wake him, he may not go back to sleep again. The night air can be injurious to—"

"It is August, my dear. The night air is positively salubrious. We are his parents," Adam said gently. "For the present, at least. We have missed him. It is only for the one night, after all. Can you not give us that much?"

"Yes, of course," she said.

"Do not look so stricken. We will bring him here tomorrow before we set off for London. I gather we are all to travel together. Marian will explain to Jamie that his *Uncle Philip* wishes to become better acquainted with him because he will be marrying Aunt Isabella, and so he will be seeing much of him once Marian and I return to Scotland."

He gave her a warning look and indicated with a nod of his head the dancing couples around them.

"That is a kind thought," she forced herself to say. Now that she was to marry Philip, she wanted to lay claim to her son. It had been torture to pretend he was another woman's child all this time. She wanted him to be acknowledged as *hers*. But she knew that she must be discreet a while longer for all their sakes.

Isabella and Philip briefly had discussed how best to handle the situation before they returned to the ballroom for the announcement of their betrothal.

They could hardly tell the world that, oh, by the by, the child the world believed was Adam and Marian Lyonbridge's son was actually fathered by his brother, and Isabella gave birth to him in secret. Now that Philip has decided to marry Jamie's mother, whom he impregnated on an aborted and hushed-up flight to Gretna Green and then abandoned, the boy would now be living with him and Isabella upon their belated marriage, and calling *them* Mama and Papa.

This would precipitate the very scandal that Isabella and Marian had worked so hard to avoid.

Instead, Marian and Adam would return to Scotland, leaving "their" son in Isabella's care, and Isabella would simply take him to her new household when she married Philip. Over time, the fact that Jamie was a permanent resident of their nursery apartments would occasion no remark, especially if Adam continued to serve with his regiment over a period of years, which he had every intention of doing.

"I cannot like this idea of taking Jamie home with you tonight," she said. "Perhaps I should go with you—"

Adam gave her a look that was not unsympathetic.

"Isabella, he lived with us for a time after our wedding. Trust me, I am abundantly aware of how much mischief Jamie can get into if one is not vigilant. You cannot keep him wrapped in cotton wool all his life."

"Adam, Jamie is two years old," Isabella said. How *dare* he patronize her! "And, trust *me,* you have no idea how much mischief that child is capable of getting into."

Adam threw his head back and laughed.

"Oh, I think I do. Do not worry, Isabella. Marian and I, between us, are capable of keeping a careful eye on one small boy for one night without your supervision."

At that moment, Isabella's maid, Betty, came into the ballroom with Jamie in her arms. His dark hair was mussed, and his eyes were round, like an owl's. He struggled to get down, looked around at all the curious eyes staring at him, spotted Marian, gave a boyish squeal of glee, and ran for her. Marian gave an answering cry, got out of her chair, knelt, and held her arms out.

Betty spotted Isabella and hurried at once to her side.

"Miss Isabella, he woke up wanting Mrs. Lyonbridge, and he cried fit to wake the dead when his nurserymaid told him he must wait to see her until the morning. I was afraid he would make himself ill."

"You did right, Betty," Isabella said as she watched Jamie run into Marian's arms.

"Mama, Mama, Mama!" Jamie cried excitedly.

Despite the irregularity of introducing a small child to a ballroom twice in one evening, a soft, collective chuckle swept the room. He looked so adorable in his little white cotton nightshirt.

Isabella felt a pang of jealousy stab her heart as Marian cuddled Jamie close. She could see the glow of happiness on his little face. Then he turned, looked right at Isabella and gave another glad cry. Isabella reached for him as he came running.

"Papa!" he cried.

Isabella's heart plummeted. She had forgotten all about Adam, who was standing right beside her.

"There's a good lad," Adam said as he scooped the boy off his feet and made him giggle. Jamie snuggled into Adam's chest, managing to avoid the medals. "Do you want to go back to bed now?"

"No! Not sleepy! I want to stay and watch the pretty ladies dance," he said.

Clearly, Jamie was wide awake and not going to go to sleep any time soon. His eyes were alert and full of mischief.

"Perhaps, instead, you would like to come home with Mama and me in the coach and stay the night in our own house."

He winked at Isabella, who frowned.

"Yes! Yes!" Jamie said, bouncing in Adam's arms in his excitement.

"Good. Go with Betty now," Adam said. When the child would have protested, he added, "She will dress you in your clothes for the trip home. Mama and I will join you directly."

"Yes, Papa," Jamie said excitedly as he went quite willingly into Betty's arms.

"I will help you pack your things, Jamie," Isabella said quickly. "You would not leave without kissing me good-bye."

Jamie gave her a sweet smile that made her heart turn over and held his arms out so she could take him from Betty.

"Isabella! You cannot leave the ballroom now," Lady Grimsby said in severe displeasure. She grasped Isabella's arm.

"Certainly we can," said Philip. Isabella started in surprise. She had not seen him approach. "I have a wish to become better acquainted with the lad. Come along, Isabella."

With that, he put an arm around Isabella's waist, and Lady Grimsby had no choice but to relinquish her hold on Isabella or embark upon an undignified tug of war.

"Hurry, Aunt Isabella," Jamie said, his eyes shining. "I am going home with Mama and Papa."

"He is too heavy for you," Philip said as he reached to take the boy from her. "Let me carry him."

"He is not," Isabella said as she tightened her grip on Jamie and quickened her pace to keep Philip from taking him.

Jamie was *hers*. Philip could wait until tomorrow to become better acquainted with him!

CHAPTER 11

"Papa! Papa! May I ride with you on your horse to London?" Jamie asked excitedly as Isabella put some of his clothes into a small traveling case for him.

Isabella's hands froze on his little shirt, the one with the tiny frill around the neck that made him look so grown-up. She looked at Adam with alarm.

"Perhaps," he said, meeting her eyes. "If you are a good boy."

"I do not see any harm in it," said Marian, who was attempting to button Jamie's coat at the time. She gave a little laugh when Jamie twisted out of her grasp to look at Adam. "Jamie, love. You must stand still. We cannot go home until you are dressed."

He stilled immediately, Isabella noted with some resentment.

She directed a glare at Marian.

"Well, it will do him no harm," Marian said firmly to her sister, as if Isabella had voiced her objection out loud. "Adam will hold him quite securely, I promise you. You know he would *never* let any harm come to Jamie."

"Thank you, Mama!" cried Jamie as he threw his arms

around Marian's neck. Marian closed her eyes and hugged back. "I missed you so much," she said softly.

There were tears in her eyes when she looked at Isabella.

I am so selfish, Isabella thought to herself. *Marian loves him, and I cannot wait to take him away from her.* But Marian had left Jamie without hesitation when she had the opportunity to follow Adam and the regiment to Scotland. It was clear that if she had to choose, Marian would always choose her husband over Jamie. Isabella *never* would have left her son behind to follow some man.

Of course, Marian, who loved them both, had known that Jamie would be safe and happy with Isabella, and that Isabella would treasure this stolen time with her son.

Adam's face was solemn as Jamie tugged on his coat. Adam picked the child up.

"Will you stay home with me for always and always?" Jamie asked.

"No, son," Adam said sadly as he glanced at Isabella. "I must go back to Scotland to be with my regiment."

"Can you and Mama not take me with you?" Jamie asked. The way his lower lip quivered almost broke Isabella's heart. "I am old enough to ride a pony of my own."

"I wish we could," Adam said as he ruffled Jamie's hair. "But let us not think of that now. We are going to London, and I will take you up on my horse for a little while." He glanced at Isabella again. "But for most of the journey, you must ride in the carriage with Aunt Isabella and Uncle Philip."

"Why?" the boy asked.

"Because they are going to take care of you once Mama and I go to Scotland. You will be a good boy, will you not?"

"Yes, Papa," Jamie said wistfully. "When I grow up, can I go to the army with you?"

Marian looked away quickly. Isabella felt tears fill her own eyes at the thought of her little boy growing up and possibly going to war.

"Perhaps," Adam said. He forced himself to smile. "But

let us not think of that. Tonight you are all ours." He turned Jamie upside down to make him giggle.

"Adam, you will make him wild, and he will not sleep!" Isabella snapped before she could stop herself.

"No matter," Marian said, looking hard at her half sister. "Tonight is a celebration." She moved closer to Adam and Jamie. Adam closed his arms around Marian and the child. "For the three of us."

Philip appeared in the doorway.

"The carriage is waiting for you," he said.

"Thank you," Adam said as he put Jamie down. The brothers looked at each other for a moment. Then Philip walked forward with his hand extended and Adam took it to give it a shake.

Marian stepped forward to hug Isabella.

"It will be all right," Marian whispered into Isabella's ear, but Isabella could hear the tears in her voice. She turned to Jamie with a bright smile on her face. "Jamie, darling. Kiss Aunt Isabella good-bye."

Jamie dutifully put his little arms around Isabella's neck when she bent to accept his kiss on her cheek.

"I love you, Aunt Isabella," he told her.

"I love you, Jamie."

"Give Uncle Philip a kiss," Marian instructed.

Surprised, Philip crouched down so he would be at the boy's level.

Unsmiling, Jamie considered Philip from behind the shelter of Marian's skirts. She gently pushed him a bit forward.

"All right," the child said hesitantly.

Philip's heart was beating hard as he took the child's shoulders. Jamie dutifully kissed Philip's cheek. Then, in that openhearted way of his, he put his arms around Philip's neck. Jamie smelled of clean linen and something sweet, like milk.

"Good evening, Jamie," Philip said solemnly. "Pleasant dreams."

"But not for a while, eh, Jamie?" said Adam. "We are going to stay up late tonight."

Jamie gave a cheer as Adam hoisted him to his shoulder. Adam put his free arm around Marian and the three of them moved away. Marian turned back and gave them a shy little wave.

Isabella returned it, and gave a sob as the three of them passed beyond the doorway. She felt Philip's hands on her shoulders, and then he rested his chin on her head.

"He did not even look back at me," she said brokenly.

"You will see him tomorrow," Philip reminded her.

She turned to face him.

"I know that. But he is going to spend the night away from me, and he will not miss me at all now that he has Marian and Adam. You have no idea what it is like for me."

"Do I not?" he asked. "He is my son, too."

"You did not even know he was your son until a few hours ago."

"Has it been only a few hours?" he asked ruefully. "It seems longer. I am a father. I can hardly comprehend it." He took her hand. "And I am going to be a husband."

She tried to take her hand away, but he held it in a strong grip.

"I intend to be a good and faithful husband to you, Isabella."

"Please," she said, looking away from him. "You do not have to say these things. I truly wish you would not. I am aware that you are marrying me because your honor compels you to do so."

"My honor and my extremely muscular brother, who has told me he will break every bone in my body if I do not," Philip said with a humorous sigh.

"Do you think he would?" Isabella asked pensively.

"Oh, yes," Philip said. "Adam does not threaten. He delivers. He would welcome an excuse to rearrange my face. He has been looking for one for years."

She actually smiled.

"That would be a great pity," she said, looking up into his eyes.

"Thank you," he said, surprised by the heartfelt compliment. Taking a chance, he offered his arm. "The ball is still in full swing. May I beg the honor of a dance with my fiancée?"

She cocked her head to one side, considering.

"Are you mocking me, Captain Lyonbridge?"

"Never."

At that, she took his arm.

"Very well, then," she said. "But I shall expect you to escort me to supper and taste every dish before I do. I strongly suspect there is at least one young lady among my former friends who would take great pleasure in poisoning me."

Isabella sat across from Philip in the coach and was almost sorry her mother elected to travel with her maid in the second carriage instead of with them in order to escape, as she put it, all the botheration of traveling with a noisy child.

The child in question was seated before Adam in the saddle of his horse, and Marian was riding at their side on a pretty chestnut mare from Lord Revington's stable.

Without the child in the coach, Isabella realized she and Philip had little to say to one another.

Or perhaps they had too much.

She looked out the window to watch her son's jubilant face.

"He loves horses," she said, worried. "The bigger and more dangerous the better. I hope Adam is holding him securely."

Philip left his seat to sit beside Isabella and watch their son with her.

"I would not give twopence for a boy who did not love horses," Philip said, sounding proud. "Adam and I were both horse-mad before we were out of leading strings. It is bred into all the Lyonbridge men."

He put his hand over hers.

"Isabella," he said.

She kept watching Jamie.

"Yes?" she said absently.

"Look at me, please."

Reluctantly, she drew her gaze from the window. In her heart of hearts, she believed that as long as her son was under her eye, nothing very dreadful could happen to him.

Philip put his arm around her shoulders, and she gave him a suspicious look.

"What is this?" she asked as she drew back to give herself some distance.

"I know nothing about children," Philip said solemnly. He sighed. "Being in disguise and in the hands of the enemy when I knew that the slightest mistake in my imposture could bring death is not nearly as terrifying as this business of being a parent."

Isabella softened and turned her hand in his so that their fingers grasped one another's.

"There is no way to prepare for it, believe me," she said. "I had six months to become adjusted to the prospect—that is when I realized that I was going to have a baby—and still it was such a shock when it happened. It is *still* a shock."

He shook his head.

"And you went through all of that alone."

"Hardly," she said. "I had Marian, thank heaven. And my maid, Betty, and the servants, of course. It was not easy to hide the truth from them. Or from my mother. Fortunately, she loathes the country and so did not come to Derbyshire often enough to discover the truth."

"You must hate me for subjecting you to that," he said.

She thought about it.

"By the time I knew that I was going to have your son, we received word that you were missing. Then we received word that you were dead. Hating you would have been rather pointless."

"And when you learned I was alive?"

She gave a mirthless laugh.

"Very well. Then perhaps I hated you a little," she admitted.

How odd life is, Isabella thought. Never during that harrowing time did she dream that someday she would be having a civilized conversation with Philip in a carriage as they watched their son laugh in the sunshine.

"I look at Jamie, and it still seems a miracle that this wonderful creature came from me," she said.

"From us," Philip said, "although I can take little credit for what he has become."

He took her hands again.

"Thank you," he said. Incredibly, she could see that his eyes were moist. "Thank you for the gift of my son."

She raised her eyebrows and withdrew her hands from him.

"You do not have him yet," she said coolly. "Look! Adam is signaling for us to stop."

Philip gave the desired order by striking his walking stick on the roof of the carriage. A footman opened the door and soon Adam was handing a ruddy-faced, pouting boy into the carriage.

"There you go, lad," Adam said as he gave the wriggling boy to Isabella. "Your mother says you have been outdoors long enough. She does not want you to become sunburned."

When he said the words "your mother," he averted his eyes from Isabella's.

"It is time for you to have a rest, Jamie," Isabella said. The child's lower lip stuck out a mile.

"Not sleepy," Jamie murmured. His eyes were at half-mast. Isabella knew very well, because Marian had told her, that Adam had allowed Jamie to stay up half the night. How like a man to permit a child to tire himself to the point of exhaustion and then hand the cranky little fellow over to someone else.

"Perhaps not," Isabella said, "but *I* am tired. I would like to rest, and I would like for you to rest with me. Will you do that?"

"Yes, Aunt Isabella," Jamie said with a sweet smile. He turned to Philip. "Will you tell us a story? Aunt Isabella would like that."

"A . . . story?" he repeated, completely at a loss.

"Jamie is in the habit of hearing a story before he goes to sleep," Isabella explained.

"Papa told me a story about when he was in the war," Jamie said. "About marching and riding his horse. Papa knows the best stories."

"We shall see about that," Philip said, on his mettle.

CHAPTER 12

The afternoon sun cast Philip's face in partial shadow as Isabella stole a glance at him. He had gone back to the opposite seat once Jamie had fallen asleep, and now he was staring straight ahead at the wall of the coach at a point just above her head.

"I had no idea," she whispered to him. "No idea at all."

He looked at her with unfocused eyes. His smile was forced.

"Few people have," he said. "Do you think my story frightened the boy? I would not want to give him nightmares."

"No," she said as she brushed the dark hair from Jamie's slightly sleep-dampened forehead. "You made it sound almost . . . humorous."

"Compared with the tales I did not tell him, it almost was."

Jamie had actually laughed at Philip's description of how he was forced to hide himself in a flour barrel in the French camp after his escape and emerged covered with flour. He had pinched his nose together to keep from sneezing as the French soldiers scurried about, looking for him. Later, a leap into a river saved him from capture, and he held his breath for what seemed to be forever. Mercifully, the French assumed he was drowned and went away. Then he nearly got shot by the British sentries when he came squelching into their camp in his ruined boots and saturated uniform, which had shrunk by a third of its size and left his bare wrists gangling at the ends of his arms.

That was when he met the colonel, who recruited him to spy on the enemy. There were not that many British soldiers available who spoke unaccented Spanish and could successfully infiltrate the enemy camp. Philip always had a gift for languages.

And so back he went to the French camp—after his mustache and a scraggly beard had grown out—to outwit the enemy by pretending to be a servant.

Quite a cheerful little adventure, the way he told it.

Except for the haunted look in his eyes when he told the tale.

"It was . . . how do I describe this? For more than a year, I did not hear my own name spoken. I did not speak my own language. I *became* a gregarious, simpleminded buffoon, and I began to doubt that Philip Lyonbridge, son and heir of Viscount Revington, had ever existed."

He gave a self-deprecating little gesture of impatience.

"You would not understand," he said.

Isabella looked down at the child resting in her arms.

"Oh, I believe I would," she said ruefully. "What do you think I was doing while your child was growing inside me? Isabella Grimsby had disappeared. She laughed. She talked. She even went to a few parties and flirted a little when she was compelled to do so. But inside was this frightened, half-wild thing who was terrified that someone would learn her shameful secret. I fled to the country and dismissed all the servants so no one would know."

"Isabella," he said as he reached out to grasp her hand. She quickly drew back out of his reach.

"Then I learned you were dead," she said stonily. She had promised herself that she would not lower herself to reproach, but she could not help it.

"Isabella," he said again.

"I could have lost him. My grief was that strong. I do not know what would have happened to him or to me if Marian had not come to take care of me. My thanks to her was the ruination of her reputation. And now I am going to take Jamie away from her."

Philip looked out the window at his brother and sister-in-law, riding side by side. Marian was laughing at something Adam had said. It almost hurt to watch them.

"They will have each other," Philip said wistfully. His eyes rested on the child in Isabella's arms. "And we will have him."

"He is all we will have," she said flatly.

"There will be more children," he said, looking straight ahead. "I will not press you for this. Not right away. But this will be a real marriage in every sense of the word."

"Naturally," she said. "But I do not expect to find my part too onerous. It will not be long before you tire of me and turn to others, after all."

He gave her a look of pure exasperation.

"Is that what you think?"

"That is what I *know*," she said. "My father. Your father. Every man in our world. Why would you be any different?"

"Because I—" He stopped and clenched his jaw. "Never mind. I might as well save my breath."

"Yes," Isabella said. "You might as well. I go into this marriage with my eyes wide open. It is better so."

"I have done this to you," he said softly. "I have made you hard."

"You have made me strong," she corrected him. "Nothing will ever hurt me that much again. You have already betrayed me, and at the time when my heart was most vulnerable."

"I know this," he said. "And I have done everything I can to make amends."

"It is more than I expected of you," she said. "I am content with that."

Philip looked at her beautiful, sad face and saw that she meant it.

At that moment, he resolved to prove her wrong.

He *would* crack the protective coating of ice that surrounded her heart and make her love him again. His greatest ally in the task lay sleeping in her arms.

General Lord Grimsby straightened from a sitting position on his bed of infirmity and by sheer will forced himself to his feet. For the moment, he lowered himself to using the hateful cane to assist his ascent, but he vowed that in a week's time he would consign the thing to the fire.

He stood, tottering, then he found his balance and gave a deep breath of satisfaction. Almost at once his lower back nearly brought him to his knees with pain.

At that moment, a fire-tressed termagant entered the room and glared at him out of wrathful green eyes.

God, she was magnificent in her anger, but she could not hold a candle for sheer temper to her mother, the late, much-lamented Annie Randall and the love of General Grimsby's life.

Too bad he had been married when he met her, and that when she learned the truth, she married another man to give their child a name.

"What do you think you are doing?" she demanded. "I *knew* you would do this the moment my back was turned."

"I have work, girl," he said. "I cannot be lying about in bed all the day long."

Her hands knotted into fists on her hips. These were not the delicate, pampered hands of a lady, but the strong, skilled, work-roughened hands of an army nurse. Of course, due to her husband's position she was not listed as such on the rolls. Officially, her role at the hospital was honorary only. However, hospital staff members who neglected their patients found her a force to be reckoned with. And heaven help the invalid on *her* ward who did not obey her orders to the letter. Her husband's celebrated ferocity in battle was nothing to it.

Lord, he was proud of her, although he could not acknowl-

edge her as his daughter. Even so, he gave her his most forbidding scowl.

"This is none of your concern, girl." He moved a bit on
his legs. He forced himself not to wince.

"None of my concern! You are my . . . my husband's commanding officer. And the physician ordered you most strictly
to stay in bed to give the bones a chance to heal. It is why
Adam and I brought you home to London, after all."

"Dashed nonsense," he grumbled. "There was no reason
for me to come back just to consult some physician of your
choosing."

"Adam agreed with me," she said almost smugly.

Moreover, Adam had threatened to forcibly put him in the
carriage to London if he would not go willingly. If General
Grimsby had not been half dead of pain at the time, he would
have had the fellow drawn up on charges of insubordination.

"There is nothing so very surprising in that," he said with
a snort of derision. "I never thought I would see the best of
my officers, a man who struck terror in the hearts of the enemy,
brought around a girl's thumb. Pitiful, I call it."

Another moment of this pain, he thought, restraining himself from putting an aching hand to his back from sheer will,
and I am going to disgrace myself by bursting into tears.

Yet he could hardly back down now. Was he a raw recruit,
to be felled by a mere tumble from a horse, or, more to the
point, a doddering old man to be bullied by a bossy female
less than half his age?

He *would* be the master in his own house!

Even if the pain in his back was about to bring him to his
knees.

"What is all this fuss about?" demanded his wife as she
swept into the room. "We can hear you shouting all the way
to the parlor."

She gave Marian a dismissive sniff.

"What are *you* doing here?" she asked the girl. "That
child is asking for you."

The boy was never Jamie to her. Or your son. Or even *the*

child. He was always *that* child. Lady Grimsby despised her husband's natural daughter only a shade more than she loathed her husband, so she never tired of making it clear how much she resented the presence of Marian and the boy in her house. Since the boy was Lord Grimsby's grandson, albeit on the wrong side of the blanket, and he had grown fond of the lively, precocious youngster, her disapproval of Jamie had the happy effect of annoying her husband, as well.

Lady Grimsby was nothing if not efficient in expressing her acrimony, for all that the beautiful matron pretended in company to be nothing more than a gracious ornament to Society. To those whom she perceived as her inferiors, she could be scathing.

Incredibly, she smiled at her husband.

"I see you are up and about, my lord," she said, looking pleased. "I am certain you are eager to return to Scotland and your regiment."

Not nearly so eager as she was to see the back of him, the general was willing to wager.

In that, they were in complete agreement for one of the few times in their tempestuous marriage.

General Grimsby noted sourly that he would have to make a notation in his journal to commemorate this rare occurrence.

"Just so, my dear. I will make arrangements this afternoon," he said. Heaven knew his life would be intolerable if he had to stay in his house in London with his wife after Adam and Marian returned to Scotland. He credited the longevity of this marriage—and the fact that neither he nor his wife had strangled the other—to the fact that he had served with his regiment far away from her most of the time.

"You cannot," Marian objected. "I *forbid* you to do this thing!"

Lady Grimsby raised her eyebrows.

"I hardly think *you* have anything to say to it," she said smugly. "He is *my* husband, after all."

"And you do not give *twopence* for him!"

"How dare you say such a thing, you little—" Lady Grimsby said, turning on Marian. Her hands opened and closed like claws.

The door came open with a bang against the wall as Major Adam Lyonbridge strode into the sickroom.

"What is the meaning of this?" he snapped. "My lord, you should be in bed."

"I will not be bullied by *you,* Adam. I was the godfather at your christening, for the Lord's sake," the general snapped right back.

"This is no business of yours, Major Lyonbridge," Lady Grimsby said triumphantly. "Kindly remove your wife from this room and—"

The major gave a snort of humor when he glanced at his wife's angry face.

"Not I!" he said. "I have no wish to have my face scratched for me."

"As you please," Lady Grimsby said smugly. "The matter is quite settled. I shall direct your valet to pack your things, my lord. Such nonsense, anyway, this flight back to London merely because you have received a minor injury."

"Marian wanted a physician from Chelsea Hospital to have a look at me," the general said. "Well, the man's come and gone, and he had nothing better to say than that I should lie about on my back for a month, and then he will return to see if he wishes to operate on me."

"A man in your position has responsibilities," Lady Grimsby said. "It is hardly appropriate for you to be consulting some person employed by Chelsea Hospital who treats officers and enlisted men alike."

"Quite so," the general said. "I will make my preparations immediately. Tell my valet I wish to dress."

At this, Marian's face crumpled and she let out a loud sob that almost caused the general to lose his precarious balance on his cane.

"Marian," cried her horrified husband as he reached out for her, but she pushed his hands away.

"Young woman, this is hardly becoming behavior," Lady Grimsby chided her. "If you cannot control yourself, I must ask you to leave this room at once."

"Yes, do come, Marian," said the major.

"No!" the sobbing woman cried. "I won't! I have just as much right to be here as *she* does."

"How *dare* you?" Lady Grimsby cried, drawing herself up in magnificent disdain to annihilate this upstart's pretensions. She could not disguise her satisfaction, however. It was never enough for Lady Grimsby merely to have won. She dearly loved to see her enemy spread dead on the floor at her feet, bleeding profusely. Figuratively, of course. And it was clear that Marian was extremely distressed by Lady Grimsby's victory.

"Love, do give over," the major whispered as he put his arm around the sobbing woman.

"No!" Marian cried out as she rushed to the general. She took his free hand, the one that wasn't wrapped, white-knuckled, on the head of the cane. "You must not go!"

"She is hysterical," Lady Grimsby said, smiling thinly. "Someone should slap her." Clearly she would have enjoyed having the honor. Her movement forward was arrested by a single, wrathful look from Major Lyonbridge.

"What is it to you, girl, whether I stay or go?" the general asked.

"I have already lost one father to a fall from a horse," she said brokenly. It was true that her foster father, Dr. Lawrence Randall, the man her mother had married to give Marian a name, had died in just such a way. "I will not lose another."

At the risk of landing on the floor in a broken heap, the general put his free arm around Marian and allowed her to sob on his chest. Over her head, he met his wife's furious eyes.

"I am staying," he said defiantly. He kissed the top of his daughter's head. "As long as the surgeon says I must."

"And you will obey his orders," Marian's muffled voice emitted from his chest.

"Yes," he said.

At that, she carefully extricated herself from his embrace and grabbed his arm.

"Help me, Adam," she said to her husband. The major strode quickly to the bed and took the general's weight so he could lower him to the bed.

Lord Grimsby could have wept in relief, and not only for the cessation of pain in his back.

"You do care for me, just a little," he said wonderingly as he reached up to touch Marian's damp cheek.

"Of course I do, you stubborn old man," she said with a tremulous smile. "You must get well quickly, so you can return to the regiment as soon as possible."

She took her husband's hand and her father's, so they were joined in a circle of affection.

"We will miss you, but we want you back in health," the major said.

None of them looked up when Lady Grimsby bared her teeth in a furious snarl and stamped her foot before she flounced out of the room.

CHAPTER 13

Isabella sighed as she regarded the cranky but wide-awake child she had been trying to pacify for the past quarter hour.

Jamie had slept long in the carriage after his ride on horseback with Adam, and although Isabella was ready to drop from fatigue, he needed to shake off the restriction imposed upon him by the close confines of the carriage to run and play or he would never sleep that night. Unless she created a diversion, he would go clattering through the halls in her father's cavernous house and make her mother even more furious with him than she already was.

She shuddered to think of what damage a small, enterprising boy with his keen talent for mischief could achieve in a large, formal, beautifully appointed house filled with treasures gathered over two decades of tasteful acquisition by one of London's most accomplished hostesses.

Even Isabella, to her surprise, felt intimidated by the sheer size of the place, even though she had been born and had grown up here. Once, as the spoiled daughter of the house, she took all this magnificence for granted.

Once she could have recited the names and manufacturers of all the china and porcelain patterns that adorned the mantels of the fifteen fireplaces in the public and family rooms of the house. Now she simply did not care about such things.

She found the whole monstrous place oppressive.

From the spotless window, she could see that the sun was well advanced in its journey toward the horizon and the late summer sky wore a blush of pink and purple. The clouds were plump and fluffy, like woolly lambs.

"Come, love," she said to the boy as she reached for his hand. "Let us go outside to the gardens."

"Pretty flowers," Jamie said as he walked between the fragrant roses whose fellows stood in tall crystal vases throughout the house. These fortunate ones would be permitted to bask in the sun and rain until their blooms were perfect. Then they would be harvested to perfume the mistress's parlor and boudoir. If they never grew perfect, they would wither and be plucked and disposed of by the gardeners so that her ladyship would not be offended by their inferiority as she strolled her domain.

Only a few stubborn blooms clung to the tulip trees, whose trunks were surrounded by fallen pink, flute-shaped flowers.

There were other flowers as well, all of them procured at great expense and trouble, and nurtured lovingly by her mother's army of gardeners, but Isabella found herself missing the simple lilies of the valley and pansies and daisies that grew in hardy clumps along with rosemary, mint, and chives on the grounds of Major Lyonbridge's house in Derbyshire. Her mother would have been appalled by the encroachment of such homely growths in her domain and ordered them plucked out at once.

"Fireflies!" cried Jamie as he ran tearing after the winged creatures that lit the early dusk with small bursts of yellow light. Isabella smiled as he pelted down one of the garden paths. She gathered her skirts to run after him so that he would remain in her sight.

When they were both winded and laughing so hard they could hardly get their breath, she sat down on the green lawn and Jamie jumped into her lap to snuggle close. Her hair had come loose from her pins and was tumbling half down her back. She kissed the top of his sweaty dark hair.

Her mother would be shocked by her hoydenish behavior, but Isabella did not care.

"We should go in," she said regretfully. "It will be getting dark soon."

He looked as if he wanted to object, but he let her take his small, sturdy torso in her hands and set him upon his feet. He took her hand and made a show of hauling her to her feet.

Laughing, they walked up the steps to the veranda, but Isabella stopped abruptly when she saw the thin wisp of smoke curl from the shadows and the glowing tip of the hidden smoker's cheroot.

"Good evening, Miss Grimsby. Jamie," he said in his deep voice. The tip of the cheroot rose, and Philip's form materialized as he stepped from the shadows.

His eyes glittered strangely as they slowly inspected Isabella's disheveled appearance, from the crown of her wildly undone hair to the tips of her shoes liberally coated with garden dirt. She had opened the bodice of her traveling costume slightly because of her exertions, and her face colored with embarrassment at the slovenly picture she must present.

"Your . . . parents are looking for you, Jamie," he said to the boy, without taking his eyes from Isabella.

"Of course," Isabella said, lowering her eyes as she prepared to pass him. "I will just take him inside."

His strong hand shot out and caught her hand as she skirted around him.

"Jamie! There you are, love," said Marian from behind her husband as he opened the door for her. She came out and bent down to touch Jamie's dirty little face. She took her handkerchief and would have spit on it, but Jamie wailed and scrunched up his face to avoid the homely mother-son ritual that would have followed, and the major put a hand on Marian's shoulder to stop her.

He glanced from Isabella's face to Philip's and gave a

small, imperative jerk of his head toward the house when Marian gave him a questioning look.

She, too, looked from Isabella to Philip, and without a word took Jamie's hand and pulled him toward the door.

"But I want to stay and play with Aunt Isabella!" the child said, looking back and reaching out for her.

"Not tonight," said Adam as he put his arms around his wife and Jamie and swept them into the house.

"That," Isabella said to Philip, "is a filthy habit."

He gave her a questioning look.

She pointed at the cheroot.

"Oh, this? A taste I picked up on the continent." Since he was in the presence of a lady, he immediately dropped it, stamped it out with his foot and kicked it under the railing of the veranda.

"I won't have you smoking them in front of Jamie," Isabella said.

"I will not, then," he said calmly as he quirked an amused eyebrow at her. "Anything else?"

"I do not like the way they smell," she continued petulantly. "The smoke gets into a man's hair and clothes and makes him smell—"

"I will not smoke them at all in the future, then," he said. "Or, perhaps, not often." He tipped her face up by putting one finger under her chin. "Why are you determined to argue with me? It is a beautiful evening. We have arrived safely in London with our son. You have seen that there is nothing wrong with your father that careful nursing and common sense will not remedy. And we are to be married."

She bit her lip.

"Will that be so terrible?" he asked. "Such a pity," he added as he captured a long strand of her hair between his fingers, "that it is not the fashion for ladies to wear their hair like this. God, you are beautiful."

He leaned forward. He was going to kiss her! Isabella gulped in alarm and averted her face.

"I am your future wife," she said, "not an upstairs maid you may maul at your will."

He stepped back.

"My most abject apologies," he said, every inch the gentleman. "I forgot myself."

She gave him a curt nod.

Bloody hell.

Philip wished he had not thrown his cheroot away. He could have used it to steady his nerves.

Isabella Grimsby, the woman he had wronged, was going to get her wedding at St. Paul's in the spring, for autumn and winter weddings were inferior affairs, and not at all fashionable. And in the meantime, he had to keep his greedy hands off of her, for he would show her every courtesy due a virgin bride of his class if it killed him.

Spring was eight months away.

His fingers tingled in memory of that one touch of her beautiful, fragrant, shiny hair.

He would go mad. Stark, staring mad.

"I am going to see your father now," he said. She gave him an anxious look.

"He knows, now, that you . . . that I permitted you to . . ." She made a helpless gesture of dismay. "My mother would have told him."

"That is to be expected," Philip said with a calmness he did not feel.

The general was fond of his daughter and would not look with kindness upon the man who compromised her, even if the world was ignorant of the fact.

Philip half expected the general to produce a pistol and threaten to shoot him with it if he did not marry his daughter without delay. The fact that he had injured his back in a fall from the horse would only make him more irascible.

Isabella hesitated. She looked as if she wanted to say something, but decided not to do so upon reflection.

"Yes?" Philip said.

"I am so ashamed. Only a lightskirt would surrender her virtue so lightly," she said. "Like your father, he will want us to marry quietly and at once."

"That we will not," he said. "All of this is my fault—entirely my fault. You will have your wedding at St. Paul's. I will pay for it, if he will not. I will not have the gossips commenting upon the haste of the ceremony."

A small, ironic smile twisted her lips.

"Whose reputation are we salvaging? Yours or mine?"

"Both," he said. He mentally braced himself. "I will see him now. I have delayed this long enough."

"Do you wish for me to go with you?"

He thought about it. Her father was unlikely to draw a pistol and splatter his brains against the wall in her presence, but he would not hide behind her skirts.

"No," he decided with some regret. "I will see him alone."

The door to the house opened, and Adam, Marian, and Jamie came out to join them.

"We are going to Father's town house to spend the night," Adam told Philip, "and we will take Jamie with us."

When Isabella would have objected at the removal of her son, Marian placed a gloved hand on her arm.

"It is best," she said quietly.

Isabella bit her lip.

"Papa is very angry, I take it," she said. "Mother told him about . . . everything?"

Marian nodded.

"We are taking Jamie with us because we do not want Jamie to overhear anything . . . disturbing," Adam said. He glanced at his brother. "The general is waiting. I should go now, if I were you."

Philip nodded.

The moment of truth was at hand, and he would face it like a man.

* * *

"Come closer," General Lord Grimsby said when Philip entered the room. "Let me see the face of the blackguard who has dared defile my innocent child."

The general was sitting up in bed with pillows propped at his ailing back, and he was wearing a nightshirt, but he was no less formidable for all that.

"Good evening, my lord," Philip said as he moved forward.

"The son of my oldest friend," Lord Grimsby said. "The brother of her fiancé."

Philip wanted to hang his head, but he knew that would only make the general despise him more.

"Even after I learned you had run off with her to Scotland, I would not have credited you with such perfidy," the old man said. "And you dare come to me, now, with a request for her hand in marriage."

"Yes, sir. A most humble request."

General Grimsby gave a snort of derision.

"And that is to return her honor to her."

"Your daughter is a courageous and virtuous young woman," Philip said. "It is *my* honor that has been lost."

The general cocked a suspicious eyebrow at him.

"And I suppose you expect to receive a generous dowry, just the same."

"Your daughter could come to me with nothing but the clothes on her back, and I would consider myself a fortunate man."

"And the child?"

"He is mine."

"What if Adam and Marian refuse to give him up? In the eyes of the world, he belongs to them. Will you withdraw your offer for Isabella if you cannot have the child?"

Philip had not thought of that. He had assumed that Adam and Marian would hand the child over to his mother eventually, despite their obvious affection for him. But seeing the three of them together made him wonder if taking him from them was the right thing to do.

"You do not answer," the general said.

"In such a case, my offer for Isabella will stand."

"Even without a dowry."

"Even so."

The general gave a long sigh.

"I do not approve of your behavior," he said dryly, "but I am hardly one to cast stones."

Philip nearly choked at this reference to the general's own amorous peccadilloes.

"Dare I hope you intend to accept my suit?"

"It is a good match. I would be derelict in my duty to Isabella if I refused it."

"Thank you, sir," Philip said in relief. He extended his hand to seal the bargain, but Lord Grimsby merely looked down his long nose at him as if he were guilty of a grave breach of etiquette.

"I accept your petition for my daughter's hand on the condition that she will have you," the general said, "but understand this—if you give her any cause to regret her decision, I will hunt you down like the miserable cur you are and shoot you dead."

"Believe me, my lord. I will make your daughter a good husband, or I will die trying."

The general gave a sniff of disdain.

"See that you do," he said. "Now get out of my sight and send my daughter to me."

"I insist that you interview her in my presence," Philip said.

"I beg your pardon," the general said incredulously.

"She is ashamed, my lord. She fears you are disappointed in her. I would not have her face you alone."

Lord Grimsby narrowed his eyes at him.

"You have courage, boy. I will say that for you, regardless of the fact that it is misplaced. I know who is to blame for her disparagement, and it is not my daughter. Now, send her in."

"Yes, my lord."

Philip left the room to find Isabella wringing her hands in the hall.

"Here I am," he said with a heartiness he did not feel, "alive to tell the tale."

"Was he . . . very unpleasant?"

"Not so bad as I expected," Philip said. "He wishes to see you now."

He could see her gather her courage with an effort.

"Very well," she said. "I am ready."

"I will go with you."

Isabella lifted her chin.

"He is my father. I do not need you to protect me from him."

CHAPTER 14

Isabella entered her father's bedchamber to see something she had never seen before. Her father was sitting up in a chair, facing the doorway, and her mother standing beside him with one hand placed protectively on his shoulder. Lady Grimsby must have entered the room through the door that connected her boudoir with her husband's suite of rooms.

They wore identical frowns on their faces as they watched her approach.

Seemingly, Lord and Lady Grimsby were united at last in their condemnation of their daughter, so Lady Grimsby's first words were a surprise.

"You have done well, daughter," she said.

"I . . . beg your pardon?" Isabella said, thinking she had not heard correctly or, more likely, that this was sarcasm of some obscure sort.

"Are you mad?" the general said, turning his scowl on his wife. "She has done *well?* She has lost her virginity to a smooth-talking rogue, borne a bastard child, and lied to us about it."

Lady Grimsby's lip curled as she gave her husband a sardonic smile.

"Imagine *you* being squeamish about such matters," Lady

Grimsby said, putting an end to the illusion of solidarity Isabella had at first perceived. It was almost a relief, for she had known from the start this state of affairs could not last, even in their shared disapproval of their daughter's grave transgression. "I will give her credit," Lady Grimsby added as she transferred her arch, sarcastic smile to her daughter. "She is even better at concealing bastard children than you are."

"Mother," Isabella reproachfully.

"That was a compliment," Lady Grimsby said. "I said you have done well, and I meant exactly that. You have managed to convince everyone that the child belongs to that person who calls herself Mrs. Lyonbridge." Even now, Lady Grimsby could not bear to say the Christian name of her husband's love child. "And you are about to marry the man who fathered the brat upon you, and thus better your position in Society. It is an even better match than the one your father had arranged for you in the beginning."

"Is that all you care about? My position in Society?"

"Yes," Lady Grimsby spat, letting the true force of her anger penetrate the mask of ice at last. "And it is a good thing for you, my girl, or I would lock you in your room for the rest of your natural life or mine! How *could* you give yourself to this man before marriage? Has the humiliation that I have been subjected to nearly all of my married life because of your father's roaming eye not been enough for me to bear?"

She gave an unlovely snort.

"Thank you, at least, for sparing me the embarrassment of having all of Society know that my daughter has borne a bastard child. The fact that *I* know it is bad enough. I would have been happy to live the rest of my life without knowing it. At least the truth may be hidden for good now, for the boy will continue to be known as that creature's son, of course."

"Only for a short while," Isabella said. "Philip means to acknowledge him."

"That insolent puppy!" growled her father. "I should take my stick to him."

"What are you talking about?" Lady Grimsby demanded of Isabella. "Why should he do such a thing?"

"Because it is the truth!" Isabella said. "The only reason I am marrying Philip is so I can have my son back."

"Isabella," the general said, "be sensible. These children who are born outside of marriage, they are not the same as those born within. It is better to leave well enough alone with regard to them."

"I wish you had thought of that before you brought that creature into my home," Lady Grimsby said. She referred, of course, to Marian.

"The girl was stranded in the Peninsula when her foster father died," the general said with great exasperation to his wife. "What else was I to do?"

"You should have left well enough alone," his wife snapped. "She would have found a protector sooner or later. Her sort always does."

"Jamie is going to live with Philip and me," Isabella said. "We are going to be a family."

Lady Grimsby gave a mirthless laugh.

"You say that as if it were some great thing," she scoffed. "Wait until *you* have a daughter!"

With that, she stuck her nose in the air and stalked from the room.

"Very fond of the last word is your mother," the general said, rolling his eyes. Then he simply stared at Isabella with a look on his face so sad that it broke her heart.

"Papa," Isabella began.

He held one hand up for silence. His eyes blazed.

"Your mother may think you have done well, but I can only pronounce myself deeply and profoundly disappointed in you, Isabella," he said.

Isabella felt tears start in her eyes.

"I freely admit I have not set you a good example," he continued in a soft voice that was worse than his bellow could ever be, "but I expected better of you. Both of us expected better of you."

"Papa, I—"

"You are the only living child of our marriage," he said, "and for that reason you have been precious to me. You were the child I could claim as mine. You were the one who was to justify my pride in my lineage. You were to give me grandsons."

"I *have* given you a grandson!" Isabella said, emerging from her stupor of self-loathing. "A *fine* grandson!"

"But he cannot inherit his father's title. What if you do not have another son?"

"Jamie is the pride of my heart," she said. "It would not matter."

"Oh, it would matter," the general said bitterly. "It did to *her.* She thought I would give her another son to replace the one that was lost, but I never could, for all that I tried. And you can see the way she has continued to hate me for it."

When Isabella gasped, he gave a sour smile of satisfaction.

"Young Philip was not the only one to anticipate his wedding vows," he said. "I was a randy young buck, and your mother was so beautiful. We used to meet in secret, and a child came of it. I married her, of course. It was early days yet when she discovered she was with child. She lost it soon after the wedding. It would have been a boy."

"Papa," Isabella said softly. "I had no idea."

"No one did. We kept it secret. At first we told ourselves we would have another son. We were sure of it when your mother discovered that she had conceived another child. Oh, make no mistake. We were delighted to have a girl. You were so beautiful, so perfect. A father's joy. But the years went by, and there was no son. She withdrew from me, and I turned elsewhere for comfort. The fact that I seemed to have no difficulty in conceiving sons with other women made it worse." He gave a bitter laugh. "I tried to hide it from her, but a wife always finds out in the end."

"So that is why she hates you so much."

"One of the many reasons, nearly all of them justified.

You may scoff at such an idea, but a lady of quality's self-esteem is never complete until she presents her husband with a legitimate son to inherit his honors. You may think your Jamie will be enough for you and your husband if you have no other son, but you are wrong."

"I am not like her," Isabella said.

"Nor was she at the time," Lord Grimsby said. "She was much like you when I first knew her. We said at first that it did not matter. I vowed to be faithful, of course. We always do. But the bed of a bitter woman is a cold place, and I transgressed. Oh, do not look at me like that. I have a strong feeling that she did as well, only she is more subtle when it comes to hiding it. You take after her in that regard."

Isabella stiffened and would have left the room at once, but the general reached out to capture her hand to prevent her from doing so. As soon as his fingers closed on hers, he gave a loud cry.

"Papa!" Isabella cried.

"My back," he gasped as tears stood in his eyes.

Isabella rushed forward at once to put her arms around him. Breathing hard, he rested his head on her bosom and she kissed the top of his head.

"I love you, girl," he whispered. "You need not marry him if you do not wish to do so. I would do *anything* to prevent your having a marriage like the hell your mother and I have lived in all these years."

"I know, Papa," she said soothingly. "I am much obliged to you for that, but you need not fear for me. Ours is not a love match, as yours must have been. I go to Philip with my eyes wide open."

She straightened and stared straight ahead. "I have no illusions about any man. Not now."

When Isabella left her father's bedchamber and went into the parlor, it was to find Philip, Adam, Marian, and Jamie, already asleep in his nursemaid's arms, on the point of departure for Lord Revington's town house. She gently touched the top of Jamie's head.

"Do you have to take him with you?" she whispered.

"It is best," Adam said. Marian, she noticed, had a set look on her face.

"Lady Grimsby made the suggestion," Philip said carefully.

"She does not want them here," Isabella said, referring to Marian and Jamie.

"So it appears," Philip said.

"I will go with you, then," Isabella said.

"That you will not, missy!" said Lady Grimsby from the doorway. "It is quite out of the question for you to spend the night under the same roof as Captain Lyonbridge with only his brother and *her* as chaperon. It is too late to undo what has been done, but you will behave properly until his ring is on your finger, my girl."

"Mother!" cried Isabella, coloring with embarrassment. "There is no danger of . . . that."

"Lady Grimsby, I must protest," Philip interjected.

"Captain Lyonbridge, you may call tomorrow to see your betrothed, if you wish."

"Marian and I will return to Scotland tomorrow. Jamie will stay with Isabella, of course," Adam said. "If you do not wish to have him under your roof, the two of them may return to my house in Derbyshire."

"What utter nonsense," Lady Grimsby exclaimed. "There are all the wedding arrangements to make, the bride clothes to be fitted, and all of that. Isabella must stay in London." She gave a martyred sigh. "And the boy must stay with us, I suppose. Unless . . ." She gave Philip a speculative look. "He could just as well stay at Lord Revington's town house with a competent nursemaid as here."

"Not unless I go with him," Isabella said.

"Stubborn girl," Lady Grimsby hissed.

"I will not have the boy left with strangers," Adam said, looking Lady Grimsby straight in the eye. "I will leave funds with Isabella. If Jamie is not welcome here, she will take him to Derbyshire immediately."

"She will not," Lady Grimsby said sternly. "Who are you to be giving orders to my daughter?"

"If Jamie goes, so will I," Isabella said. "And you can make all the wedding arrangements without me."

"I do hope it does not come to that," Philip said with an arch look. "Or I shall have to leave London as well to hang on my father's hospitality to be near my fiancée, and Derbyshire can be devilish dull at this season. I should much prefer to go to Brighton. What say you, Isabella? Shall we all go to Brighton? We can plan a wedding just as well from the seaside. It might be difficult to find lodgings at the height of the resort season, but I could try. And perhaps I can find rooms for you and your mother at the Castle Inn."

"But what about Papa?" Isabella asked, although she liked the idea of going to the seaside very much. Jamie would adore chasing the gulls about on the beach and digging into the sand with a sweet little bucket and shovel.

"Best thing in the world for him," Philip said. "Invalids are always going to the seaside."

"All of us together?" Lady Grimsby asked in disbelief.

"Why not?" Philip said. "You can return to London next month to begin preparations for the wedding."

Adam gave Philip a grudging nod of respect for having employed a diversionary tactic that seemed to have defused Lady Grimsby's acrimony completely as she contemplated the prospect of going to Brighton.

"I will give it some thought," Lady Grimsby said. Lest anyone think she had forgotten the issue under discussion, she added, "But Isabella will stay here tonight. You can send the child here with his nursemaid after you depart for Scotland."

"I will bring Jamie to you," Philip said, "for I mean to see the two of them off, and Jamie will want to bid them farewell." He glanced at Isabella. "Miss Grimsby is welcome to accompany us, if she, too, wishes to see the stagecoach off."

"I should like that," Isabella said.

"I shall call for you in the morning, if that would be convenient."

"Quite," she said gratefully. "Thank you. I should like to see my sister off."

Lady Grimsby compressed her lips until they formed a thin line of displeasure.

"She is *not* your sister," she said, stomping out of the room.

"Well, that was pleasant," Marian said humorously after a moment.

"Marian, I am so sorry for—"

"Do not bother to apologize to me for Lady Grimsby," Marian said. "I do not care enough for her good opinion to permit a few rude words to hurt me. I *am* your sister, and there is nothing she can do about it. Let us take our departure. We must arise early tomorrow."

Isabella placed a wistful caress on the sleeping Jamie's head.

"You will have him to yourself soon enough, Isabella," Marian said softly. She turned away, but not quickly enough to hide the sheen of tears in her eyes.

CHAPTER 15

Marian was brushing her short auburn hair in her husband's old bedchamber at Revington House when his handsome face suddenly appeared above her own in the mirror.

He kissed her on the side of her neck and took the brush from her hand. She closed her eyes as he took up the rhythm of her strokes to perform this office for her.

"I am glad, now, that you did not hire a maid when I told you that you could do so," he said softly. "She would be very much in the way."

He put down the brush and placed his hands on her shoulders. His eyes met hers in the mirror.

"What is wrong, my love?" he asked.

She bit her lip.

"Am I a monster for not wanting to give him up? He is her child, after all."

"No, of course not," Adam said. "I do not want to give him up, either. I had grown quite accustomed to the idea of being his father. I thought my brother dead, and Isabella was unwed. It seemed best for the child that we take him." His voice hardened. "With her blessing, I might add. And now she wants him back."

"He is such a sweet boy," Marian said as her chin quivered. "And we left him to go to Scotland."

"I forced you to choose," Adam said. "Will you ever forgive me for not resigning my commission?"

"But I *wanted* to go with you. I am no better suited to be a country gentleman's wife than you are to be a country gentleman. And I knew Isabella would take excellent care of him. Indeed, she was eager to spend the time alone with him at your house."

"*Our* house."

Marian smiled as Adam kissed her cheek.

"Our house," she conceded. "It still does not seem real." Her smile faded. "I only want Isabella and Jamie to be happy. What if your brother will not be kind to them?"

Adam's smile grew hard.

"I will simply have to put a bullet through him," he said. "Jamie deserves a proper father. And Philip *will* be a good father to him, or I will know the reason why."

"Isabella is an excellent mother," Marian said ruefully. "He minds what she says. Most of the time. She does not find him nearly as exhausting as I do."

"As *we* do," Adam corrected. "I had no idea that one small boy could get into so much mischief."

"Did we do the right thing by going to Derbyshire to demand that Philip make an honest woman of my poor sister? Would it have been better for all of us if we had not told him that he was Jamie's father?"

"He deserved to know," Adam said stonily. "And, although I have never been overfond of Isabella, he has wronged her grievously. It is his duty to make it right by her."

"What if he makes her a wretched husband? What if he does not want Jamie?"

Adam gave a long sigh.

"No fear of that. What man would *not* want Jamie?"

Marian bowed her head to avoid her husband's eyes in the mirror. Then she stood and put her arms around his neck.

"I am sorry, my love," she said. "If you cannot be Jamie's father, you will be his fond uncle. And I will be his aunt."

"It will not be the same," he said.

"No."

Adam smiled and touched her cheek.

"Let us go to bed, wife. I am persuaded Jamie will arise early tomorrow. I will take him riding before breakfast. You will join us, I hope?"

"I would not miss it," she said. Her face crumpled. "Oh, Adam. Did we do the right thing?"

"Yes," Adam said simply. "For Jamie, for Isabella, and for Philip." He bent and put his forehead against hers. "As for the two of us, we are the most fortunate of all, because we have each other."

With that, Marian raised on tiptoe to kiss him, and he led her to the bed.

The next morning, Isabella went into the breakfast room to find Philip and Jamie waiting for her. She gave a glad cry and bent down so Jamie could run into her arms.

"Thank you for bringing him," she said to Philip, who had stood at her entrance. He was wearing a well-tailored uniform and had his headdress tucked under his arm.

"It was my pleasure. We are a bit early, so we will wait for you in the parlor while you eat breakfast."

"Do not be silly," she said. "You must join me, of course."

"We have already eaten—"

"Marmalade!" cried Jamie. Isabella hurriedly caught his coattails to keep him from falling face first into the bowl. "May I have some?" He gave her a heartrending look. "Mama gave me porridge for breakfast." The look of disgust that accompanied this information made Isabella feel a bit smug. *She* normally gave Jamie eggs and toast and marmalade for breakfast, for could not abide porridge, despite Marian's insistence that it was good for adults and growing children alike.

"Of course," she said, laughing as she spread some of the thick, fragrant marmalade on a piece of toast for the child. Like her, Jamie never had liked porridge. "Philip? Will you join us?"

"I should be delighted," he said, gazing into her eyes.

She looked down self-consciously.

"Why are you staring at me like that?" she asked softly.

"Because you are so beautiful." He gave her a teasing smile. "You certainly have turned yourself out in fine trim to see my brother off. Should I be jealous?"

"Do not be absurd," she said, blushing. The pink walking gown was certainly becoming to her, but she would not admit to wearing it in order to impress *him* for the world.

"Aunt Isabella loves *me* best," Jamie said with a pout.

"Of course, I do, darling," Isabella said at once as she wiped a smear of marmalade from the boy's chin. "Now, Jamie, you must be careful. It would not do for you to get marmalade all over your new suit. You will want to see—" She hesitated and met Philip's eyes. "You will want to see Mama and Papa off in style."

Jamie looked up at Isabella.

"I told Mama not to go, but she said she had to take care of Papa. And I had to stay and take care of you."

Isabella bit her lip.

"She is right," she said. "I do not know what I would do without my Jamie."

"Maybe when I am big, I can go to war," he said.

"No," Isabella said vehemently. She looked straight at Philip. "I forbid it."

"A man has to do his duty to his country," Philip said quietly. "A man has to do what he knows in his heart is right."

"I want to wear a uniform and ride a big horse like Papa," Jamie said.

"Perhaps you will," Philip said as Isabella gave him a look of disapproval, "but not for some time. You need to grow a bit first."

"Never," Isabella whispered.

Jamie, by this time, had returned his attention to the toast as Isabella spooned some marmalade on a piece of toast for Philip, and then for herself.

"Thank you," Philip said, gazing at her lips. "I have always been partial to sweets."

He was *flirting* with her, and there was no audience to observe him except for Jamie. What did he mean by it? He knew that theirs was no love match.

"Have you given any more consideration to Brighton?" he asked.

"Brighton," she repeated.

"About your going there with your parents, Jamie, and me. I wish you would do so. I think I missed summer in Brighton the most when I was at war." He gazed soulfully into her eyes. "I have always had a special attachment for it, especially after a certain memorable ball at the Castle Inn."

"We shall see," she said noncommittally. "I am not certain it would be good for my father to travel."

"He has already come all the way from Scotland."

"True. He is to consult his doctor about it. I should be happy if Father would stay away from his horrid regiment for a little while. When I was Jamie's age, I rarely saw him, for he was always away. Such is the life of a soldier."

Jamie looked up at that.

"Papa says when I get old enough I can travel with the regiment, just like Papa and Mama."

No doubt Adam had told him this when he expected to be Jamie's father. Just what she needed was for her darling son to grow up to be exactly like Adam!

Over her dead body.

Her son was going to be a gentleman. Since he could not inherit his father's title and estate, he would go into some gentlemanly profession, perhaps law or the church. *Anything* was preferable to the military. She would thank Adam Lyonbridge not to put such ideas into his impressionable young head.

"My papa is bigger than you," Jamie said proudly to Philip.

Isabella gasped at this innocent rudeness.

"Yes," Philip said dryly. "My brother is bigger than just about everyone."

Philip sat back and wiped his lips with a serviette.

"I told Isabella and Adam we would be back in time to drive them to the stagecoach," Philip said. "So if you are quite finished . . ."

"Quite," said Isabella, getting up at once. She found that she had no appetite for anything more than the marmalade and toast. "We would not want them to miss the coach to Scotland."

"If they do, will they have to stay with me?" Jamie asked wistfully.

"No, lad," Philip said sympathetically. "There will always be another coach."

Marian's green traveling costume, the only one that was fit to be seen, had been cleaned and pressed, and so she was ready for another journey. It must be so easy, Isabella thought, to be Marian. She came out of the house on a gurgle of laughter at something Adam, who was right behind her, had said.

Adam's batman, an elderly but still spry Irishman named Morgan, had materialized sometime during the night, apparently, from the bachelor lodgings he occupied in the city when Adam had no need for him. Now he followed the couple to the carriage with a satchel containing his belongings in one hand. A liveried manservant followed him with two larger, more substantial bags, which he and another servant strapped to the roof of the carriage. The batman got up on the seat next to the driver.

"There. Let us be off," Adam said as he handed his wife into the carriage and got in himself.

Jamie immediately jumped down from Isabella's lap, and Adam picked him up to place him between himself and Marian.

"But . . . what about your trunks?" Isabella said, astonished. She knew the regiment would be in Scotland for at least two months.

"There are no trunks," Marian said, laughing. "I have no need for fine clothes where I am going, except for one evening gown and a decent morning gown for taking tea with the other officers' wives on occasion."

Marian's laughter contained no derision at Isabella's question, but she felt chastened, just the same.

"My wife," Adam said pointedly, "needs no trunks full of fine feathers to lend her consequence."

Isabella thought of the many trunks she once thought essential when she moved from capital city to summer resort to country house party and stiffened. She had adopted a simpler mode since Jamie's birth, but she still considered herself ill-provisioned if she did not have several changes of clothing for each social situation at her disposal during a journey.

"Exceedingly convenient for you, is it not, Adam?" Philip said archly.

"Exceedingly," Adam said as he gave his wife's shoulders a squeeze.

"Mama is the most beautiful lady in the world," Jamie said loyally.

Adam ruffled the child's dark hair.

"That she is, lad," Adam said.

"Aunt Isabella is very beautiful, too," Marian said.

"Yes, Mama," Jamie said as he clutched Marian's hand. "I wish you did not have to go."

Marian kissed the top of his head. *You do not have to go,* Isabella thought. *I would never leave him if I had a choice, not for any man.*

"It is only for two months, love," Marian said.

Two months. Without Jamie. Isabella knew *she* would die.

In the beginning, Isabella knew, Marian had intended to stay in London to supervise her father's convalescence. While he was unlikely to obey the doctor's orders, and even less his wife's, General Lord Grimsby did obey Marian, more or less. In the end, though, the general's condition was deemed not as serious as Marian had at first supposed. Still, she could have stayed with Jamie, if she chose.

If Isabella were feeling charitable, she might believe that Marian had elected to follow Adam back to Scotland to give Jamie some time to become accustomed to Isabella and Philip as a couple. But Isabella was hardly feeling charitable at the moment. Marian simply put her husband before Jamie, and that was hardly surprising.

Jamie was *her* son, not Marian's.

"Oh, look, Jamie!" cried Marian just as her feet touched the ground at the inn. "Is it not exciting?"

The yard of the inn was full of coaches and ostlers and passengers rushing for their seats. There was a good deal of cheerful shoving and shouting and hefting of trunks as the guards registered passengers and made sure each was on the right coach.

Exciting? Hardly.

Isabella had never traveled by mail coach or stagecoach. Her mother would have been horrified at the thought of herself or her daughter being jostled by any chance person who happened to have purchased a ticket to the same destination. Isabella had always traveled by private coach with at least two trunks strapped to the roof and her maid in attendance, even on short journeys.

"Barbaric," Philip said in her ear.

Isabella agreed wholeheartedly.

Adam, who had overheard the comment, raised one brow.

"And how was it that you got from Spain to Lisbon when the hostilities were over, Philip? By post chaise, perhaps?"

"On the bleeding stumps of my own bare feet," Philip said with a dramatic shudder. "And I am *never* doing so again. It will be only private coach for me from now on, with frequent stops along the way for fortification."

Adam snorted with manly derision, but Isabella could only applaud Philip for his common sense.

Poor Marian.

Marian and Adam rushed on ahead with the batman, who was burdened with all three bags of luggage, to leave Philip, Isabella, and Jamie to scurry in their wake as best they might. They were a few minutes past the appointed time, and there was every chance that the coach had left without them.

As it turned out, however, there was no danger of this.

"Father!" exclaimed Adam as he spotted Lord Revington standing next to the guard to the Edinburgh coach, scowling ferociously at the man.

"Here they are," his lordship said to the man. "You may prepare to depart now."

Both his sons shook their heads in admiration. Only Lord Revington could manage to hold up the Edinburgh coach by sheer force of will.

"I am surprised to see you, Father," Adam said as he reached for his father's hand and got a hearty hug instead.

"You should not be. How could I not see my own son and his wife off to Scotland?"

The old man kissed Marian on the cheek, much to Isabella's surprise. It was common knowledge that he had not approved of his son's choice of a bride, but it appeared he had resigned himself to it. He gave Philip and Isabella each a careless nod.

He ignored Jamie completely, even though Jamie looked curiously at him.

Isabella hugged the boy closer.

If that disgusting old man thought he was going to slight her boy after she married Philip, he was much mistaken!

"Be a good boy for Aunt Isabella and Uncle Philip," Marian said as she sank in a circle of green skirts, heedless of the dirt in the yard, to hug Jamie. "We will be back before you know it."

Sad Marian might look, Isabella observed, but her excitement at the prospect of returning to the regiment was still apparent.

"We'll miss you, lad," Adam said as he shook hands with

the boy, and then picked him up to give him a hug so fierce that Jamie gave a laughing little squeak of surprise. He tweaked the boy's nose and handed him to Philip. Jamie's chin trembled, but he did not cry. Isabella could see Adam's eyes were moist.

"This dashed cold wind," Adam said, perceiving that Isabella had noticed this. His eyes dared her to contradict him.

Then he patted Jamie on the head, shook hands with Philip, took his wife's arm, and was gone.

CHAPTER 16

After the Edinburgh coach was out of sight, Lord Revington brushed by Isabella and Jamie to address his son.

"You had better have your man pack your gear at once when you return to the town house," he said gruffly. "I wish to be on the road to Derbyshire before noon."

"I am not going to Derbyshire, Father," Philip said. "I intend to accompany Isabella, Jamie, Lady Grimsby, and General Grimsby, if we can persuade him to join us, to Brighton until the end of the month."

"The devil you will!"

"Lady and child present," Philip murmured as he watched Isabella's jaw stiffen. She made a move to distract Jamie, but the lad was all eyes and ears as he soaked up Lord Revington's profanity like a little sponge.

"The devil you will," the boy echoed softly before Isabella could shush him. She looked daggers at Lord Revington.

"Beg your pardon, Miss Grimsby," the older man said to Isabella at once, but with no real apology in his voice. He ignored Jamie completely. "Why do you think you need to accompany the Grimsbys to Brighton?"

"I do not need to. I want to," Philip said as he took Isabella's arm. "I have been through hell. I want to spend some time at the seaside with my fiancée and my . . . brother's stepson."

"Supporting the character of a lovesick swain, are you?" Lord Revington said with a huff of impatience. "*She* has no right to expect it."

Philip bared his teeth in a fierce smile.

"She has *every* right to expect it, Father," Philip said. "I know what you want me to do in Derbyshire. Follow you about and stuff my head full of corn and milk yield and your endless accounts. There will be time enough for that when the summer is over and the rest of the world is in Vienna for the Congress. I will resign my commission then and give myself over to your tutelage."

"Resign your commission? Are you *mad?* You will, of course, go to Vienna to enhance your reputation among the delegates there. Everyone who is anyone in social and political circles will be in Vienna for the Congress."

"Vienna," Philip said consideringly. "I should quite like traveling to Vienna. You are quite correct. Everyone who is anyone will be there." He turned to Isabella. "What say you to Vienna, Isabella?"

Before she could answer, Lord Revington cut in.

"*She* is not going to Vienna!" he exclaimed. "She will have all of the *ton* laughing behind their hands at you! It was not so long ago that she was playing the role of loyal fiancée to your brother, and all the world knows how well *that* ended."

"Pity," Philip said as he reached for Jamie and placed him inside the carriage. "I am afraid, then, I must stay in England to be near my bride. Come along, Isabella. We do not want to keep my father standing in this hot sun."

With that, he assisted Isabella into the carriage, got in himself and slammed the door. From the window, Isabella could see Lord Revington's furious face raised to her.

"What was that noise?" Philip asked as a thud hit the side of the carriage.

"Your father just struck it with his walking stick," Isabella said. "It is his own carriage, too."

Philip sank into the corner of the seat, closed his eyes, and gave a long sigh.

Before long, Jamie plucked at his sleeve, and Philip opened his eyes.

"Are you and Aunt Isabella going to leave me, too?" he asked plaintively. His chin trembled.

"No, no, no, no!" Isabella cried as she scooped him up and held him to her bosom. "Never, my darling. Pay no attention to the mean old man."

"Isabella!" Philip exclaimed.

"Well he *is,*" she said defiantly. "The manipulative old goat! I know very well why he won't have me in Vienna, and it has nothing to do with the fact that I was once betrothed to your brother! That little affair was explained away practically before I removed his betrothal ring from my finger."

"Isabella, it is quite unnecessary—"

"He wants you to go to Vienna to find a more worthy fiancée, of course," she said.

"There *is* no more worthy fiancée," Philip interjected.

"Kind of you to say so," she said. "He hopes that when you are away from Jamie and me, you will come to your senses and marry someone like his precious Lady Anne."

"Well, he is doomed to be disappointed," Philip said. "Vienna would be very pleasant, I must admit. But not without you. I promised I would never leave you again, and I mean it."

"You will not go without me, and I will not go without Jamie," Isabella said.

"Certainly not," Philip said, ruffling the boy's hair. Jamie looked up at him with solemn eyes. "We are a family now. The three of us. And we are going to be together forever."

"That is what Mama and Papa told me," Jamie said sadly, "but they did not mean it."

General Lord Grimsby tried shouting, grumbling, and finally he even lowered himself to attempting to *reason* with his wife, but it was to no avail.

"Believe me, my lord husband," she said. "I would as soon go to Brighton with the Gallic monster himself than accompany you, but your physician insists that a holiday by the sea is just the thing to hasten your recovery, and so you are going to Brighton, and there is an end to it."

"It is strangely unlike you, my dear, to take such an unprecedented interest in my health and well-being," he said with heavy irony. "I must say I am gratified beyond words."

"Do not be," she said sweetly. "The sooner you are recovered, the sooner you will return to your dreadful regiment and leave me in peace."

"Well, that's frank," he said. "Why not leave me alone here, then?"

"Because you will be out of that bed and disobeying the doctor's orders before my carriage has left the front door, that is why," she said as she put her hands on her hips and glared at him. "And if you make your condition worse, I will have that creature back down from Scotland, moving into my house and ordering my servants about on the pretext of supervising your care."

"Ah. Now all this solicitude makes sense," he said.

"Do not think," she said, "that I will derive any satisfaction whatsoever from your company."

"In that case, then," he said with a big, insincere smile, "it will be my very great pleasure to accompany you to Brighton."

Since the general's valet had almost finished packing his master's clothing at the mistress's order, this capitulation was not as effective as it might have been, but Lady Grimsby gave a nod of satisfaction.

"Excellent. I shall send one of the footmen with the Merlin chair."

"That you will not, my lady!" he snapped. "I am not going to be trundled from one place to the next like some antiquated old invalid taking the waters at Bath."

"That is just what you are," she said. "An antiquated old invalid who has no one to blame but himself for falling off his own horse. You could have been *killed,* you old fool!"

Her bosom heaved, and her husband looked at her in absolute astonishment.

"Phoebe," he said. "Do you mean you would have . . . cared?"

"Of course I would have cared," she said fiercely. "I would have had to see to your burial, and I would have had to stand there in a black dress and *pretend* to be desolated, and I would have had to listen to all those stuffy old bores from the War Office recite platitudes over your dead corpse, when all the time they were thinking what an *idiot* you were to make it alive all through the war and then fall off your *horse!* Have I not endured enough of your neglect and your mistresses and your sheer perverseness all these years without *that?*"

"You are right," he said sarcastically. "How could I have been so inconsiderate?"

"You can use the Merlin chair or hobble outside on your cane, whichever you prefer," she said. "But we are leaving. Immediately. Isabella, Captain Lyonbridge, and that child are waiting for us."

Grumbling, the general levered himself out of the bed to sit on the side of it and nearly toppled over in a sudden dizziness.

With a sigh of exasperation, his wife steadied him by catching one shoulder. He practically screamed with the jolt to his spine. She jumped back and flounced from the room with a curt, "I will call your valet to assist you."

Lady Grimsby took a deep breath and went out to the garden to steady her poor nerves. The carriages were pulled up to the front door, but she needed a moment alone before she subjected herself to her husband's company in the close confines of a carriage all the way to Brighton.

Everyone in her life seemed to be involved in a conspiracy to drive her mad!

First, her husband sent his grown love child from Portugal

and announced that it was his responsibility—but they both knew *she* would be the one to fulfill it if she wanted the creature out of her house—to find her a husband, which she did, only to have the creature refuse to marry him.

Then her maddening husband fell off his horse and she was saddled with his broken body to nurse back to health.

Then, as if *that* were not bad enough, she found that her only daughter had been impregnated by some man and given birth in secret to a bastard in turn, and now the child's father was back—thankfully willing to marry her, but insisting upon claiming her daughter's bastard as his own.

And now she must plan a wedding for Isabella—again. This would make—Lady Grimsby counted them in her head—four, counting the three that would have been to Adam Lyonbridge if they had come to fruition.

Once this girl was married—*if* she went through with it this time—Lady Grimsby was of half a mind to take herself off to the continent, change her name, and live in anonymity.

And her husband and daughter, for whose sake she had borne more humiliation than any woman alive, would care not at all.

She sat upon the stone bench before the statue of Diana the Huntress that she had purchased at great expense only last month. The serene countenance of the goddess mocked her. All Lady Grimsby wanted was some peace and elegance in her life. Was that too much to ask?

"Why are you crying? Are you sad?"

Lady Grimsby jumped and clutched her heart.

"What are you doing out here?" she said, turning on the small, dark-haired boy who was regarding her from curious blue eyes.

"Because if you are sad, I can ask Aunt Isabella to read you a story. That is what she does when I am sad."

Her eyes narrowed at him.

He was, indeed, the very image of Philip Lyonbridge, but about the eyes and mouth there was a bit of Lady Grimsby's own daughter in him.

How could she have been so blind? She should have seen it at once.

"I have had quite enough stories from your precious Aunt Isabella, thank you very much," she said bitterly.

The imp cocked his head to one side, considering, in that way Isabella had sometimes.

"Uncle Philip says we shall go to the seaside and gather shells. Will you go with us?"

"No," she said, sighing as she heard sounds of disruption emit from her once serene house. The rotting corpses of Viscounts Grimsby long past were probably turning over in their graves at this desecration of their town house.

The boy got a mischievous grin on his face and prepared to run out further into the garden. The little devil had escaped his handlers once again, Lady Grimsby surmised, and was about to lead them on a merry dance.

Before he could do so, she reached out and captured his small hand. Instead of wriggling for escape, the boy's small fingers turned within her grasp and clung to hers. Lady Grimsby swallowed painfully. She remembered thinking, so long ago, that her daughter's two-year-old hands were a miracle—so tiny, but so strong like this boy's. There had been no children in her life since then, no matter how much she longed for another child. She had hoped Isabella would give her grandchildren.

Instead, her daughter had given her . . . this. A child she could not claim as her grandson and hold her head up in Society.

If he had been born on the right side of the blanket, Lady Grimsby would have presided at the birthing. She would have been the one to present the newborn to his father. And if she had been given a voice in the rearing of him, he would not have grown so pert!

"Go inside, child. They are looking for you," she said. She tried to extricate her hand from his, but he clung obstinately to it.

"Aunt Isabella is taking my favorite book so she can read it to me," he said. "It has monkeys in it."

"How appropriate," she said dryly.

"Mother!" cried Isabella as she appeared at the entryway to the garden. She rushed down the path and gathered Jamie into her arms. "What were you doing out here with Jamie?"

"I was doing *nothing* with him," she said resentfully. The girl behaved as if she were about to drown the little nuisance in the garden pond.

"Lady Grimsby needs a story, Aunt Isabella," the boy said. "She is sad."

Isabella gave her mother a considering look.

"Are you well, Mother?" she asked. "Is there anything I can do?"

"I think you have done quite enough already, my girl," Lady Grimsby said stiffly as she led the way into the house.

CHAPTER 17

Philip loved the seashore.

It had been so long since he had been to Brighton. The last time, in fact, had been almost three years ago, when Isabella told him that she must return to London at once with her mother to prepare for her wedding to his brother.

The magic that was Brighton had lulled him into believing that the oft-postponed wedding would never take place, so his whole world had come crashing down when Isabella admitted she loved him, but would marry his brother out of duty.

Until then, he had thought it was the worst thing that would ever happen to him.

Now he sat across from her in his father's coach and wondered if he could look forward to decades of marriage with the woman of his dreams, knowing that the only reason she endured his touch was for the sake of her child.

He might never be able to reawaken her love for him.

She might even come to love another man—one who had never betrayed her—and night after night she would lie unresponsive in Philip's bed, wishing he were someone else.

Now *that* was the worst thing that could ever happen to him.

Isabella had removed her hat, and at that moment she was dozing against the cushioned seat with her head thrown back to reveal her long, graceful neck. She wore a dainty necklace of amethyst beads to compliment her stylish blue traveling costume and tiny pearls at her perfect ears.

God, she was beautiful.

And between them was their son, who was becoming quite cranky within the close confines of the coach.

"I want to get out," he said, looking mulish. "Papa always rides his horse, and he lets me ride with him. Why did you not bring your horse, Uncle Philip?"

"Because I do not wish to arrive in Brighton looking hot and dusty and smelling like a horse," Philip said. He leaned confidentially toward the boy. "Ladies don't like it."

"Mama does," Jamie said. "And the ladies like Papa. It makes Mama angry sometimes. My papa is a hero!"

So am I, Philip almost said.

"Uncle Philip is a hero, too."

Startled, Philip turned to see that Isabella had awakened and straightened her clothing.

"Thank you, Isabella," he said, surprised and touched.

"He does not *look* like a hero," Jamie protested.

"That will do, young man," Isabella said sternly. "Just because Uncle Philip does not bellow at people and smell as if he lived in a barn does not make him any less heroic."

Jamie hung his head.

"Jamie is merely bored, my dear," Philip said. "Perhaps we should order a halt so we can get out of the carriage for a bit."

"We will *never* get to Brighton at this pace," Isabella said ruefully. "My parents are confined in a carriage together. Neither may emerge alive if the journey goes on much longer."

"I have every confidence in the general's resilience," Philip said, smiling. He tapped his walking stick on the roof of the carriage. When it stopped, he explained to the coachman that they wished to get out of the carriage for a little while, and the driver of Lord and Lady Grimsby's coach, after inquiring as to the delay, went on around them and continued to Brighton.

"Here you are, lad," Philip said as he lifted the child from the carriage but kept a firm grip on his hand as he extended his other hand to Isabella to help her down the steps. It was a warm day, and her cheeks were deliciously flushed. Little tendrils of her hair escaped to flutter in the breeze.

"Will I see a whale at the seaside?" Jamie asked his uncle. He was all smiles now that he was out of the carriage.

"No, lad. It is too shallow for whales on the beach. Fond of whales, are you?"

"Mama read to me about whales in one of my books. Have you ever seen a whale, Uncle Philip?"

"No," he said wistfully. "When I was a young man I wanted to go to sea, but my father forbade me. All of the military Lyonbridge men are in the army, and he could not permit me to break tradition. I wanted to fire a cannon from the bow of a ship, like General Nelson."

Isabella looked quite amazed.

"I never knew that about you," Isabella said.

"There is much you do not know about me," he said, turning to her. He only relaxed his grip on Jamie's hand for an instant, but the next thing he knew, the boy was pelting down the road. Isabella gave a faint scream and ran after him. Philip joined the pursuit and passed Isabella almost at once. He scooped Jamie up under one arm and carried the giggling child practically upside down back to the carriage.

"Jamie, how *could* you!" Isabella scolded. She had one hand pressed to her heart.

Philip dumped the boy back into the carriage. Instantly Jamie poked his head out the door.

"I do not want to go in yet."

"That's a pity, then," Philip said. "For I cannot trust you not to run away."

"I will be good," Jamie said.

Philip looked at Isabella.

She had already climbed the first step, so she stepped back onto the ground with a rueful smile.

"If you will promise to hold onto my hand, I suppose you may get out again, Jamie. Just for a little while, mind," she said. "We want to be in Brighton before dark."

"May I go to the seashore right away to collect seashells?" he asked.

"The best time for gathering seashells is in the morning, at dawn," Isabella said. "We shall get up very early and go out on the beach together. Will you like that?"

Jamie clapped his hands with glee.

"Of course, if we get to Brighton too late and do not go to bed early, you will awaken too late to get the best seashells," Philip said.

"Let us go right away!" the child said as he disappeared back into the carriage.

"Clever man," whispered Isabella as he handed her inside. She actually smiled at him the way she used to, before she found out he was merely human.

One smile, and his heart nearly burst with pleasure.

He smiled back, but then she colored and looked away.

"There *must* be another room," Lady Grimsby said in dismay when she found that she and her husband would have to share a single bedchamber with sitting room.

"But, my lady," the flustered landlord said, "it is the busiest time of the summer season. Captain Lyonbridge was most fortunate to procure two rooms at such a time. Three is simply impossible."

"It will not do," Lady Grimsby said. "We must go to another hotel at once."

"No," Lord Grimsby said. His face was gray with pain and fatigue. The journey from London had taken such a toll on him that he was sitting in the Berlin chair. He lowered his voice. "Madam, you have dragged me all the way from London. *You* may go to another hotel, if you wish. I am staying here."

Lady Grimsby gave a sniff of displeasure.

"It will be vastly inconvenient," she said.

"We can make other arrangements tomorrow," Philip said. "Why not rest here tonight?"

"I could stay in Isabella's room with her if it were not for that child," Lady Grimsby said.

Isabella looked quickly at Jamie to see that he was sound asleep.

"Jamie can come with me to the Old Ship," Philip said.

"There. A perfectly sensible solution," Lady Grimsby said.

"Absolutely not!" Isabella cried. "I will not spend the night apart from Jamie. Heaven knows what *you* will give him for breakfast. Beefsteak and cigars, I have no doubt."

Lady Grimsby regarded her husband with a sigh of resignation.

"I suppose it cannot be helped for tonight," she said.

"Thank you, my lady," the innkeeper said in relief. "I will show you to your rooms."

"I have bespoken a private parlor here for dinner," Philip said. "I would be honored if you would join me."

"That is very thoughtful of you, Philip," Lady Grimsby said as she went off to see the accommodations that had been reserved for her and her husband.

Because of Lord Grimsby's infirmity, he and his wife were given a spacious, beautifully decorated room on the first floor.

"I believe it will do," Lady Grimsby said.

Once the innkeeper was gone, the general gave her a grin through his pain.

"Are you going to share a bed with me, Phoebe, for the first time in years? I see no other here."

It was true that the only bed was a large, four-poster affair that dominated the bedchamber.

"You may sleep on the sofa," she said. "You should be comfortable enough."

"It looks too soft for my ailing back," he protested. "You are a cruel woman to expect me—"

"Oh, very well. *I* shall sleep on the sofa," she said irritably.

Lord Grimsby hobbled over to the bed and tested it with his hand.

"Plenty of room for two," he pointed out.

"Do not be disgusting, you old goat," she snapped.

"Never mind, then," he said. "I daresay the inn has a parlor maid or two who would not mind a bit of entertainment."

Lady Grimsby's hands curled into claws.

"If you *dare*—"

"You have a touching faith in my powers of recuperation if you think I could do any such thing in my condition," he said dryly as he lowered himself to the bed with an audible creak. "I can hardly *walk* without whimpering. You would be as safe as the ugliest nun in Christendom in my bed tonight."

She gave him a look of pure loathing.

"I know what is wrong with you, and it isn't this room or my proximity," he said. "You are always in bad temper when you are hungry. Let us have dinner brought to the room. It has been a long time since we dined alone together."

"Are you mad?" she asked incredulously.

"No. Merely in too much pain to hie me to a private parlor for dinner."

"Very well," she said. "I suppose it will do me no harm to dine in your presence."

"Gracious, as always," he said with a lift of his eyebrows.

And so it was that Isabella arrived at the private parlor after changing out of her dusty traveling clothes to find Philip waiting for her alone. He stood at once when he caught sight of her.

Philip quickly moved to pull a chair out for her.

"I told the waiter to begin serving as soon as you arrive," he said. "How pretty you look."

Isabella bit her lip. She had worn the pink gown precisely because it became her well, but now she felt a bit silly for having changed into fresh clothing. He was dressed in the same uniform he had worn all day for, of course, his trunks already had been conveyed to his hotel.

"Thank you," she said, hoping she did not appear too obvious in dressing up. A waiter entered the room and at once began serving the soup. "Should we not wait for my mother and father?"

"They are not coming," he said. "Your mother was kind enough to send me a message."

Isabella pushed her chair back and stood as soon as the waiter left the room. Was it her imagination, or had the man given her a knowing look as he served her?

"I am afraid I cannot dine alone with you, Captain Lyonbridge," she said with all the dignity she could muster. "It would not be at all proper."

"My good girl," he said, smiling, "we are betrothed, and there is no one to witness this grave breach of propriety. We could always have Jamie down to chaperon."

"He is still asleep," she said with a rueful smile. "I adore my son, but he is absolutely exhausting."

"So I noticed," he said with an answering smile. "What a miracle he is." He took a spoonful of soup. "And what a miracle *this* is."

Isabella also took a spoonful of soup.

"Lobster bisque?" she asked in surprise as the voluptuous richness made her want to sigh with pleasure. "I have not had lobster bisque in . . . well, in a long time. Not since before Jamie was born."

"There will be filet mignon and strawberries as well," he said, "with asparagus in cream."

"All my favorites," she said with a sigh. Her eyes widened as he poured a sparkling beverage from a bottle. "Champagne?"

"French," he said.

"For no occasion at all?"

"I am dining with my affianced bride. Alone. For the first time since our betrothal," he said.

He was so much like the man she had once loved to distraction that she felt tears sting her eyes.

"My dear," he said in concern.

Blast him!

"You must not weep into the lobster bisque," he said. "Too much salt would make it inedible."

She gave a watery gurgle of laughter.

"I am just *so* tired," she said helplessly. "I cannot fight you tonight."

"Do not, then," he said as he put his hand over hers. "Relax and enjoy your dinner. I shall leave as soon as the last morsel is consumed."

His beautiful dark blue eyes were huge with compassion.

"You have nothing to fear from me, my dear," he said. "Not ever again."

Isabella remembered well the last time they were in a private parlor together. It was at an inn on the Great North Road, and they were eloping to Gretna Green to be married. Jamie had been conceived during that romantic interlude.

And the day had ended in betrayal and abandonment.

Isabella hardened her heart. Then she caught sight of a silver plate on the table.

"Caviar," she exclaimed.

"Russian," Philip said as he scooped some of the rich, black eggs onto a small piece of bread and held it before her bedazzled face.

Isabella's lips parted on a sigh as she closed her eyes in surrender.

CHAPTER 18

Oysters followed the caviar.

Isabella looked at Philip with dawning suspicion in her eyes.

All right. Perhaps he had been a bit *too* obvious.

It was a dinner designed for seduction. He had presided over many such in his wild bachelor days.

Odd.

When did he stop considering himself a bachelor? He strongly suspected it was when he made love to Isabella that first and last time.

"I am not going to let you bed me," Isabella said, even as she tilted the smooth, rich oyster meat into her mouth. She swallowed and closed her eyes with that voluptuous look on her face again. Was she *trying* to drive him mad?

Then, to his horror, her lower lip trembled and she hid her face in her hands.

"My dear," he said at once as he stood and rounded the table to put his hand on her shaking shoulders. "Are you ill? Good God! I shall have that chef's head on a plate if the oysters were—"

Isabella sniffed and raised her tear-drenched eyes to his.

"No. The oysters are *wonderful*. It is just that it has been so long since—" Her lips trembled again, and she could not seem to continue.

"Since you have eaten oysters?" he asked.

"Since I have felt like this."

He must have looked his confusion, because she pulled herself together with an effort and tried to smile at him.

"It has been a long time," she said, "since I have felt like a desirable woman. My life since before Jamie's birth has been one of exhaustion and anxiety for him. Thank you, at least, for this."

He could not help himself. He bent his head and kissed her, even though he expected to have his ears boxed for his pains. Instead, to his surprise and delight, she gave a sigh of pure pleasure, and he pulled her up out of her chair and into his arms. When they had to break off the kiss to breathe, he held her close and inhaled the perfumed softness of her hair.

"Roses," he murmured. "You always smell of roses."

"I should probably try a more appropriate scent. Rose," she said, "is for innocent young virgins."

"Ah, and you are a woman of the world, having been bedded by at least a score of men since the day you lost your virginity to me."

She pushed against his chest. Hard.

"How dare you? You are the only man who—"

"Precisely," he said as he tightened his grip to prevent her escape. "You have been bedded *once*. And by me. That makes you an innocent in my eyes, Isabella."

He kissed her again, and she gave a little moan of capitulation and put her arms around his neck again.

"You are so beautiful," he murmured. He started to lift her into his arms to carry her to the sofa. "So sweet."

Then he froze, and almost dropped her.

This was *precisely* how the mischief had started on that fateful day.

A private parlor. A beautiful woman. And a convenient sofa.

Did the same thought occur to her? He practically held his breath.

"And how many women have *you* bedded since that day, Philip?" she whispered into his ear.

"I cannot recall a single one," he said with perfect truth.

She laughed without mirth.

"What a fool I am," she said, still breathing hard as he set her on her feet. "I almost succumbed to your practiced seduction again."

"Not so practiced as you seem to think," he said ruefully. His hands were trembling, and he quickly put them behind his back so she would not notice. "At least, not at all lately."

"Are you going to tell me that was the last time for you, too?"

"Would you believe me?"

"No," she said. "I know rather more about men now than I did then."

"Then I will not tell you that," he said. In point of fact, it *had* been the last time he bedded a woman, but it was pointless to pursue that avenue.

She would not believe him.

"Well, now that we have established that you are not mine for the taking merely for a few oysters, do let us return to the table to see what else the chef has provided," he said. "I ordered dinner most carefully, I promise you."

With all the polish at his command, he ushered her to her seat and pulled the chair back for her.

"Come, Isabella," he said. "If you are determined to resist my advances, what have you to fear?"

After a moment of hesitation, she gave him a regal inclination of her head and seated herself.

He let his hand rest on her shoulder for a moment. She turned her head.

"Is something wrong?" she asked.

"No. Nothing," he said.

Yes. Everything.

"Actually," she said, "I am quite famished." She gave him one of those pert smiles that he had missed so much during the years of their separation. "Let us see what else the master of seduction has provided."

She removed the cover from one of the silver dishes and laughed out loud.

"Pâté de foie gras!" she crowed. "You used to have more subtlety."

"The stakes are higher now," he said seriously.

"You appear to have forgotten that I detest the stuff," she said.

"No, I have not. The pâté is for me. Like the caviar and the oysters, it is a symbol of what I could not have in my days of deprivation during the war. I told myself that one day I would be back in England, dining in a private parlor with a beautiful lady, and having all my favorites."

"This was a beautiful lady dressed in scarlet satin, no doubt," she said archly, "with a beauty patch at the corner of her mouth and masses of brassy blonde hair."

"Masses," he mused as he gazed at her.

Actually, in those daydreams, the beautiful lady was always Isabella, but he would not tell her that.

In that perverse way of women, she felt safer with the hardened rake than she did with the man who sincerely loved her.

"In fact," she said playfully, "all of this is not a clumsy attempt to break down my virtuous inhibitions, but a much delayed reward for your fortitude."

"You have caught me out," he said, smiling.

If she wanted to think of it that way, so be it.

"Shall I help you to some pâté, since it is closer to me than to you?"

"Please," he whispered.

She put a generous dollop of the creamy substance on a round of bread and placed it on a small silver plate that she passed across the table to him. He popped it into his mouth and licked the excess from his lower lip.

"Now we are safe from temptation," she said as she helped herself to some more of the caviar.

He had been watching the voluptuous expression on her face as she anticipated her taste of the caviar, and he must have missed something she said, for her words made no sense to him.

"I beg your pardon?" he asked bemusedly. "I was . . . distracted."

She gave another of those delightful peals of laughter that her mother would no doubt consider vulgar.

"If you were determined upon a seduction, you would have had strawberries and cream instead, for now my breath smells of fish eggs and yours of liver."

"Is that a challenge, my dear?" he asked with one upraised eyebrow.

"Certainly not," she said hastily. She indicated another covered dish. "What is under that one?"

He peeked under the cover.

"A rare sirloin of beef and asparagus with cream sauce."

She grinned.

"Is that for you or for me?"

"Oh. Did you want some, too? I had planned to feed you only caviar and pâté so that you would be too weak to resist my advances."

She shook her head and handed an empty plate to him, which he obligingly filled with meat and asparagus.

"I suppose there is a sweet?" she asked.

Sheepishly, he lifted the last cover to reveal a bowl of strawberries and one of cream.

"You rogue," she said as she reached for a succulent fruit and popped it into her mouth.

"They are better this way," he said as he dredged a strawberry through the cream. He stood, walked around the table and held it before her lips. She looked into his eyes and took a dainty bite. Without breaking eye contact, he turned the strawberry and popped the rest into his mouth.

And choked on the stem. For a moment, as he gasped for breath, he thought he was going to die.

"Oh, good heavens! Are you all right?" she cried as she stood and pounded smartly on his back.

"Perfectly," he croaked. His eyes were streaming with tears and, to his everlasting humiliation, his nose had started to run. "You do that very well. It is plain that motherhood has taught you at least one useful skill."

"You are too kind, Captain Lyonbridge," she said as he re-seated her.

"But, my poor dear," he said, "do you mean to say you have given up all thought of romance?"

"Of course I have," she said as she helped herself to more caviar. "This really is delicious. Romance is an illusion." She popped the caviar into her mouth. "An illusion fostered by men to get what they want from a woman."

"Isabella! I am shocked," he said.

"Oh, I do not mean *that*. If *that* is all they want, they can hire it for money and no fuss to the matter. No, what a man wants from a woman is a brood mare to give birth to his children, a hostess to manage his household, an ornament for his arm when he chooses to visit the best houses. In short, romance is that cunning device a man employs when he wishes to lure a woman into lifelong servitude."

"And a woman? Are her motives so pure when she exerts herself to please a man? From him she gains a roof over her head, the clothes she places upon her body—"

"And his name for her children," she said softly. "Do not forget that."

"No, Isabella," he said soberly. "I have not forgotten."

He smiled at her, hoping to lighten a conversation that had suddenly taken a too serious turn.

"There is champagne as well," he said, "unless you do not trust yourself to partake in my company."

"I will risk it," she said as he expertly popped the cork. Thank heaven there were *some* skills that stayed with a man forever.

"To your health, then, my dear," he said, toasting her.

"And yours as well," she said with perfect cordiality.

So Isabella thought she was dead to romance, he mused as the bubbly liquor slid down his throat.

Well, he would see about *that*.

CHAPTER 19

It was just dawn, and although Isabella had indulged in rather too much champagne the night before, she awakened with a clear head and a smile of anticipation on her lips.

She and Jamie had stolen out of the hotel before the servants were awake. Now they stood on the beach in their bare feet with their shoes in their hands as they enjoyed the perfect pink and violet sunrise. White gulls flew before the fiery orb of the sun and the air smelled of morning, promise, and salt.

"Aunt Isabella! I found a shell!" Jamie said excitedly as he bent to pick up a perfect scallop shell of white and lavender gray.

"That is lovely, sweetheart," she said, still transfixed by the glorious dawn.

"And here's a wiggling one, with long hair! I can see the sand through it."

"What? No!" she cried in alarm as she dropped her shoes and scooped him up in one arm. "Leave that one alone. It could *bite* you!"

"Why?" he asked. "I only want to pet it."

"It does not want to be petted. It is not a dog," Isabella explained. Imagine wanting to *pet* a jellyfish. "It is stranded on the beach, far from its home in the sea."

Jamie nodded in understanding.

"He misses his mama and papa," he said. "Like I do."

When Isabella put him down again, he walked over to the jellyfish, but kept to a safe distance when Isabella moved to scoop him up again.

"Do not worry," he said to the jellyfish. "Your mama and papa will come back for you."

Then he skipped off further down the beach with Isabella in pursuit.

She felt young again, suddenly. Young and hopeful and in—no! She was *not* in love. Not with *him!* Never mind that her blood sang in her veins, and in her mind a thousand images of him made her smile at the thought of seeing him again today.

He did not, as a rule, rise before noon. There was a time when she had not, either.

Then there was Jamie.

Isabella could only pity those pampered ladies who would not be sipping their chocolate and eating sweet biscuits in bed for at least another four hours. They were missing the most glorious part of the day.

Jamie skipped to the edge of the water and splashed into the lapping waves.

"Jamie! That is far enough!" Isabella called as she ran after him.

He splashed, causing his rolled up pants legs to become damp.

"Eeeeee!" he squealed. "The water is cold."

Isabella reached him and took his hand. She gave an involuntary squeal of her own.

"It is like *ice!*" she cried, laughing. "It looks as if it would be warm, does it not, the way the sun shines on it?"

"I like it!" Jamie said.

"So do I, sweetheart," she said solemnly.

"Look! A horse! It's Papa!" Jamie cried excitedly.

Isabella looked up to see the muscular horse prancing through the water along the beach and a horseman dressed in a scarlet uniform.

"No, Jamie. It is some other officer—"

"It is Uncle Philip!" Jamie cried. Isabella gave a shriek and took off at a run when the boy went pelting toward the horse, splattering his clothes and small, precious person in the water as he drew close to the horse's dangerous hooves.

Philip reached down and grabbed his arm. In one graceful movement, he drew the laughing child up to sit before him on the saddle. In response to his signal, the horse pranced backward. Philip's hands were around Jamie, so he guided the horse with the pressure of his knees.

Isabella put her hands on her hips and squinted up at him. The sun was behind him, and it was like looking into the face of some pagan sun god.

"Do not *dare* ride away with him where I cannot see you," she said.

He reached for her with one imperious hand.

"Come with us," he said.

"But I am not dressed for riding," she said inanely.

He threw back his head and laughed.

"My dear Isabella, you are not even dressed for *walking*," he said. It was true, she realized. Her shoes were back on the beach where she had dropped them. "Come," he said again.

"Please, Aunt Isabella," Jamie said. He held his hand out to her as well.

Isabella bit her lip and looked around her, but there were no members of fashionable society to notice her bare feet and soaked skirt. The thought of taking that well-shaped, muscular hand and being swept up behind him on the horse made her blood pound.

Still, if her mother found out . . .

She gave a guilty glance toward the windows of the hotel.

"No, I cannot," Isabella said regretfully. "It would be most undignified." She stepped closer and held out her arms for Jamie. He shook his head and turned away.

Philip leaned closer, so his handsome, smiling face was out of the glare.

"She cannot see you, Isabella," he said, reading her mind. "The windows are too far away."

"But someone may see me and tell her—"

Philip shook his head as if in disappointment at the recital of an unsatisfactory student.

"My dear girl, you are a grown woman. Surely you can go for a ride on horseback with your betrothed husband without answering to your mother," he said.

Isabella looked at him askance, teetering on the brink of capitulation. The sun was so bright. The water was so blue. And Jamie was bouncing on the saddle in his eagerness for the ride to begin.

She placed her hand in Philip's, and he gave it a squeeze.

"There is the girl who longed for romance and adventure," he said exultantly. "I knew she could not have disappeared completely."

With that, he hoisted her up with that one strong hand so she could put her legs astride behind him. Her body was placed intimately against his back. She leaned back to give herself distance.

"No, it is safer to hold on tightly," he said as he took her arm and placed it firmly around his waist. "You do not want to fall off."

"This is most unseemly," she said. "I cannot sit astride a horse. You must stop and let me get on—"

"Do not be so missish, Isabella," he said. "I cannot let you sit sideways on the horse. You will fall off and break your neck, and then your mother will have to cancel the wedding, and I will never hear the end of it."

She gave a shriek as the horse trotted through the water and shining droplets of water splashed all about them. She wrapped her arms around Philip's torso so tightly that the side of her face was pressed against his strong, muscular back.

"Hold on to Jamie!" she cried out.

"Do not worry about Jamie. I have the lad," he shouted back. "*You* hold on to *me!*"

"Go faster!" Jamie said excitedly.

"No! Do *not!*" Isabella screeched.

"You are riding like a sack of meal, Isabella," Philip said as he turned his head toward Isabella. She looked up into his laughing dark eyes. His mischievous grin was pure Jamie. "Your seat used to be impeccable."

"You may keep your opinion of my seat to yourself, thank you very much," she said, but she could not help being amused.

"There. That was a smile," he said. "I saw it."

"Should you not be watching where you are guiding this great beast?" she snapped.

"Papa's horse is bigger," Jamie said loyally.

"But can he leap like a rabbit over fences?"

"Not with Jamie on his back, he will not," Isabella shouted.

"Certainly not," he said, "but when Adam comes home I shall take great pleasure in challenging him to a contest of horsemanship. We shall see whose horse is the best."

"I think we should stop," Isabella said.

"Why should we?" Philip asked. "You cannot fool me. You are *enjoying* this."

"Because my bare legs are exposed and I think my skirt is riding up my, um—please stop, Philip."

"Good God," he said as he drew back on the reins. She leaped from the standing horse at the peril of a broken ankle and quickly smoothed her skirt down over her limbs.

"I should like to know what *you* are laughing at, sir," she demanded.

"I am laughing at the delightful spectacle of the exquisite Miss Grimsby, barefoot and misted with seawater and her hair loose about her lovely shoulders," he said.

"I look a fright," she said.

"You look glorious. I wish I could commission a sculptor

to take your likeness just as you are and place it in my garden."

"You do not *have* a garden."

"We will have, my dear. Eventually."

Something in his eyes made her blush and turn away. They promised all sorts of wicked adventures.

She felt a tingle of pure joy go through her at the thought of possessing a garden—and presumably a house—with this man. They would live together and perhaps have unexpected adventures like this one. The three of them.

But what was she thinking?

He was attentive now, and would be until they were wed. Then when the novelty wore off, he would seek entertainment elsewhere.

It was the way of men.

The thought of Philip turning to other women while she tried to maintain her pride in the face of the gossip his defection would cause effectively put a damper on the sunny morning.

"Isabella?" he said, frowning as she reached out for Jamie. Jamie was clinging to Philip because he did not want to get down from the horse. "Is something wrong?"

"Jamie is soaking wet," she said curtly. "Hand him over this minute so I can have his nurse dress him in dry clothes."

"Of the two, I would say you were the one most in need of dry clothes," Philip said, appreciatively eyeing her from top to toe. "A wonderful fabric, muslin. It practically disappears when damp. Now if you only had red shoes with laces tied up the leg, you would be right at home at Napoleon's court during the Directoire."

Horrified, she looked down to see he had exaggerated only slightly. She quickly crossed her arms over her bosom as Philip nearly fell off the horse, laughing.

"Since you do not have two more spare arms to take Jamie," he said, "I shall take him into the hotel for you."

She gave him a cross little nod of her head and turned her back to stalk back down the beach.

"I do not want to get down," the child sulked.

"Then you may sit on the horse and I will lead him," Philip said as he dismounted and put Jamie on the saddle. He led the horse by the bridle and kept a firm hand on Jamie's leg as he walked beside him. Soon Philip's long legs and the horse's overtook Isabella.

"Much as I am enjoying the sight of your . . . charms swaying before me in that damp muslin, perhaps it would be more seemly if you join Jamie on the horse," he said when he had drawn abreast of her. She still had her arms across her bosom. "Then you may use Jamie as a shield."

"I am going to sit sidesaddle," she said.

"Certainly," he said. "I will be alongside to steady you."

He took a protesting Jamie off the horse and lifted Isabella to the saddle. She itched to slap the smirk off his face as he took that opportunity to stare at her bosom.

"You cannot blame a man for looking, my dear," he said, "when there is so much worth looking at." He gave her a comic leer. "Here, love. Your shield." He handed a frowning Jamie to her, and she settled him securely in front of her.

"I do not want to ride like a baby in front of Aunt Isabella," he said with a pout.

"Aunt Isabella needs a gentleman to look after her," Philip said, "because she is afraid of horses."

Jamie turned his sweet face to her.

"You can ride with me, Aunt Isabella. I will take care of you."

She gave Philip a fulminating look that promised retribution. It made him laugh out loud.

"Thank you, love," she said to the child. "I feel much safer now."

They had almost reached the hotel when Isabella gave a faint shriek of alarm.

"Turn back," she cried.

"Turn back? Why?" Philip asked. Then he halted his progress to give her an apologetic look as the figure of a woman strode imperiously and angrily toward him. "Perhaps she has not seen us yet."

"She has seen us," Isabella said despairingly.

"Captain Lyonbridge!" Lady Grimsby shouted when she got close to them. "What is the meaning of this disgraceful performance?" Her eyes raked Isabella. "And *you,* missy. Get down from that . . . animal and go to your room in the hotel at once. I shall have plenty to say to you presently."

"Yes, Mother," Isabella said as she lowered her eyes and made as if to get off the horse. It was always better to obey Lady Grimsby when she was in one of these humors.

Instead of helping Isabella down, to her surprise Philip moved to prevent her from dismounting. He looked Lady Grimsby straight in the eye.

"Isabella merely was taking a morning ride with her betrothed husband on the beach," he said. "She is a grown woman and does not need your permission or, indeed, the permission of anyone else to do so."

"Captain Lyonbridge," Isabella whispered. "You are making it worse. Let me down now." Instead, he kept her on the horse without taking his eyes from Lady Grimsby.

"I will not have my fiancée scolded like a naughty child because she went for a ride with me at my request."

"Until your ring is on her finger, she is *my* daughter, and how she behaves in public is my affair and not yours, sir. Get *down,* Isabella." She glared at Jamie. "And take that little brat with you."

Jamie's lip quivered again, and he burst into tears. Isabella clutched him to her bosom and glared at her mother.

"Mother, how *could* you?" she demanded. "He is only a child, and you have frightened him."

Lady Grimsby's lip curled.

"He is just another little b—"

"Don't you *dare* say it," Philip snapped. He glared at her until her gaze faltered. He took Isabella by the waist as she clutched a sobbing Jamie to her chest and set her on the

ground. Then he deliberately stepped between her and Lady
Grimsby, who had already stretched out her fingers like claws
toward her daughter, as if she intended to leave bruises on
her arm. He caressed the side of Isabella's face. "Go inside,
love, and take Jamie with you. Lady Grimsby and I have matters to settle between us, and I think it would be better if
Jamie did not hear."

Love. How sweet it sounded.

"Yes, Philip," she whispered gratefully as she forced herself to walk away with shoulders back, chin held high, and
cheeks burning with mortification.

CHAPTER 20

How dare he look down his nose at *her,* this perfect stranger who had stained the honor of her only daughter—for all that no one in Society knew it—and now made a spectacle of her on the beach at England's most exclusive resort?

Lady Grimsby had known Philip Lyonbridge from the cradle and had watched him grow into a suave, exquisitely groomed, sophisticated young man who knew how to behave in good Society. Once she would have been thrilled by the prospect of Isabella's becoming his wife and assuming the role of Society ornament and hostess for which she had been bred.

But he had changed.

He had become this great brute, riding his huge, over-muscled horse and treating *her* daughter in public with a familiarity that a decent man would not use in handling a trollop. And the way the both of them fawned over that ill-begotten little bastard was positively sickening.

She had thought she knew him! She had frequently permitted him to squire a young Isabella about in Society—with her chaperonage, of course—certain that he would never overstep the boundaries of propriety with his brother's fiancée. In truth, while he was politely and correctly attentive to any personable female, she had rather suspected that he was not overly interested in the opposite gender.

Once she could have intimidated him into compliance with one mean look.

Now he looked the complete barbarian—worse than his brother, the hardened warrior, in fact, because he towered over her with his face set and his eyes blazing with anger. The Philip Lyonbridge she had watched grow from a polite, well-schooled child into a sophisticated man would never have behaved so churlishly to a lady of her wealth and position in Society before he had joined his accursed cavalry regiment.

Be damned to the war! Be damned to the army!

It had ruined every good man she knew.

Well, he was *not* going to intimidate *her!*

She put her hands on her hips and faced him defiantly.

"What have you to say for yourself, Philip Lyonbridge?" she demanded. "If you were not betrothed to Isabella, my husband would have you *whipped* for daring to make a trollop of our daughter!"

He took a menacing step forward. He knotted, then forcibly relaxed his fists. Good heavens! The creature actually looked for a moment as if he might strike her!

"Madam, if you were a man *I* would horsewhip *you,*" he said in a deep, perfectly controlled voice. "Be grateful that I have been bred to show respect for all women, regardless of how little they deserve it."

"Respect? Is that what you call what you have shown my daughter? You have impregnated her, sir, with a . . ." Her eyes fell before the anger in his. "And you have shown her, virtually naked, to every occupant in Brighton. Gentlemen from every window in the hotel were most probably ogling her from their spy glasses. Her and the fruit of your perfidy."

"The fruit of my perfidy," he repeated with a wondering shake of his head. "Lady Grimsby, Jamie is a *child.* Merely a *child,* like any other. And your own grandson."

"No," she said, shuddering. "That *creature* is no flesh and blood of mine. He should have been taken from her at birth. Or rather, he should have been destroyed when he was still in the womb. If I had known the truth, I would have seen to it. You *monster!*"

"You would have endangered her life to destroy her innocent child. *I* am not the monster here, madam."

"It would have been better," Lady Grimsby said, unashamed. "There are far too many bastards in this world, and I do not thank you for adding to their number."

"I thought at first that Isabella had been foolish not to take you and my father into her confidence. I assumed that your first concern would be for *her,*" he said. "I was the one who was foolish."

"My first concern *is* Isabella! She is my only concern."

"Her reputation, you mean."

"Of course. It is everything to a woman of quality. Even you should understand that. And you have made a spectacle of her before all the *ton.*"

"Only a few idlers who have chanced to see a young lady from a distance on the beach," he said impatiently. "You make too much of an innocent early morning excursion."

"She is no longer the girl I reared, thanks to you."

"If that warm, vital woman I was with this morning is the one who has come of it, I am heartily glad. She shall make me a delightful wife, and a devoted mother to Jamie and our other children."

"You will have her following the drum, I suppose," Lady Grimsby said with a sigh of resignation. "She will be miserable. She has no great love for the army, I can tell you. It took away her father for all her childhood, and now it will take away her husband, for I do not deceive myself that you will not leave her and that brat with me and go blithely off to your regiment."

"There you are wrong, Lady Grimsby," he said. "It is peacetime now, and I have had my fill of war. I intend to marry Isabella and turn myself over to my father, Lord help me, for training in managing his properties in preparation for my eventual inheritance. Your daughter will have a rented house in London for the Season until I inherit the town house. She will have a position in Society as a political hostess, because I intend to go into government. In short, she will have everything for which you have bred her and more."

She gave him a look of suspicion.

"You will not go haring off to the army as soon as the wedding is concluded? I do not believe you."

"Believe me," he said dryly. "I have no love for the life."

Lady Grimsby gave an unlovely snort.

"All men talk of how much they want peace, but they go haring off to war at the first opportunity, just the same. Whether it be against Napoleon or a collection of smugglers off the coast in peacetime, it makes no difference." Her eyes grew distant with remembered pain. "And she will be compelled to endure your mistresses, for a man must have his pleasure, and why should you be faithful to her once she has sold herself to you so cheaply and has borne your child into the bargain?"

"You are speaking," he said with clenched jaw, "of my betrothed wife. If she is not treated with every respect in your household, I will remove her and place her and Jamie elsewhere."

"Under your own roof? I forbid such a thing!"

"Certainly not. At a hotel in London or Adam's house in Derbyshire with a hired companion, whichever she prefers," he said. "I would marry her out of hand, but she *will* have her wedding in the spring at St. Paul's, as I have promised, with all the *ton* in attendance. I refuse to deprive her of that, when I have already deprived her of so much."

"I prefer to keep her under my eye," she said.

"And so you shall, as long as we understand each other. You will never again refer to Jamie as a bastard. You will never again give Isabella a dressing-down in public as if she were ten years old. If you have anything more to say of her behavior this morning, you will address those remarks to me. It was *I* who practically forced her to go riding this morning. I wished to give my son a treat."

Lady Grimsby gave a scornful laugh.

"You wished to appear to advantage on horseback so he will transfer his hero worship of your brother to yourself," she said.

"Am I so transparent?" he asked with a sigh.

"Abundantly," she said with satisfaction. "It will not work, you know. Adam Lyonbridge is a warrior born and bred. You cannot keep up this imposture for long, convincing as it may be at the moment, for you are nothing like him, and it is the best thing I can say for you."

"Perhaps," he said dryly, "but, most unfortunately, Jamie does not have your superior taste in such matters."

"I shall not have you horsewhipped after all, I think," she said with satisfaction. "I believe that after this whole affair is over, you will have suffered enough."

With that, she turned on her heel and stalked off to the hotel as Philip let his breath out all at once.

His future mother-in-law, heaven help him, had the tongue of an adder, but she was right, devil take the woman.

Well, he had given his son his dawn ride on the beach. With luck, he was suitably impressed.

Now he must turn his attention to the more important task of impressing his fiancée.

As it turned out, he had not done as badly at this as he thought.

He returned his horse to the stable where it was lodged and returned to the hotel in proper calling attire in order to subject himself to Lord Grimsby's anger, for he had no doubt that Lady Grimsby, for all that she professed to detest her husband, had told him of Philip's infamy. When he was being escorted to Lord and Lady Grimsby's room after being announced by a hotel footman, he found Isabella lying in wait for him just before he came to their door.

"She is very, very angry," she said to him. Her dark eyes were luminous with concern. "What did you say to her?"

"Nothing that did not require saying."

"Papa is beside himself. I shudder to think what she told him. I will go in with you. Perhaps it will defuse their anger."

He smiled at her.

"I have been through this ordeal before, my dear. He cannot be more angry about such an innocent transgression than he was after learning the truth of Jamie's parentage."

"He was weakened by pain from his injury then," she said. "Today he is much better, and more himself."

"You alarm me, Isabella," he said mildly.

"Philip, this is no laughing matter," she said impatiently.

He tipped her face up with one hand under her chin.

"My love, you are concerned for me," he said. "I am touched."

She drew back and placed her hands on her hips in exasperation.

"You are *touched* all right—in your upper works! You do not know what he can do."

"*He* can do nothing," he said, "but send one or two of his minions after me to give me a good thrashing." He bared all his teeth in a defiant grin. With her pretty, concerned face before him as inspiration, he felt he could slay a thousand of her father's whipping boys. "Very well. I will be ready for them."

She almost fell back with horror.

"Philip!" she cried, wide-eyed. "You looked just like Adam when you said that! Pray, *never* do so again in my presence!"

"Forgive me," he said, equally horrified. Whereas he would like nothing better than to have his son's allegiance transferred from Adam to himself, he was abundantly aware of how repulsive Isabella found his warrior-brother's positive relish of a good fight. "I do not know what came over me."

"See that it never happens again," she said. Was that a glimmer of a smile in her eyes?

"Very well, then," he said with a lighter heart than he would have imagined possible under the circumstances.

He gave her a quick kiss on the mouth. She drew back

and stared at him, but she touched her lower lip with one finger, as if to savor the sensation.

"What was that for?" she said breathlessly.

"For courage, love," he said, "as I go off into the lion's den."

"Men," she said in mild disgust, but he did not miss the way her lips turned up ever so slightly at the edges.

She caught his arm when he would have passed on.

"I will be right outside the door if you want me," she said earnestly.

If he wanted her? She would be terrified if she knew how much.

"Thank you, my dear," he said instead as he left her to face his doom.

CHAPTER 21

General Lord Grimsby was, indeed, much more the formidable ogre Philip had secretly feared in his childhood. They had seemed implacable gods then, his father and the general. Even so, he squared his shoulders and advanced into the room.

The general sat in his chair, swathed in a gorgeously patterned silk dressing gown from India. His thick white hair had been combed back from his brow, and his eyes were blazing.

Incredibly, Lady Grimsby was standing behind her husband's chair with one hand on his shoulder. She wore a smug, brittle smile on her face with the avid eyes of any violence-loving spectator anticipating a good thrashing. Lady Grimsby was beautifully turned out, as always, in a pearl gray gown with amethysts at her throat and her dark hair arranged in little curls at her forehead and temples, a mocking touch of femininity that did nothing to soften the severity of her strong cheekbones and jaw.

All of the world knew Lady Grimsby positively despised her husband, but she was not above using him to keep her future son-in-law in line.

"There he is," she said with grim satisfaction, "the creature who has dared insult your daughter before all the *ton*."

She sputtered with indignation when Philip surprised himself by bursting into laughter.

"I see no humor in this situation, young man," the general said with narrowed eyes.

"Forgive me, Lord Grimsby." He gave a polite nod of acknowledgment to the lady. "Lady Grimsby. But her ladyship looked exactly like a handler at a cockfight, ready to launch her champion into the ring with some molting scrap of poultry she expects to give a poor showing."

"How *dare* you," she breathed, "you insolent puppy? My lord, are you going to permit this man to insult me so?"

"Um, no," the general said. "Of course not. Perhaps you should remove yourself, my lady. This is best handled between men."

She gave an indignant huff and stalked out of the room.

"She will probably listen at the door," the general said with a sigh, "to be sure I do not waver in my resolve to blister your ears."

"Blister away, my lord," Philip said. "I am at your disposal."

The general gave him a look of aristocratic displeasure, a look that would have set Philip to cowering in his boots two years ago.

"Your levity at my daughter's expense is most unbecoming, sir," the old man said.

"I have every respect for the young lady who is about to become my wife," Philip said. "My intent this morning was to become better acquainted with her and with our son, not to insult her. Or you or your wife, for that matter."

The general gave a painful grunt as he shifted position in a vain search for physical comfort.

"If I were not a broken man, you would not dare to take liberties with my daughter," he said. He gave a grimace of distaste. "Or *additional* liberties, I should say. Do not make the very grave error of believing that just because I have been injured, I will not exact painful retribution if you do wrong by Isabella. I have not been a good father to her. I freely admit it. But you will be a good husband if I have to thrash you within an inch of your life. Do I make myself clear?"

"Abundantly clear, my lord, and I thank you for your bluntness, for now I can be equally blunt. I will be a better husband to Isabella than you have ever been a father. You will *not* say a word of reprimand to Isabella about this business. If I have any cause to believe you have bullied or mistreated my future wife or my son, I will thrash *you* within an inch of your life."

He approached the general, who got up from his chair to meet him on his feet, even though he obviously found the process painful.

"You dare threaten me?" he snarled to Philip. "Do you have any idea with whom you are dealing?"

"I am dealing with my future father-in-law, heaven help me," Philip said wryly. "This relationship with you and your wife is the *only* thing I did not envy my brother during his betrothal to Isabella, I assure you."

The general gave a snort of mirthless laughter.

"Pretty words," he said. "One would think you actually cared for the girl."

"I do. I will protect her and Jamie with my life, once they are mine."

"You have ever been a cowardly man milliner, Philip Lyonbridge. Your father used to say it was a pity that Adam was not the elder instead of you, because he is twice the man you will ever be. This show of defiance does not fool *me*. The only reason you played your part in spying for the enemy was to save your own skin, and you know it. A real man would have drawn his sword and taken ten lives for his own. Your brother would have done so without hesitation."

"If so, he would have been dead," Philip said coolly, even though the general's words illustrated his inadequacies with excruciatingly painful clarity.

"Adam would have gone down in a blaze of glory instead of masquerading as a peasant and licking the enemy's boots while he sneaked about looking for papers. Like a sneaking coward."

"So he would, my lord. And he would have made Isabella a terrible husband, for he would have left her to follow the drum without the slightest hesitation. As you did your own wife, my lord."

"My wife is my business," the general said wrathfully. "Kindly leave her out of this."

"Leave her out of this?" Philip said with one mockingly upraised eyebrow. "If only one could, my lord."

The general let out all his breath at once.

"Too true," he said ruefully. "Very well, then, Philip. We understand one another. I will accept your word that you intended no insult to my daughter's reputation today. But I must insist that in the future you behave more circumspectly."

"I will, my lord," Philip said with a bow.

His conscience smote him. He *had* been careless, and not only at the seaside. He had come very close to seducing Isabella last night despite his good intentions. And he had wanted nothing more than to ride off with that lovely water nymph of this morning to some secret cove and have his way with her. He was only flesh and blood, after all, and she was so beautiful.

Isabella's parents were right.

He must be more careful from now on. A man could take only so much temptation.

"May I go?" he asked Lord Grimsby.

"Yes," the general said. He seemed to sag into age and infirmity all at once, although his voice was withering. "Get out of my sight."

"I do not believe the two of us are standing here with our ears at the door like a pair of chambermaids," Lady Grimsby said bitterly to Isabella.

"*You* have *your* ear to the door, Mother," Isabella pointed out. "I am merely waiting here for father to finish with Philip so I may speak to him."

Lady Grimsby made a moue of displeasure and a hushing movement with her hand. Then her expression dissolved into one of disgust.

"Just as I feared," she said with an unladylike growl. "He means to let him off easy."

She would have opened the door and stalked into the room to whip her husband into a lethal frenzy if Isabella had not caught her arm.

"It is not *your* reputation that is at stake here, Mother, but mine," Isabella said firmly.

"There you are wrong, girl," Lady Grimsby said with a snort of derision. "A son is a mother's pride, and a daughter is her respectability. Just wait until *you* have daughters. I hope you have a dozen. Exactly like you."

At that, Philip strode from the room and Lady Grimsby gave a small shriek of pain as the door connected with her forehead.

"Lady Grimsby," he said. Was that a *smile* lurking in his eyes? "Your pardon. I did not see you there."

The general's wife colored at being caught listening at the keyhole. She straightened to her full height and gathered the shreds of her dignity around her.

With a single mean grimace, she stalked away.

Isabella turned to Philip. Now his lips were smiling as well. He put his hands on her shoulders.

"I am glad you can smile," she said.

"Your father is not an unreasonable man," he said.

"What he said is not true. You are not a coward simply because you used your wits to survive instead of slashing all about you with a sword or whatever other nonsense he said."

"You heard *that*?" he asked. He sounded absolutely appalled.

"Of course. He was shouting it at the top of his lungs. *Men!* I will never understand the way they think."

"Me, either," he said with a rueful smile.

She had to smile, too.

"Will you take breakfast with Jamie and me, Philip?" she asked.

He cleared his throat.

"Um, no. I pray you will excuse me. It was wrong of me to dine with you alone last night."

"You . . . regret it," she said, feeling hurt.

He tipped her chin up and looked into her eyes.

"Not at all," he said. "I enjoyed it very much, just as I enjoyed our excursion on the beach. I will not apologize to you for that, or to *them*. But neither will I give the gossipmongers more cause to criticize your behavior or mine."

"I . . . see," she said stonily. There were to be no more intimate dinners. No more stolen kisses. No more magical rides on the beach.

"It is just as well," he said ruefully. "You are far too beautiful, and I am not a strong man."

Pretty phrases poured from this man's lips as wine flowed from a tilted bottle.

She gave a dismissive wave of her hand.

"Yes," she said derisively, "I feel very beautiful just now."

She had changed her clothes, of course, and her maid had tried to tidy her hair, but it was partially dried stiff with saltwater, and her skin felt stretched tight—no doubt from contact with the same saltwater—and feverish, for the rays of the sun in the summer morning had been hot. If she didn't sunburn, she would probably *freckle,* which would be a catastrophe of no mean order.

He laughed out loud, which made him look even more handsome and heroic, the irritating man. She had *worried* about him, and now he was laughing at her.

"There is a ball tonight," he said. "May I escort you to it? And your mother, too, of course."

"A ball?" she said inanely, for all the world as if she had never heard of such a thing.

"It is Wednesday," he reminded her. "There is always a ball at the Old Ship on Wednesday."

"Oh, yes," she said. "How . . . kind." She could feel herself blush.

Good heavens, girl. It isn't as if you have never attended a ball before!

Isabella pulled herself together.

"I should be pleased to attend the ball," she said politely. "With you and my mother."

"Until then," he said with a small, correct bow.

To her consternation, she felt his hands briefly touch her hair. She closed her eyes in pleasure at his touch. Then he showed her the limp sprig of seaweed that was suspended between two fingers.

"I will throw it away," she said, mortified, as she tried to take it from him.

He removed it from her reach.

"Not on your life," he said. "You are the first water nymph I have encountered in all my years of coming to Brighton. I intend to press it between the pages of a book."

She had to smile at that.

"Tonight," he said. "I will call for you and your mother at nine o'clock."

"I . . . *we* will be ready," she said. She touched her hair ruefully. "If you will excuse me, Captain Lyonbridge, I had better start making ready at once."

With that, he laughed, bowed again and sauntered out the door, looking more gorgeous than any man had a right to, blast him!

CHAPTER 22

The prince!
The prince!
The prince!

The sibilant whisper swirled all around Isabella as she stood to one side of the ballroom with her mother.

Brighton was the Prince Regent's personal playground, but his appearance at a ball at the Old Ship was still cause for excitement.

He was in his cups, of course. He most usually was at this time of the evening, but he was still an impressive figure as he appeared in the archway of the room with his entourage.

Isabella froze with horror as the corpulent but gorgeously dressed first gentleman of Europe came sauntering forward, wreathed in smiles as he accepted the bows, curtsies, cheers, and well-wishes of the onlookers. Only a few months ago, she had stood before this same prince, pretending to be every inch the proud fiancée as he pinned a medal upon her erstwhile betrothed, Major Adam Lyonbridge. She turned slightly to the side in the hope that he would not recognize her.

The affable prince, however, never forgot a face.

Especially not a pretty one.

"How delightful to see you," he said, smiling at Isabella

as she and her mother sank into deep curtsies. Courteously, he raised Lady Grimsby. "Is your husband present, my lady? I would enjoy exchanging war experiences with him."

In point of fact, His Royal Highness had never participated in a battle in his life, but *he* seemed to believe he had, and no one in England would have had the bad manners to contradict him.

"My husband is recovering from an injury, your highness," Lady Grimsby said. "He is staying at the Castle Inn to recuperate, but he did not feel equal to a ball tonight."

"A pity," the prince said graciously. "But I have no doubt he will be dancing a jig in high style before long with such a nurse to take care of him. You will convey to him my very best wishes for his recovery."

Lady Grimsby's social aplomb would never cease to amaze Isabella. She smiled, for all the world like a devoted wife, even though she detested her husband and did not make a secret of it to anyone.

"Thank you, your highness," Lady Grimsby said, smiling. "He will be grateful, I am sure."

"And Major Lyonbridge?" the prince said, turning to Isabella. "Is he in Brighton as well?"

"Major Lyonbridge is in Scotland with his regiment, your highness," Isabella said carefully.

"And you are not with him?" the Regent asked. "You had better join your husband in Scotland without delay if you are to breed all those little soldiers for England." He laughed merrily at his own jest, and Isabella and her mother had no choice but to laugh as well. "I did not see the notice of your marriage in the newspapers. Major Lyonbridge is well, I hope."

"As far as I know, your highness," Isabella said uncomfortably.

The sprightly middle-aged gentleman accompanying the Prince Regent discreetly whispered in his ear. The Regent's brow furrowed as he regarded Isabella, who could have sunk through the floor with embarrassment.

"They did not marry?" the prince exclaimed indignantly

in what he probably thought was a lowered voice. "What nonsense is—" The gentleman whispered further. The Prince
Regent's eyes rose almost to the middle of his forehead. "He
married another girl instead?" Obviously the prince disap-
proved of what further confidences the gentleman made to
him. He looked a bit flustered as he regarded her with a sheepish look, and Isabella could have expired from sheer humiliation. Even her mother's tongue was stilled as the onlookers
watched with bated breath to see what would happen next.

Wonderful. Now the Regent *pitied* her, and she had no
doubt he was puzzling upon how he could extract himself
from her presence without causing himself further embarrassment.

Philip, at that moment, approached with two glasses of
champagne in his white-gloved hands. He wore the dress uniform of his regiment and could not have looked more handsome.

She could have kissed him for providing this much needed
distraction.

"Isabella, my dear. I am sorry to have been detained. I
hope you are not quite parched." He smiled and nodded pleas-
antly to her companion as he handed one glass of champagne
to Isabella and the other to Lady Grimsby. Then he glanced
back quickly as he recognized the Prince Regent. "Your highness," he said. "Forgive me."

"Your highness," Isabella said. "May I present my fiancé,
Captain Philip Lyonbridge."

"Ah. Major Lyonbridge's younger brother," the Regent said
as he leaned forward with an expression of interest on his
face.

"Older brother, actually," Philip murmured. "It is an honor,
your highness."

"Yes, I remember now. Clever fellow, are you not? Disguised
yourself as a Spaniard and stole papers right out from under
the French officers' noses. Excellent work." He looked from
Philip to Isabella and back again. "It appears that is not all
you made off with," he said as he gave Philip a sly wink and

chuckled at his own wit. He lowered his voice in an attempt at discretion. "Pretty girl. Glad to see she isn't wearing the willow for the fellow. When is the wedding?"

"May, your highness," Philip said, looking awed.

"My felicitations," the prince said. "We will have a glass of wine together in the card room a bit later."

A bit stunned by this royal condescension, Philip bowed as the prince moved on.

"He did not know I did not marry Adam," Isabella said as she put her hand to her fevered brow. "I thought I would die of embarrassment."

"And that odious little man whispering in his ear the entire time," Lady Grimsby said, now that she had finally found her tongue. "He will probably dine out on this story for months."

"Would you like to dance?" Philip asked Isabella. "Or shall I send for your maid and your smelling salts?"

"Do not be silly. I would much prefer to dance," she said tartly. She handed her half-full champagne glass to a passing servant. "If you will excuse us, Mother."

Lady Grimsby nodded and went to converse with another matron as Philip led Isabella onto the dance floor.

"We seem to have weathered that business rather well," Philip whispered into Isabella's ear as other dancers turned to smile at them. From not far away, the Regent raised his glass in a mock toast to the couple and Isabella smiled at him. "If you keep smiling at him like that, he is going to come over here and demand to marry you himself."

"He thinks Adam broke off our betrothal to marry another woman, and I am consoling myself with you," Isabella said.

Philip gave a careless shrug.

"Does it matter what he thinks?"

"No," she said, looking up into his eyes. "Not at all."

"I have news," he said, suddenly serious. "The Congress will begin in a few weeks, and if we are to attend, we must make arrangements for our transportation. My father has procured two cabins for you and your mother aboard ship. My dear, we cannot take Jamie."

"Cannot take Jamie?" Isabella echoed in disbelief. "Whatever do you mean?"

"Think, Isabella. What will we do with him? The crossing is difficult even for a seasoned traveler. Space will be cramped. And once we are there, we will have many social obligations. He will have to stay with a nursemaid most of the time, anyway, and there is no room for a boy's entourage and nursery staff on ship. Not if all you and your mother have is two small cabins." He gave her a rueful smile. "All the world wants to go to Vienna just now, my dear. I am sorry."

"It never occurred to me . . . I did not think . . ."

"I know," he said. "I have tried to procure accommodations aboard another ship, but none are available. There is not enough space left on any of them for all of us to travel together."

"I cannot leave Jamie," she said. "Marian and Adam are in Scotland. If we could not even take his own nursemaid, he will be left with strangers most of the time."

"I know. We would have to hire a nursemaid when we arrive."

"No," she said. "I will not leave him. I will stay in Adam's house in Derbyshire until the wedding instead."

He bowed his head.

"If you will not go, neither will I," he said. "My future as your husband and Jamie's father is more important to me than my future as a politician."

"You would do this for me?" she asked wonderingly.

"For us," he corrected her. "For all of us."

Her lips parted, but no sound came out.

He laughed.

"Speechless, my dear?" he said. "I shall have to remember this clever method of rendering my wife mute after we are married. Did I not tell you that nothing is as important to me as your happiness and Jamie's?"

"Yes," she whispered. "But I did not think you meant it."

She could not have conceived of such a sacrifice on the part of a man simply because a mere affianced wife and a child required it. All of her life, she had been surrounded by men who put duty first and their families second, even though they paid lip service to the ideal of home and family when it suited them.

Philip *did* care for her more than he did his military rank and his political aspirations. And perhaps he truly did love her.

Isabella felt her heart swell nearly to bursting. Tears stung her eyes.

"Here, none of that, my girl," he said, sounding concerned. The dance ended at that moment, so he put his hand at the small of her back to escort her off the dance floor while he carefully shielded her from the curious eyes in the rest of the room with his body.

Philip knew his father would be furious when he told him he would not go with him to Vienna for the Congress, but he did not care. When Isabella looked at him like that, with tears trembling on the ends of her impossibly long lashes and her smile lighting up her face, he would do anything for her.

He escorted her through the anteroom of the ballroom and out into the cool gardens illuminated with torchlight. As soon as they were away from curious eyes, he turned her to face him and put his hands on her shoulders.

"You are trembling," he said. "Are you cold?"

"No," she said as she looked up into his face. She was, at that moment, the Isabella he had known of old. The shy, innocent one who had thought he was a god. He had never expected to see that particular look on her face again.

He gathered her into his arms and kissed her forehead.

It had been so long since she had loved him.

"I wish we could be married tomorrow," she whispered.

This from the girl who had dreamed from the time she was a child of a lavish wedding at St. Paul's that would make her the envy of all her friends.

He couldn't help himself, even though he had vowed to avoid such moments with Isabella for fear he could not stop himself from crossing the bounds of propriety. He bent his head and kissed her. The fragrance of roses surrounded him and almost made him dizzy.

It had been so long, too long since she had kissed him like this, with all the fervor in her innocent heart.

Suddenly she drew back.

"But what if you are called back to serve with your regiment?" she said. "They will *make* you leave me."

"I am going to sell out," he said. "I was going to do so after the Congress, anyway. It is peacetime, remember. The army can get along without me. You and Jamie cannot." He smiled. "As for marrying you tomorrow, I want nothing more. But I have promised you St. Paul's in May, and St. Paul's in May you will have."

"Thank you," she said as she threw her arms around his neck and pressed light, ardent kisses along his jawline. She rested her head against his chest as if, at last, she had found safe harbor.

"Isabella," came an urgent whisper in the darkness beyond them.

Philip gave a long sigh and had to smile when he heard it echoed by Isabella.

Her mother.

Of course.

"We are here, Lady Grimsby," he said.

"What are you doing out here together in the dark?" she demanded. Then she lowered her voice, mindful of other listeners who might have come out into the semidarkness for a breath of air.

"Nothing, Mother," Isabella said.

Philip could feel Lady Grimsby's accusing eyes upon him. He held up both hands to show they were empty, as if that signified anything.

"Come along now," Lady Grimsby said. "His Royal Highness has sent a footman looking for you, Captain Lyonbridge, so you may share a glass of wine with him. A signal honor. Do *not* fail to take advantage of it."

He would have liked nothing better than to consign the ruler of his nation to the devil at that moment, but he would soon be a family man and he had obligations.

He offered his arms to the ladies.

"Certainly I will not," he said with a wry smile at Isabella.

"Your Miss Grimsby is certainly a delightful young lady," the Prince Regent was pleased to say to Philip later, as they sipped on claret in the cardroom. "She will make you a charming wife."

"I thank you, your highness," Philip said.

"See you do better by her than your brother did."

The Prince Regent obviously was laboring under the misapprehension that Adam had done Isabella an injury in preferring Miss Randall's charms to hers, and thereby did Philip's brother a great disservice. However, since this mistake made him think kindly on Isabella, Philip was not about to rise in defense of his glorious brother.

Adam had a reputation for ferocity in battle; he could take care of himself.

"Still in uniform, I see," the prince said. "Too many of our men are selling out now that peace has come."

Perhaps now was not a good time to confide to the prince that he intended to resign from his commission.

"Too true," Philip murmured.

The prince's eye brightened.

"Now *there* is a charming lady."

Philip looked to see which lady the prince's eye had lighted upon and was surprised to see he was looking at Isabella's mother. There was no mistake. She was standing quite alone. She smiled when she saw the two of them looking at her.

"Do you mean . . . Lady Grimsby?" Philip asked.

"Indeed. That fortunate dog, Grimsby, snatched her out from all the men's noses. Your Miss Grimsby, pretty as she is, cannot match her mother for beauty and spirit. When she was in her youth, that is, although she is quite beautiful even now."

"I find that hard to believe, your highness," Philip said. When the prince frowned slightly at him, he added, "But you must excuse me. As the young lady's future husband, I cannot allow any woman to be more fair than Miss Grimsby."

"That's as it should be," the prince said, nodding in approval at this sentiment. "Pity the wedding will not be until May, but the two of you plan to go to Vienna with the rest of the world, I trust."

"That had been our plan," he said, "but as it happens, we will remain in England after all."

The prince's brows drew together.

"Is it your bride's father?" he asked. "Lady Grimsby had said his injuries were not extensive."

"And so they are not," he said.

"Well then," the prince said, clearing his brow. "There is no reason why you may not go."

"We will take it under consideration, your highness," Philip said. "Miss Grimsby has never been abroad. If we do not go to Vienna now, I shall certainly take her abroad on our honeymoon."

"Do so," the prince said cordially. "I should like to tour the continent. The architecture! The music! The paintings! It is unsurpassed. As regent and someday as king, however, I am not permitted to leave England. It would be too dangerous."

"The continent's loss, your highness," Philip said as he bent his head in the suggestion of a bow.

"By Jove, I like you, young Lyonbridge," the prince said. "Too bad you are the younger."

"As you say, your highness," Philip murmured.

Never mind that he was still cast into shadow by the reputation of his magnificent brother. He was not immune to the jealous looks of other men, who would have committed murder for the privilege of sitting alone with the First Gentleman of Europe for the space of a quarter of an hour. Philip's father would have been delighted to see it for all that he deplored the excesses of the so-called Carleton House set, composed of the prince's raucous cronies.

He and the prince took cordial leave of one another, which elevated Philip's status—and therefore Isabella's—immeasurably in Brighton.

Now he could look to his own pleasure.

He had danced once with Isabella. He grew dizzy as a young boy with delight that he could dance with her as often as he chose without calling down the censure of Society upon her head, for now they were formally betrothed and he had already claimed her as his own.

He walked across the room and took her hand. He knew there must have been others in the room, but he saw none of them. Then he led her onto the ballroom floor where a waltz had just been struck up by the orchestra.

"I missed you," he said inanely as they whirled around the floor. "Never has a glass of wine lasted so long."

"And I missed you," she said, sounding almost giddy. "Mother wanted to go back to the hotel to make sure Father is behaving as he ought, for now that he is feeling better he is quite determined to vex her to death, but I told her we could not until I danced again with you. She took a hired carriage back."

Isabella's eyes shone. They would be alone in the carriage as he escorted her back to the Castle Inn. A day ago Lady Grimsby would not have trusted him to be alone with her precious daughter. An *hour* ago she would not have trusted him so much. What a difference the favor of a prince makes.

It was unfashionable behavior in the extreme, but Philip and Isabella stayed and danced every dance until the orchestra members had begun putting away their instruments. Neither wanted the evening to end.

But end it must, and Philip felt his hands tremble like those of an unfledged boy as he placed Isabella's patterned silk wrap over her creamy shoulders and led her into the darkness of the fragrant late summer night.

CHAPTER 23

"Will your father be very angry with you for not going to Vienna?" Isabella asked just as Philip gave the coachman the signal to start by rapping his walking stick on the roof of the carriage and prepared to take her into his arms. He let out a shuddering breath. The thought of his father was certainly enough to dampen his ardor, temporarily at least.

"Very angry," he said ruefully. "He was certain that my appearance in Vienna during the height of the Congress would be sure to command all sorts of preferment for me. Let us not talk about him."

But Isabella was not to be deterred.

"Perhaps you should go anyway," she said carefully.

"No," he replied firmly. "Not without you."

He could feel her eyes upon him in the darkness.

"I do love you," she said after a moment.

"Isabella!" He took her into his arms, but she drew back to look at his face. He could barely see the glitter of her eyes in the muted glare of the carriage lights outside the window.

"I tried not to," she said. "I had suffered such pain when you abandoned me that I thought I could never trust you again. But I love you. I will *always* love you. I cannot help myself."

"You have made me the happiest of men once again," he said, smiling. He kissed her then, certain his heart would burst from sheer ecstasy.

She hesitated, then she gave him a beatific smile.

"We need not go to the Castle Inn just yet," she said. "You have a room here, do you not? Where we may be private?"

He drew back and took in her drooping eyelids and her lopsided smile.

She had drunk three glasses of champagne at the ball, probably more wine than she had ever drunk in her life. He *did* have a room here. And he knew if he took her there in her vulnerable state, the inevitable would happen. He would not be able to stop himself.

But he *could* stop now, before the temptation became too great.

"My dear, it is late," he said. "You must go back to your hotel now."

"I want to be with you," she said with a pout of those pretty lips.

He could not help himself. He kissed her.

"I want to be with you," he said. "And I will be. For the space of the time it takes to drive to the Castle Inn."

"You do not want me, then," she said sadly.

"I want you too much," he said. "But your honor and mine forbid it."

"I do not care," she said recklessly.

"*I* care," he said. "You are my future wife and the mother of my son. If I do not show you the respect you deserve, who will?"

He thought she might argue. He *prayed* she would not, for he was not as strong in this resolution as he pretended to be.

"Too sleepy, anyway," she murmured.

After that, she rested her head against his chest and he just held her in his arms until they reached the hotel.

* * *

"There you are, Phoebe," the general said when his wife walked into the sitting room. Only one lamp burned, so his form as he sat in an armchair near the window had been cast in shadow. She gave a faint scream.

"What are you doing there?" she cried as she held one shaking hand over her heart. "Where is my maid?"

"I sent her to bed," he said, standing.

He did not use his cane, she saw as her eyes adjusted to the dark. He had been recovering rapidly from his injury and had been using the cane less and less often. At his insistence, the hated Merlin chair had been relegated to a storage room in the hotel for shipment back to London. He stumbled a bit, and she rushed to his side to prop him up with a shoulder under his arm.

"You foolish man," she said as they walked into the bed-chamber. "How am I to prepare for bed without my maid?"

"I was once quite adept at undoing your gowns," he said wistfully. To her astonishment, he tightened his grip around her shoulders and kissed the top of her head. "Still heart high," he murmured into her hair.

Her eyes misted.

He used to tell her that often when they were first married. Before he betrayed her. He always said she was just heart high, the perfect height for him.

"Are you in your cups?" she demanded. She would have wrenched herself out of his arms, but then he'd probably fall down without her support and injure himself again.

"Not at all," he said. He positioned her so she was standing in front of him as he leaned with one leg against the bed for support. She felt his warm hands on the bare skin of her upper back as he started to undo the fastenings of her gown.

"What do you think you are doing?" she demanded.

"Preparing my wife for bed," he murmured into her ear.

"Stop this nonsense at once," she said, all in a huff. "Do you honestly think I am going to . . ." She turned and glared at him. "What is the matter, my lord husband? Could you not find any accommodating chambermaids in this hotel?"

"My lady wife," he said with a sigh. "I outgrew my taste for accommodating chambermaids long ago." His voice held a glimmer of humor. "Besides, they are all too young and spry, and I am slower since I fell off my horse."

"How vastly unfortunate," she said, but she couldn't help smiling. His fingers released another hook from the back of her gown and she trembled. It had been so long, but her pride would not permit her to give in so easily. The two of them had grown too old for this sort of thing. Her body had sagged in certain places since he had last seen her without her clothing, despite the fact that she had been careful to limit her intake of food to avoid running to fat. Even if she insisted they extinguish the lamp, he would know by touch that she was not the young girl who once thrilled to his caresses—and had not been for some time.

She extricated herself and faced him defiantly from just beyond his arm's reach.

"Do you think I am going to roll over on my back for you, now that you have deigned to come home to me at last? When I was young, you left me without hesitation to follow your ambition!"

"It was your ambition as well, my dear," he reminded her. "You liked being the wife of a general and playing hostess to the greatest men in the land very well. You certainly did all you could to enhance my status and yours."

"Yes, I entertained every stuffy old bore in England so that you could go off to foreign lands and have wonderful adventures! Did it ever occur to you that *I* might have wanted to have adventures?"

"You?" he scoffed. "I could see *you* living in a tent in the middle of a battlefield."

"And why not?" she asked defiantly. "You were so dashing! So romantic! A hero! And so I *marry* you, thinking that I am going to have all these wonderful adventures, but instead I am confined to London running a household all alone while *you* are off having adventures without me."

"You could have come with me," he said, "but you never wanted to do so."

"Come with you! Have you forgotten I had your daughter to rear properly? Was I to go off with you to please myself and leave Isabella to her own devices? She has ever been headstrong. You have no idea what it has been like for me."

"She is all grown-up now and about to be married," he said.

"Then there is the wedding to be got through," she said with a sigh. "I do not suppose you plan to be of any help whatsoever in that."

"Phoebe," he said, taking her shoulders. "You have done enough, do you not see? Your obligations have all been discharged. As have mine." He stumbled a little, and she quickly gripped his elbows to steady him. "I am an old man, worn out by my duty to my country. And the country is now at peace, at long last. We are free, my dear. Free to live the rest of our lives as we please."

Lady Grimsby gasped at the enormity of this idea.

To be free of obligation at last.

The general laughed heartily.

"Phoebe. If you could see the look on your face," he said. He started to wipe his streaming eyes but lost his balance instead and went pitching toward the bed. She grabbed him and succeeded only in landing beside him. He put his arm around her and pulled her on top of him so she was braced with her forearms against his chest. "Still light as a feather," he said gallantly, even though he was wheezing a little.

"You wretch," she said. "You did that on purpose."

When she would have extricated herself, he tightened his grip.

"The question is, my lady wife, now that your daughter no longer needs you and my country no longer needs me, are we going to continue our war of bitterness, or are we going to make the best of our liberation?" His voice deepened. "We could have a real marriage now, my dear, with all the intimacy that entails. What say you?"

She narrowed her eyes at him.

"I shall have to think about it," she said, striving to gather the shreds of her dignity.

The general flipped his wife over on her back so he could lean above her on one elbow.

"Think later," he said softly as he started to kiss her.

She gave a snort of amusement.

"Very pretty, my lord. I should be more impressed, however, if the gesture had been a little less practiced."

"Ingrate," he said, grinning mischievously. "You have no idea how much pain I am in at this moment."

She rolled her eyes at him.

"Get *off*, you great ox," she said.

"I cannot," he said, unrepentant. "My spine seems to have locked on me. And my legs, of course. We shall have to stay like this until morning."

She was rendered mute by the sheer audacity of the man, and he took advantage of this by placing a kiss on her slightly parted lips. Good heavens! Was that his *tongue?*

"I shall call for my maid," she said.

"Pray do not," he said as he deftly continued to unhook her gown with one hand, "unless you want to shock the poor woman and provide every busybody in the hotel with food for gossip."

"You are *far* too good at this business of undressing women one-handed," she said wryly, even though her lips were already pursed for his next kiss.

"You inspire me," he whispered.

"Did you say so to all the others as well?"

"Others? I do not remember any others," he said.

His tongue was probably turning black after uttering such a lie, but, heaven help her, she did not care.

Her blood was pounding in her ears from sheer excitement.

Pride demanded that she reject him, but she could not.

It had been so long!

She never dreamed when she left the ball early that she would find her husband waiting for her, randy as he had been in their youth. He had her gown around her waist now. She moaned her surrender as her husband's warm hands caressed her pliant body.

Later, when it was over, she rose from the bed. The lamp by the bed was still burning. She looked down at her sleeping husband. His face in repose looked younger and free from pain for once. He was smiling in his sleep and snoring softly.

A man in her bed after all this time. *This* man in her bed after all this time.

There had always been only one man for her. Him. And now he knew it, blast his eyes! She had told him so, over and over. She could not help herself.

And now he was in her bed, snoring, and she could not bear for him to find her there beside him, defenseless, in the morning.

She shuddered.

She had surrendered every bit of her pride to him, and he would *laugh!* She just knew it. She put on her dressing gown and went into the sitting room. The pink glimmer of dawn was just a suggestion at the windows. She frowned when she heard a bit of a clatter in the hall outside her room and the drone of a soothing masculine voice. Something struck the door.

Servants trysting, more than likely. Or some inebriated guest staggering toward his room with some trollop.

Disgraceful!

A feminine giggle emitted from the hall and the sound of a man's lowered voice in response. Lady Grimsby frowned and went forth at once to admonish whoever it was to have the decency to be silent. Isabella's room was near Lord and Lady Grimsby's, and if this irresponsible couple awoke that wretched child, he would keep poor Isabella up all night.

Purposefully, she opened the door and was horrified to see Isabella leaning with her back against the door to her room and Captain Lyonbridge with his hands on her shoulders.

"Isabella!" Lady Grimsby said in utter horror. "What is wrong?" She turned to Captain Lyonbridge. "Is she ill?"

"No," he said. "Isabella, my dear, you must go into your room now. Have you a key?"

"I do not want to," the girl said petulantly. "I want you to kiss me again."

"Captain Lyonbridge!" Lady Grimsby said accusingly. She was absolutely scandalized, for her daughter, she could see now, was drunk and clinging to him like a wanton! "It is plain you cannot be trusted alone with my daughter."

"Not his fault," Isabella said. "I *wanted* him to kiss me. I wanted him to take me to his room, but he would not."

"Lady Grimsby, she is not herself. She had too much champagne and—"

"Enough," Lady Grimsby said. She took her daughter's elbow and knocked softly on the door. Isabella's sleepy maid opened the door, gasped, and quickly took Isabella's other arm to draw her inside.

"I will take care of her, my lady," the maid said.

Lady Grimsby gave a nod of her head and turned to face her daughter's fiancé as the door closed.

"I assure you that nothing happened," Captain Lyonbridge said. He had his shoulders back and his chin thrust forward as if he expected her to hit him and was steeling himself for the blow.

"It better not have, young man," she said sternly. "Now go back to your hotel. I shall have plenty to say to you—and to her—tomorrow. I am seriously displeased with both of you."

"My lady—"

"Go!" she said. She turned and started back to her suite to sleep on the sofa in her sitting room.

What a hypocrite I am, she thought.

To her horror, her husband opened the door and peered out.

"There you are, Phoebe," he said, smiling. His hair was mussed and his dressing gown loosely tied so one could see the front of his nightshirt and his big feet and hairy legs. She had rarely seen her husband less than impeccable in appearance. Military men, as a rule, considered dishevelment some sort of weakness. Strangely, he looked even larger now than he did in uniform with every hair in place. He held his hand out. "Come back to bed."

Phoebe looked from her husband to Captain Lyonbridge and found his astonishment equaled only by her embarrassment. She looked down at the floor.

"I will not, you silly man. I only stayed with you tonight because you were ill," she said.

"What are you doing here, Lyonbridge?" Lord Grimsby asked, frowning. "Not in your cups, are you?"

"No, my lord. Of course not," the younger man said.

"Very well. Carry on," he said with a stiff, military nod to his head. Captain Lyonbridge gave the suggestion of a bow. The general then put his arm around his wife in a suggestion of intimacy and she would have wrenched herself away except for the fact that just then he stumbled, and she could hardly let her husband fall on the floor in front of another officer, could she? Instead, she braced her shoulder under his arm and grasped him around the waist. His skin was warm under his nightclothes.

"Now he knows we have been together," she said. "How *could* you make such a spectacle of me, and in front of our daughter's fiancé?"

He peered into her face as they entered the sitting room.

"Phoebe, are you *embarrassed* at being caught in bed with your own husband?" He sounded amused, the wretched man.

"You make it sound so vulgar. It was no such thing, thank heaven! You should have ordered him not to tell Isabella."

"You are! You are embarrassed," the general said almost gleefully. "You are adorable with your color high like that. One so rarely catches you at a disadvantage."

"I am at a disadvantage most of the time with you, you irritating man," she said.

"And I would take advantage of you again," he said softly.

"Do not be ridiculous," she said. "I have no intention of—"

When she would have extricated herself from their clumsy embrace he held on to her with a firm grip.

"Neither had I, my dear. But I intend to enjoy this madness while it lasts. Come. Where is your spirit of adventure?"

Her lips quivered, but she lost the battle and smiled at him.

"There it is," he said. "The smile I used to love from when you were a girl. I vow I will make you smile some more this night."

CHAPTER 24

"Aunt Isabella!" Jamie called as he pelted into the bedchamber and plucked on a suffering Isabella's nightrail in an unspoken plea for her to pick him up. His legs were too short for him to get onto the bed unassisted.

She managed to open one gummy eye and peer down at him.

He was holding both arms toward her, and some of her self-loathing receded. She pulled him into the bed with her. His warm little body gave her instant comfort . . . little though she deserved it.

"Aunt Isabella? Are you sick?" he asked. His little eyebrows were furrowed in concern.

"No, darling. I only have the headache a little."

Liar! She was sick at heart for having made a fool of herself with Philip. Had she really asked him to take her to his rooms in the hotel? Whatever must he think of her? To her intense disappointment at the time, he had been a perfect gentleman. Now she could only thank heaven that he had not accepted the invitation she so eagerly had pressed upon him.

"Miss Isabella," her maid said as she entered the room and pulled back the curtains to let in the morning sun. Isabella winced. "A footman just delivered this note from Lady Grimsby."

"Thank you, Betty," Isabella said as she received the note. She read it with a sinking heart. Her mother was seriously displeased with her, Isabella knew, because she had seen her disgustingly inebriated state last night. She had been clinging so tightly to Captain Lyonbridge that one could not have wedged a single sheet of writing paper between them. Lady Grimsby had been thoroughly shocked. Now Isabella was about to pay the piper. As if her head did not ache enough already, her mother was about to give her a rare dressing-down. *No one* had a tongue like her mother's when her blood was up.

"I do not think I can go down to breakfast, Betty," she said. Betty, too, had witnessed her disgusting state last night. Her loyal maid had helped her undress and listened to her inebriated raptures about Philip's handsome face and sweet kisses before she fell into a drunken stupor.

The maid took in Isabella's apparent suffering and Jamie's bright, curious eyes.

"Chocolate and biscuits for two in bed, Miss Isabella?" she asked.

Jamie's eyes gleamed with anticipation, and he began bouncing on the bed in delight.

"Yes, I thank you, Betty."

"When I grow up," Jamie said, "I am going to have chocolate and biscuits for breakfast every day instead of that old porridge."

"That old porridge is good for you," Isabella said, smiling. "You have had your breakfast already, have you not?"

"Yes, Aunt Isabella," he admitted. "But I would like a biscuit, please."

More likely a dozen biscuits, knowing her Jamie's love of sweets, Isabella thought. But why should she not make him happy with this small treat? Indeed, she could use some cheering up herself.

"Captain Lyonbridge is talking to Lord and Lady Grimsby,"

Jamie said. He frowned. "I asked him to help me find shells again, but he said all the shells are gone now. And he did not bring his horse today."

It was plain that Captain Lyonbridge had sunk several levels in Jamie's esteem, and Isabella was sorry for it. The arrival of the chocolate and biscuits restored Jamie to his usual sunny humor.

Once the evidence of their indulgence had been cleared away, Betty came to the doorway of the bedchamber.

"Come, Master Jamie," the maid said. "Your nurse is waiting to take you for a walk."

"I want to go with Aunt Isabella," he said. He looked up at Isabella with a confident smile. It was true that she rarely denied him anything. She hated to disappoint him.

"Go with your nurse, Jamie," she said. "Betty is right. I must dress now. I will see you later."

"Yes, Aunt Isabella," he said as the corners of his lips turned down in a pout. His imposture of a mistreated child was somewhat compromised by the smear of chocolate on his upper lip and the crumbs clinging to his cheeks.

"Here, Master Jamie," Betty said fondly as she wiped the boy's face with a serviette. She took his small hand and started to lead him from the room. The child turned back.

"I love you, Aunt Isabella," he said.

Her heart turned over.

"I love you, sweetheart," she whispered. Sentimental tears rose in her eyes.

Betty returned to find her sitting dejectedly at the side of the bed, regarding her bare toes in sad disapproval.

"None of that, Miss Isabella," Betty said bracingly. "Put a smile on your face and hold your chin up or Lady Grimsby, if you'll pardon the liberty, will have your head for washing. Not one to tolerate weakness is Lady Grimsby."

This was frank, indeed, but Betty was not an ordinary servant. She had seen Isabella at her worst—spoiled, selfish, jealous, pregnant without benefit of husband, disgustingly inebriated, and now maudlin. Isabella felt like a veritable parade of the seven deadly sins. She had no secrets from this maid. None at all. Betty had been present at Jamie's birth and helped propagate the deception before the servants of the household that the child was Marian's and not hers.

Here was one human soul with whom Isabella could be completely honest.

"Oh, Betty, I do not know how I can face him," she said as she put her head in her shaking hands.

"Your father or the captain?"

"The captain," she said wryly. "My father's disapproval is such a usual condition that I am well acquainted with it. And then there is my mother. I shudder to think what they will do."

"Stop it, Miss Isabella," Betty said soothingly as she took Isabella's elbow and made her stand up. She took the fabric of the nightrail and Isabella obediently lifted her arms so she could remove it. "You are frightening yourself. You have done nothing so very bad after all."

"You do not know the half of it," Isabella said bitterly. Betty's hands froze on the fabric.

"There is more?" she asked. "Last night you said you danced with him at the ball, and he took you home alone in the carriage and you exchanged some kisses, then he escorted you to your room and Lady Grimsby caught you at it, and then I opened the door and brought you inside and put you to bed."

"Is that not enough?"

"Not enough for all this carrying on," Betty said with a smile. "Come now, what will you wear?"

"How can I think about *that* at a time like this?" Isabella asked pettishly. "Oh. The blue, I think. With the yellow kid shoes."

It was her most demure day gown, and Philip had complimented her on it several times.

"Your gold locket?"

"And the small pearl earrings," Isabella said as she fell into the soothing routine of her toilette.

"An excellent choice, Miss Isabella," Betty said with satisfaction. "Do not worry. If he was lashed to the stake with the flames licking at his ankles, your Captain Lyonbridge would not reveal a word about your behavior—no matter how wanton you think it—to his lordship."

"No, he would not," Isabella agreed, but it gave her little comfort.

"There you are, Isabella," Lord Grimsby said as Isabella entered the sitting room of her parents' suite. Philip was already there, with his dark hair brushed to a high gloss, dressed meticulously as always with spotless white gloves on his hands and his boots polished.

He looked wonderful, while the signs of dissipation were no doubt written clearly upon her face. Still, she held her chin up and marched into the room. To show weakness, as Betty had said, would be a grave error. Philip stood at once, and his blue eyes searched hers.

"You are well, Isabella?" he said just under his breath as he put his arm on the back of a chair and settled her in it.

"Quite well," she lied in response to this confirmation that she must look absolutely dreadful. She was thankful he could not see her knees knocking together under her skirts. "I thank you."

"Good morning, Mother. Father," she said in greeting as she turned to her parents.

"Isabella," Lady Grimsby said stiffly. Her face was severe, but Isabella had expected that. "My lord?"

Lord Grimsby cleared his throat.

"Yes. In view of what happened last night—"

"Mother put the worst possible interpretation on that, I imagine," Isabella said bitterly. "She is right. I behaved badly. I admit it and I am sorry for it. She could not begin to understand—"

"I was young once," Lady Grimsby snapped. "Be still

now, and listen. Captain Lyonbridge has seen quite enough bad behavior from you, my girl, without listening to you contradict your father."

"*You* contradict him all the time," Isabella could not help saying.

"Silence!" Lady Grimsby snapped. After a moment she nodded to her husband and he took up his words.

"As I was about to say," Lord Grimsby continued, "in view of what happened last night, Lady Grimsby and I think it would be best if you and your fiancé are chaperoned at all times to prevent the repetition of such an incident in the future. To be frank, it is months until May, and although regrettable accidents happen —and *did* happen—we do not want you having a six-month child shortly after your wedding to provide meat for the gossips."

Isabella felt her jaw tighten at this unveiled reference to Jamie's birth.

"I will not have my son—"

"*Our* son," Philip growled. His eyes were blazing in anger at the general.

"*Our* son," Isabella said as she met his eyes, "referred to as a 'regrettable accident.' Jamie is my heart. I will *never* regret bringing him into the world."

"That is as may be," Lord Grimsby said dryly. "But one child born on the wrong side of the blanket is quite enough, I am certain even you will agree. Captain Lyonbridge has accepted the blame for what happened last night. He should never have permitted you to drink so much champagne. And he should never have taken advantage of your condition—"

"He did *not* take advantage of my condition," Isabella snapped. "I am a grown woman. I make my own decisions. I *chose* to drink too much champagne, and I have suffered for it."

"I will not tolerate these impertinent interruptions from you, my girl," Lord Grimsby said sternly as he stared right into her eyes. "Captain Lyonbridge took advantage of you last night. He has admitted as much and apologized for it. He assures your mother and me that it will not happen again. We have taken steps to ensure that it will not."

"What have you done?" Isabella breathed. She looked to Philip, but he was looking down at the floor.

"You will stay with the child at our house in London until the wedding in order to be available to your mother while she is making arrangements for the wedding," Lord Grimsby said. "Captain Lyonbridge will go to Vienna to join his father. Perhaps you did not know that he has been given a very flattering appointment to a position on Lord Castlereagh's staff in Vienna, and I have convinced him that he must accept it."

"Philip!" Isabella cried. "How *could* you agree to such a thing?"

"I am sorry, my dear," he said woodenly. "It is for the best. And it is only for a few months until this whole thing cools down."

"You promised me you would not go to Vienna," she said, hurt to the bottom of her soul. He was going to leave her after all.

"Yes, and for no other reason than to remain accessible to my daughter," Lady Grimsby said angrily. "Once a rake, always a rake." She gave her husband a fulminating look as if he were somehow to blame for the incident. "Well, here is an end to *that* precious plan."

"If I do not comply," Philip said, "they will send Jamie to my brother's house in Derbyshire with his nurse and a nursemaid while you remain in London to prepare for the wedding. You know they have the power to do it, and there is nothing we can to do stop them."

So *that* was why he had agreed to such an outrageous condition. They were going to take Jamie away from her!

"After all," Lady Grimsby said in triumph, "he is known as your brother's stepson. It is entirely appropriate for him to stay at his stepfather's house rather than mine. This would be the most suitable arrangement all around, and your father and I will put it into execution without hesitation if Captain Lyonbridge refuses to comply. In addition to that, it is his duty to exert himself to the fullest to establish himself in the esteem of those who command the most power at Whitehall. It was a romantic and extremely foolish gesture for him to offer to turn down such an advantageous appointment. Social status is *everything,* Isabella." She looked at her husband and held his eyes as she continued. "This animal lust you feel for him will pass, I assure you. In the end, your position in the eyes of the world is all you will have to give you comfort when this temporary insanity has passed."

Isabella bared her teeth in a snarl.

"*You* would not understand how I feel about Jamie or about Philip," she said. "You have a lump of coal for a heart. I do not believe you have ever loved anyone in your entire life. Not your own husband and certainly not me. Perhaps he would not have strayed if *you* had been a true wife to him!"

The general rose and glared at his daughter.

"You will apologize to your mother at once," he said in a voice so quiet that it sent prickles up Isabella's spine. He used that tone of voice only when he was very, very angry.

"I do not care," she said. "She has no idea what it is to love a man. To yearn for him. To *burn* for him."

Lady Grimsby's face was ashen.

"Isabella, my dear, as your betrothed husband I really must insist that you apologize to your mother," Philip said unexpectedly. He rose to stand beside her chair and put his hand on her shoulder. She looked up at him, but he was looking at Lady Grimsby who, oddly, colored under his regard and lowered her eyes. "I feel certain that is not true."

Isabella put both hands to her mouth. She wished the floor would open beneath her chair and swallow her up.

"Mother, I do not know what possessed me to say such a cruel thing," she said softly.

"I do," her father said grimly. "It is the aftereffect of strong drink."

"You should know," his wife snapped. Lord Grimsby merely

lifted one eyebrow in her direction and she looked down at the floor again.

"Isabella, you must trust your mother and me to know what is best for you," Lord Grimsby said.

"I am not a child," she said quietly. Philip's hand on her shoulder tightened bracingly.

"I am severely disappointed in you," Lord Grimsby said, "as is your mother. There is nothing more to be said. Lyonbridge has given his word on it, and so it shall be."

Isabella stood.

"I will never forgive you for this," she said to her father. "Or you," she added to her mother.

"Will you ever forgive *me,* Isabella?" Philip asked.

Isabella turned to him and took both his hands in hers. Lady Grimsby started forward with a frown, but the general caught her arm and shook his head at her.

"You have promised this to keep them from taking Jamie away from me, even though you knew it might cost you my love," she said softly. "For that, I can forgive you anything."

She put a shaking hand to her throbbing head.

"You must excuse me," she said. "I am unwell."

Philip's eyes were full of concern as he put an arm around her waist to steady her.

She gave him a wry smile of reassurance.

"I am not going to faint, Philip," she said. "But if you do not release me at once, I may desecrate the carpet in a way that will send Mother into strong convulsions."

As Lady Grimsby gave a shocked gasp, Isabella put one hand to her mouth and made her escape. As she did, she could have sworn she heard Philip laugh.

Pride and admiration swelled within Philip's heart as he regarded the disgusted faces of future mother- and father-in-law.

"You look rather pleased with yourself under the circumstances," Lord Grimsby said sourly.

"She loves me," Philip said. He could not stop the silly smile from spreading all over his face. "She truly does. The effect of the champagne has worn off, but she may as well have shouted it to the world just now."

"Get out of my sight," Lady Grimsby snarled. But she was looking at her husband, not at Philip.

"You would have preferred that I lash him to a tree and have at him with a horsewhip, I suppose," the general said. Incredibly he smiled at Philip. "Remember this, boy. If the enemy ever captures you, do not let them give you to the women."

He put his hand on Philip's shoulder.

"This separation from Isabella will go hard, I know." He looked at his wife. "But that will make your reconciliation all the sweeter."

The old goat, Philip thought admiringly as Lady Grimsby's face turned a becoming shade of pink.

"Run along, lad," the general said as he put one arm around his wife. "Lady Grimsby and I have other matters to discuss. And you have packing to do."

Philip felt the temperature in the room rise a few degrees as Lady Grimsby raised her head and gazed into her husband's eyes.

"Yes, my lord," Philip said as he removed himself in some haste from the room. Once out of their sight, he allowed his shoulders to sag. The last thing he wanted was to go to Vienna, but go he must.

"Philip," said Isabella as she stepped out of her room. She walked forward and took his hands. "It is only for a month or two," she said bravely. "I can stand it for that long. I think."

He raised her hands in his. He kissed the back of one and then the other.

"I will miss you and Jamie. So much," he said softly. "But they left me with no choice."

"They have no hearts. Either of them," she said bitterly. "Not like us."

Philip remembered that smoldering look exchanged between Lord and Lady Grimsby and bit his tongue. His sense of honor had been strongly tested that day.

"No," he said. "Not at all like us."

She smiled up at him, although her eyes were sad, and he kissed her cheek.

"I must go back inside," she said with a wry smile. "It would not do for them to catch us talking alone in the hall."

"No," he agreed, even though, if he were any judge of the matter, it was unlikely that either Lord Grimsby or his wife would emerge from their room before noon. "I must go."

Her fingers clung to his for a moment, but he hastily let go of her when the door to her room opened and Jamie emerged.

"Captain Lyonbridge!" he said. "Will you get your horse now?"

"No, lad, for I will be very busy today," Philip said. "I must go to London tomorrow, and then to Vienna to join my father. I am sorry."

"It is all right," the sweet child said wistfully. "I miss my papa, too."

He meant Adam, of course. It hurt Philip more than he had a right to expect. He swallowed against the lump that had risen to his throat.

"Right," Philip said as he gazed into Isabella's sympathetic eyes, not caring that she saw the regret in his own. A tugging on his leg made him look down to see Jamie with his arms open, his eyes closed and his lips pursed.

Philip's heart swelled as he bent to receive his son's kiss. His arms tightened around the boy as he just held him close.

"Farewell, lad," he said softly. "Take care of your . . . aunt."

"Yes, Captain Lyonbridge," Jamie said as Philip rose, met Isabella's eyes, and formally kissed her hand.

"Safe journey," she whispered.

With that, he turned to go. His last glimpse of Isabella was with her back ramrod straight, her eyes clear, and her hand resting protectively on her son's head. He knew at that moment that she could do without Philip perfectly well for the space of a few months, but not for two days could she live without her son.

He had done the right thing, although it brought him little comfort when he faced the prospect of being separated from both of them for so long.

CHAPTER 25

It was almost eleven o'clock, and a ball was in progress at the Old Ship.

Philip hesitated before the entrance to the ballroom. He knew Isabella was within, dutifully chaperoned by her mother, for it would not do for Miss Grimsby's absence from a ball in Brighton to occasion remark. Her absence would declare to the world that she was ashamed of her behavior the night before.

One must never permit the creatures who would feed upon one to smell fear, for that would surely bring them slavering down upon their victim. The rule was the same whether one was on the battlefield or in the ballroom.

He looked down at his dress uniform and suddenly longed for his dark evening kit, the one he had worn before he joined the army, instead of this garish scarlet. How ironic that in those days he would have given his eyes for the right to trick himself out in military glory.

He would leave for Vienna the following morning. His passage already had been booked. It would be kinder for both himself and for Isabella if he would go without seeing her again. They had already said their farewells. But he *could* not do so.

When he was announced, he spotted her at once. She had turned her face in his direction as if she were a flower seeking the rays of the sun. A smile trembled on her soft lips. Lady Grimsby was at her side, and the older woman's jaw clenched, but she thrust out her chin at his approach. Incredibly, Lord Grimsby was present as well, although he carried an ivory-headed cane.

For a moment, the general tightened his grip on the cane as if it were a sword. Then he relaxed his stance and smiled grimly at Philip.

"There you are, Lyonbridge," the general said. "Off tomorrow, are you?"

"Yes, my lord," Philip said, but his eyes were fastened on Isabella's. "Will you dance with me, Isabella?"

"With all my heart," she said softly as she held out her hand and he took it in his.

"We were about to leave," Lady Grimsby said, frowning. The general touched her shoulder. The merest touch, but it made her look down. "I suppose it will do no harm for you to have one dance together. No slipping off into the gardens, mind."

"Of course not," Philip said. "Isabella?"

It was a waltz, which gave him an excuse to hold her in his arms. The gods were kind, for once.

"I am glad you came," she said, smiling sadly into his eyes as he whirled her onto the floor filled with dancers.

"I could not stay away," he replied. He rolled his eyes heavenward. "I sound like one of those silly chubs in those dreadful romances girls are always reading. What an unfortunate effect you have on my powers of address."

"I like it," she said. She bit her lip. "I will miss you. So much."

"And I, you," he said. "Let us not think about that now. The time will fly, for Lady Grimsby will put you through your paces over the wedding plans. And I will be back from Vienna before we know it."

"My mother has planned so many weddings for me that

she could do this one in her sleep," Isabella said wryly. "I am surprised the shopkeepers can receive us with a straight face by now."

Philip had to laugh, and she gave him an answering smile.

"Everything must be of the best," he said. "Order away with a lavish hand. I will stand the nonsense for whatever your father will not."

"That would be excessively improper," she said primly. "Besides, my mother will see to it that we are wed with ample ceremony to support her lofty opinion of herself and her status in Society. It will be a tedious affair, I warn you. All of the weddings she has planned have been shockingly elaborate, and she will outdo herself this time to dazzle the skeptics. It is a lowering thought that even the most critical mouth can be stilled when its owner has been royally fed and entertained."

"The Prince Regent has suggested that he may attend the wedding," Philip said.

Isabella's eyes widened.

"Mother will be in transports," she breathed.

"So she will. We have only to behave ourselves for the space of a few months, and then you will be mine and we may do anything we please."

Isabella blushed under his regard.

"Stop looking at me that way, you little hussy," he whispered. "Or I will not be able to stop myself from kissing you right here in the middle of the ballroom floor for the edification of all the *ton* and both your parents, no matter what I have promised them."

Isabella looked adorably pleased with herself.

"Yes, Philip," she said demurely.

The dance was over too soon, and he forced his arms to release her. She accompanied him in silence to her waiting parents, who regarded the two of them with identically grim expressions on their faces.

"Thank you for the dance," Philip said solemnly as he relinquished her to them. "I will take my leave of you now."

He kissed her hand and bowed to Lord and Lady Grimsby, who acknowledged this courtesy with regal inclinations of their heads in perfect unison.

Then he turned and walked away, glad, after all, that he was wearing his uniform and the eyes of the females present followed him as he crossed the ballroom.

It was small comfort that he should make a brave showing of her last sight of him, but it was something, at least.

Philip Lyonbridge, you are a sad, vain creature, he chided himself as he passed through the anteroom and made his way to his lonely chamber.

Isabella crept from the hotel at first light. She had not even awakened Betty to tell her where she was going. If the maid were questioned, Isabella did not want her to know the truth, for Betty, despite her unquestionable loyalty, was terrified of Lady Grimsby and would not be able to lie to her face.

Isabella had awakened Jamie and now held him closely in her arms, for his little legs could move with neither the haste nor the stealth that the occasion demanded as she bundled him into the hired carriage she had secretly arranged to have waiting for her.

She and Philip had said their farewells. Twice. But Jamie had cried last night when he learned he would not be permitted to see his Uncle Philip off in his carriage, and Isabella had decided it was his right. Besides that, she wanted to bid him a safe journey without the prying eyes of her parents and all of the *ton* upon them. Her parents would stop her if they found out she planned to steal out of the house with her son to see Philip off.

So they would not find out until it was too late.

Isabella recognized Lord Revington's carriage, all prepared for a journey with Philip's trunk strapped to the roof and the driver waiting upon the box. Then Philip emerged from the house dressed in ordinary traveling clothes. He looked different without his uniform, more like the man with whom she had first fallen in love. His eyes were sad and weary until he saw them. Then his face lit up. He stepped forward quickly as his valet unobtrusively moved toward the carriage to wait for him.

"My dear," Philip said as he approached her. "What a delightful surprise." He ruffled Jamie's dark hair. "Good morning, lad," he said.

"Good morning, Uncle Philip. Where is your horse?"

"He is already at my father's house," he said. "My groom took him there yesterday evening. I did not wish to take him to Vienna with me. Horses never complain, but they must stay below deck with all the other horses aboard ship, and it makes them lonely."

Jamie nodded solemnly, and Isabella's heart swelled with love for Philip. He knew exactly how to talk to Jamie so he would understand. What a wonderful father he would be. *Will* be, she corrected herself.

"Farewell, my love," Isabella whispered as she threw herself into his arms, which made Jamie give a surprised squeak at being crushed, as well, against Philip's coat. Philip smelled deliciously of bay rum, as always. He tightened his arms around both of them for a moment, and Isabella felt totally at peace.

"Farewell, my dear," Philip whispered into her hair. He smiled at the child. "When I return from Vienna, I will be looking about for a pony for you, Jamie. You are not too young to sit a horse."

"Papa already bought me one," Jamie said proudly. "It is at home." His brow furrowed. "I miss him, but Lady Grimsby said I could not bring him to her house, because there is no room in her stable."

"She will have to make room," Philip said tightly. "I shall see to it that he is brought to London as soon as I return."

Jamie smiled at him.

"Will you bring Papa and Mama with you?"

"They will come home for the wedding, surely," Philip

said patiently. "But they are in Scotland now, a place far away from Vienna, and I will not see them there. Farewell, lad."

Jamie gave him a kiss on his cheek as Philip bent to put him down. Then Philip enclosed Isabella in his arms and kissed her until she was breathless.

"I will return the moment I am permitted to do so," he promised. "Farewell, my love."

With that he got into the carriage, opened the window and raised his hand in salute to them as the carriage drove off. Isabella stood watching the carriage for a moment after it had disappeared around a corner and the dust it had raised in its wake settled once more.

Isabella looked up to see the sun peek out from a cloud and the heavens blush with rose and lavender. It would be a glorious morning.

"It is a new day. Let us go to the beach and gather some seashells," she said recklessly to her son as she returned to the hired carriage that had been waiting for them.

"I see Miss Grimsby did not accompany you," Lord Revington said by way of greeting as Philip stepped off the ship and the porter followed with his trunk. "Dare I hope that the faithless little jilt has put an end to it?"

Philip gave a long-suffering sigh.

"Now, Father. I told you what would happen if I heard one word of censure about my fiancée," he said. He accepted the hand his father had extended to him. "Farewell. I am for England again."

At that, he turned sharply and started back toward the ship.

"Come back here!" Lord Revington shouted. "You are dashed touchy all of a sudden."

"Apology accepted," Philip said as he looked over one shoulder. He looked around. "Delightful day."

"If not to escape from the girl and her mother and all the

wedding preparations, why are you here?" Lord Revington said.

"The matter is somewhat delicate," Philip said. "Lady Grimsby misinterpreted something she saw at the hotel, and she and Lord Grimsby decided it would be better for me to remove myself from . . . temptation, as it were. So I am here to accept the vastly flattering post on his staff that Lord Castlereagh offered to me, after all."

Lord Revington's brows drew together.

"Do not tell me you were caught diddling the girl!"

"Certainly not! I was merely escorting her to her room from a ball at the Old Ship, during which she had a glass of champagne too many and—"

"You were caught in a compromising condition. Fully clothed, I trust."

"As was she," Philip said. "*Nothing* happened. Nothing *would* have happened. Most unfortunately, Lady Grimsby was awakened by Isabella's giggling as we passed by her door and came to investigate."

Lord Revington gave a skeptical snort.

"And so you have come so tamely to Vienna merely because Lord Grimsby gave you your marching orders. How did he persuade you to do it? I wish you obeyed me so well!"

"Lord and Lady Grimsby threatened to keep Isabella confined in London and send Jamie to Adam's house in Derbyshire with his nurse if I would not comply. I did not want to come to Vienna, but Jamie is a two-year-old child and he needs Isabella more than she needs me at the moment, so here I am."

Lord Revington gave him a sideways look.

"Lady Anne is in Vienna. Still as well-bred, rich, and unwed as when you saw her last."

"I have not the least interest in Lady Anne," Philip said, "other than to express the wish that she is in tolerable good health, along with her father and mother, of course."

"The marquess could be instrumental in having the government appoint you to a highly desirable diplomatic post. What say you to Paris or Brussels or Russia?"

Philip thought about being a diplomat. He spoke several languages and his lovely Isabella was *born* to be an international hostess. Jamie would travel with them all over the world. So Adam had purchased a pony for Jamie? Philip would take him to India and have him mounted on an elephant before he was a year older, by heaven!

"Highly tempting," he admitted.

No more war. No more being bear-led by his father. He would take great pride in presenting his beautiful Isabella to all the crowned heads of Europe, those who were left in power.

"Excellent! All you need do is be conciliating toward Lady Anne and her parents, and there are no heights to which you may not climb."

"I am not going to marry Lady Anne," Philip insisted as his pretty dream faded.

"She has been wearing the willow for you ever since that ill-fated house party," Lord Revington said. "Her parents brought her to Vienna primarily to give her thoughts a new direction."

"They will be wishing me to the devil, then," Philip said wryly.

"No, they are wishing Miss Grimsby to the devil. Your appearance in Vienna without her will lead them to believe the marriage is no settled thing. All I am asking is that you do nothing to disabuse them of that notion for a little while."

"Surely you are mistaken," he said. "If not, I will have to tell them the truth of the matter myself. It is not the act of a gentleman to lead a young lady on when he intends to marry another."

"When did you become so stuffy?" Lord Revington asked in disgust.

"Fatherhood has a way of taking the frivolity out of a man."

"You have got that right, boy," Lord Revington said with a sigh. "Just try to be conciliating."

"I will try," Philip said. "But I am going to marry Isabella

Grimsby in May, and nothing that happens in Vienna will change that fact."

"It is a long time until May," Lord Revington said as he signaled for the porter to follow. He took Philip's arm and led him away. "No one makes pastry like the Viennese, my boy. You must be famished." He clapped Philip on the back. "By Jove, it is good to have you with me."

Philip gave his father a surprised look. He had been a dutiful rather than affectionate father. But he saw Lord Revington was sincere. He looked . . . happy. Philip's mood softened. After all, two years ago the old man thought his eldest son was dead. Perhaps now, during this interlude in Vienna, they would grow closer. Now that he was a father, Philip appreciated the bond between parent and child a bit more than he had during his rebellious youth.

"Thank you, Father," Philip said. "It is good to be here."

"We will stop at a coffeehouse for a bit of pastry," Lord Revington said, "and then we will go on to the hotel. There is a ball tonight. I had not thought to attend, although I received an invitation, of course. It will be a splendid opportunity to show you off. You have brought your dress uniforms, I trust."

"Every one of them," Philip confirmed.

"Excellent," Lord Revington said as he clapped Philip on the back again. "The Congress has not yet officially begun, but most of the important men have already arrived."

He quickly bundled Philip into an open carriage, and Philip leaned back gratefully against the seat. It had been a long voyage, and although Philip did not suffer from seasickness, it was good to be free of the pitching and swelling of the waves. His skin felt stretched across the bone, so dry it was from the salt air.

"There, that one!" Lord Revington said when they had been traveling for a short distance. "The best pastry in Vienna, upon my word! Driver! Stop here!"

Obediently, Philip followed his father into the coffeehouse, where the two of them were ushered quickly to a table by an obsequious waiter. Obviously Lord Revington was well known there. Two cups of hot chocolate topped with cream and sprinkled with cinnamon were placed before them immediately. Lord Revington and the waiter debated the rival merits of various kinds of pastry while Philip sat back and marveled at his father's cheerful mood.

When the waiter had left, Lord Revington leaned forward and lowered his voice.

"Have I mentioned how good it is to have you here, boy?"

"You have, Father," Philip said, smiling, "and I am glad I came."

He already missed Isabella and Jamie like the very devil, but he would make the best of the situation.

Lord Revington looked past Philip toward the doorway and rose at once to his feet. Philip looked over his shoulder and stood as well.

"Is that Lady Anne?" Philip asked in disbelief as he regarded the pale, languid young lady who seemed to require her mother's assistance to walk across the room. What happened to the vibrant horsewoman who had come to his father's house party to enchant the heir? "What ails her?"

The shop was crowded, and the young lady did not seem to see them at first. Suddenly she was before them, and she raised a trembling hand to her forehead when she came face to face with Philip.

Now, this was deuced awkward!

"Lady Anne," Philip said politely. "I hope I find you well."

To his consternation, Lady Anne's eyes rolled up in her head and she would have fallen in a swoon at his feet if he had not caught her. He quickly seated her in the chair and called to a waiter to bring water as he chafed her wrists. Her head fell back and her hat fell off. Lord Revington retrieved it as the marchioness waved her smelling salts under her daughter's nose. Lady Anne sniffed and opened her eyes wonderingly as a concerned Philip touched her cheek.

"Captain Lyonbridge?" she said weakly.

"Lady Anne," he said, relieved that she seemed to be somewhat recovered. The waiter brought water, and he held it to her lips as she sipped it.

"I am so very sorry," she said faintly. "I do not know what came over me."

"You are not well," he observed.

"No," she agreed faintly. "Mother, I think we should go back to the hotel."

"I will escort you," Philip said automatically.

"No," the marchioness said sternly. "You have done enough."

With that, she took her daughter by the elbow as Philip helped her to stand. With an arm around the stricken girl's waist, she guided her out of the shop. Lady Anne turned back once to give Philip a heartrending look of appeal, and then she was gone.

Philip frowned toward the doorway.

"What is wrong with her?" he asked in concern. "Is she ill of some wasting disease?"

"You might say so," Lord Revington said. "It appears the girl is deep in love with you, and wasting away because of it."

"What utter rot," Philip said. "There must be some other reason for her decline. A girl like Lady Anne could have any man she desires."

"Obviously not," his father said dryly. "Her parents brought her to Vienna to provide her with a distraction, but it does no good. If you had any pity, you would be . . . kind to her."

"I *will* be kind to her," Philip said. He took a sip of the hot chocolate. "I intend to introduce her to every eligible man of my acquaintance residing in Vienna at present. This is quite delicious."

"Yes," Lord Revington said as he sipped his own chocolate. "You will ask her to dance at the ball tonight, will you not?"

Philip gave a sigh and bit into a pastry.

"Of course I will," he said. "I have no intention of cutting the poor girl merely because she has had the execrable taste to convince herself that she is in love with me."

CHAPTER 26

The marquess summoned Philip to his lavish apartment in the Minoritzplatz the very next day. The elder statesman did not keep him waiting, but ushered him at once into his study, closed the door, and began pacing before his fireplace.

Philip was not invited to be seated. This was not a good sign.

"You are wondering," the marquess remarked, "why I have asked you to come here."

"I suspect you wish to discuss your daughter, and the silly rumor that she is wearing the willow for me."

"It is not a silly rumor," the marquess said. "Her mother and I have been at wit's end. We have promised her Paris. We have promised her a new carriage. We have promised her horses. Jewels. A prince of the blood from among Europe's most prominent royal families, and I promise you I am rich enough to purchase one or two. To no avail. She wants you. And we are afraid she will die if she does not get you."

Philip sat down rather abruptly, even though he had not been invited to do so. The marquess sat down across from him at the desk and poured them both a generous measure of liquor from a cut glass decanter on the desk.

"Lady Anne does me too much honor. I am not so great a prize," Philip said glumly.

"But *she* is," the marquess said. "My daughter will bring to her husband my wealth upon my death and all the preferment it is in my power to bestow during my life."

Philip choked on his first sip of the fiery liquor.

"My lord," he sputtered. "Are you proposing to me on behalf of your daughter?"

"You do rather like the branch with no bark on it, do you not, young Lyonbridge?" the marquess said sardonically. "Excellent. So do I."

"You were at my father's house. You heard the announcement of my betrothal to Miss Grimsby."

"But you are in Vienna without her."

"I am here as a member of Lord Castlereagh's staff. I regret the separation from Miss Grimsby, but I am about to become a married man and I have my future to consider."

The marquess gave him a thin smile. His round, pale blue eyes were as cold and hard as pebbles.

"Yes. Let us talk of your future," the marquess suggested. "Castlereagh speaks well of your abilities. Moreover, your father is not without influence, and if you continue in the way you have begun, you can look forward to a decent government post and a respectable career with the diplomatic service. You have your war record to draw upon, your talent for foreign languages, the attractiveness of your address and of your person to recommend you for such a position."

Philip gave a wary nod of acknowledgment.

"It is true that I wish to pursue such a career," he said guardedly.

The marquess steepled his hands before him on the desk.

"Miss Grimsby's father is a very good sort of man. Excellent war record with many years of service to his credit. A quite respectable fortune, and the girl is an only child, so she can expect to inherit it all. There can be no objection to the girl herself. Good looks. Good lineage. On the whole, a good choice for a young man of ambition. But only a fool would choose her over my daughter Anne."

Philip started to get up from his chair, and the marquess reached out a hand to clutch his arm.

"I will bid you good day, my lord," Philip said grimly as he freed himself. "It is plain we have nothing more to discuss."

To Philip's consternation, the old man's face crumpled and he gave a sob of despair. A tear rolled down his cheek.

"My lord! See here," Philip said as he rushed to circle the desk and put a hand on the man's shoulder. "Are you unwell?"

"I have made a botch of it, have I not?" the old man said with a sniff as he took out his handkerchief and blew his nose. "I am wealthy enough to buy half the world, yet I must stand by and watch my only child wither away to nothing." The marquess clutched Philip's sleeve. "She is pining away for love of you. Do you not understand? I am afraid my Anne is going to die, and there is nothing I can do about it."

"Well, good God, man. Have you not taken her to a doctor? There must be something else wrong with her," Philip said with some asperity. "A healthy young woman does not die for love."

"Of course we have taken her to see a doctor. A score of them," he said. "But she wants you. Only you."

"Well, as much as I like and admire your daughter, my lord, she cannot have me," Philip said. "My heart and my name are promised to another."

Good Gad. He was beginning to sound like an actor in a bad play.

"I am only asking that you be kind to her until she recovers from this infatuation for you."

"Have you been talking to my father?" Philip asked suspiciously.

"Yes."

"You have talked terms for the marriage settlements as well, no doubt."

The marquess gave a negligent wave of his arm.

"Only in the most preliminary and general terms, I assure you," he said. "Naturally you will have the final say in the matter."

"You relieve my mind," Philip said dryly.

At that moment, Lady Anne herself burst into the room. She was wearing an elegant green dressing gown done up with tiny bows on the bodice and at the edge of her sleeves. Her eyes were bright and feverish, and her auburn hair was wild about her face. Her cheekbones stood out in sharp relief. She held one hand to her heaving bosom.

"Anne!" the marquess said. "This is most unseemly."

"I knew you were here," she said to Philip as she ran forward and clutched his hand. Her fingers were as thin and sharp as the claws of a small bird. "I felt it. Here," she added as she put her free hand over her heart.

Philip directed a helpless look at the marquess. The older man merely gave him a look of great sadness. He had been dismayed by Lady Anne's altered appearance at the coffeehouse, but this excessive behavior shocked him to the core. Whatever had happened to the vibrant young woman he remembered? How *could* this change have been wrought for unrequited love of him?

Still, it was plain the girl was suffering.

"It is a great pleasure to see you, Lady Anne," he said.

The girl's maid hovered in the doorway, uncertain of her welcome.

"My dear, go with your maid now," the marquess said gently as he put his hand on his daughter's shoulder. "Captain Lyonbridge and I will take tea with you in the parlor before he leaves."

"Oh, but—" she objected.

"I will not leave the house without seeing you. I promise," Philip said as he encircled her small, cold hands with his.

"Very well, then," she said as she allowed her maid to shepherd her to the doorway. She looked back and gave him a wistful smile. "You will not be long, will you?"

Philip forced himself to smile, when he would rather have wept at this sad deterioration.

"Of course not," he said.

"She has forgotten all about you, your Miss Grimsby," Lady Anne said as she moved closer to Philip on the gold brocade sofa in the sitting room of her parents' apartment in the Minoritzenplatz. It was the night of the Metternichs' Peace Ball and she was wearing a white gown sewn all over with crystal beads.

Lady Anne's physical condition was much improved in the weeks since Philip had arrived in Vienna and, coerced by her father and his, began dancing attendance upon her. Her auburn hair reflected the light of the chandelier and Philip thought, dispassionately, that her ethereal loveliness should have every man in Vienna panting at her feet.

Unfortunately, *he* was the one she wanted.

"Possibly," he said as he gently removed her gloved hand from his arm. "But *I* have not forgotten *her.*"

"You are cruel," she said with a pretty pout, but no tears. He considered this progress of a sort.

"I am honest," he said. "Really, Lady Anne. I am not so remarkable a fellow."

"I know it," she admitted angrily. "But my heart is so stubborn."

"Then we are at an impasse, my lady, for mine is, too."

"You love her," she said wryly. She leaned forward again and slowly drew her finger down the side of his face. "Is there nothing I can do to change your mind?"

"Nothing," he said. "And if my affections were so easily swayed, they would not be worth having."

"True," she said with a sigh. "It is good of you to escort me to the ball."

"It is my very great pleasure."

"You do it for the preferment my father can give you, no doubt," she said.

"I do it because I enjoy your company and you, for some obscure reason, seem to prefer mine."

"There has been gossip in the newspapers about us."

"I know. But I have written Isabella and told her the truth of the matter."

Lady Anne smiled at him as if he were the most callow of youths.

"And she believes that there is nothing between us," she said almost pityingly.

"Isabella is very sensible."

"No woman is that sensible," Lady Anne said with a smug, superior smile. "If I read such things in the newspapers about my fiancé and another woman, I would scratch her eyes out. Oh, why could you not love me instead?"

"Because I love her. I will always love her. Come, Lady Anne," he said as he stood and held out a hand to assist her to her feet. "All of Vienna awaits a glimpse of you in that dress. You will dazzle everyone at the ball."

"You will spend the whole time introducing me to other men and persuading me to dance with them, when I want only to be with you," she said with a pout. But when she looked up at him, it was not devotion he saw in her eyes but obsession. He was a pretty toy beyond the reach of a spoiled child who would not rest until she possessed it—and would carelessly discard it an hour later when she grew bored with it.

"So I will," he said, smiling. "And they will be much obliged to me."

"See here?" Lady Grimsby said as she proffered the newspaper before Isabella's nose. They were now established in their London house. "The man was not out of your sight for a month before he was making up to that Lady Anne. If *this* wedding does not proceed as planned, I shall have to change my name and move to . . . India or China."

"Lady Anne is very ill," Isabella said. "He is only being kind to her."

"Kind! The newspapers are saying they will marry before the Congress is over."

"Everyone knows the newspapers are full of lies and exaggerations," Isabella said with a creditable show of indifference. "He will be back in plenty of time for the wedding."

"You are too trusting," Lady Grimsby said. "All men are beasts!"

"Mother, that is not true. Naturally Philip is exerting himself to be pleasing to everyone while he is in Vienna. If he had wanted to marry Lady Anne instead of me, he had the perfect opportunity to offer for her in Derbyshire at the house party last year."

"Perhaps he has changed his mind."

"He has not, Mother," Isabella said defiantly. "I will not hear a word against him."

"Your father has gone to the war office again. As soon as his back is healed, he is off to his old pursuits," Lady Grimsby said bitterly.

"He is a general. When he is summoned to the war office, he must go." She put a glass of milk in front of Jamie. "Here, darling. Drink it all. It will make you strong."

"If he were a good father to you, he would go to Vienna and drag your faithless fiancé home at once."

"He would do no such thing," Isabella said. "Philip has given me no reason to doubt his intentions toward me, and I trust him completely. Besides, you and Father are the ones who insisted that Philip go to Vienna in the first place." She could not stop some of her resentment from coloring her tone. "*You* were the ones who feared the consequences if we lived in one another's pocket until the wedding."

"We did not know that Lady Anne would be there, making sheep's eyes at him."

"And why not?" Isabella asked. "Everyone else seems to be there."

"Everyone but us," Lady Grimsby said bitterly. "All of the world is in Vienna, and here I am in England, planning yet another wedding for you."

Isabella smiled at Lady Grimsby and patted her on the shoulder.

"This is the last wedding you will have to plan, Mother. I promise you. Come, Jamie. It is time for your walk."

Lady Grimsby frowned at Isabella as she picked up Jamie and started to leave the room.

"Wear a hat if you are going out in the sun," she called after Isabella. "Just because everyone who matters is going to Vienna does not mean you can afford to let yourself freckle."

"Yes, Mother."

"And put that great child *down*," Lady Grimsby snapped. "He is ruining the line of your gown."

"Yes, Mother," Isabella said again as she put Jamie down and took his hand instead.

Once outside, Isabella put a hand to her temple and closed her eyes.

"Aunt Isabella?" Jamie asked. "Does your head hurt?"

She smiled him.

"Just a little, sweetheart."

While Jamie ran in exuberant circles around her, Isabella took one of Philip's much read letters from her pocket and smoothed it out.

Vienna continues to be dreadfully dull without you and Jamie, despite the fact that I cannot leave the hotel without encountering one royal or another. My father is in excellent spirits, however. He appears to think that there is some sort of diplomatic post in my future if I ingratiate myself with the right persons. How should you like to be a diplomatic wife stationed in Russia or Paris, my dear? Until I am re-

*leased from exile, I remain your loving and obedient
servant . . .*

Not a word about all the balls at which the newspapers
accounts placed him with Lady Anne.

Not a word about the extravagant medieval tournament to
which he escorted her or the exclusive dinner parties he and
his father attended with her and her parents at Lord Castlereagh's lavish apartment.

Not a word about being presented with Lady Anne to the
Tsar of Russia and his sister, the Duchess of Oldenburg, who
complimented them on the pretty picture they made, he with
his hair as dark as a raven's wing and she as fair as an English
rose.

Of course, she reminded herself firmly, everyone knew
the newspapers printed nothing but lies and exaggerations!

The fact remained, however, that Philip had not returned
in a month or two as he had originally promised. His work
on Castlereagh's staff had been exemplary, and he had been
asked to stay on. According to the newspapers, he had celebrated the Christmas season in Vienna at a succession of
house parties given by influential English nobles, including
the marquess, Lady Anne's father.

He had sent thoughtfully chosen gifts and affectionate
letters to England for both Isabella and Jamie throughout his
absence, but still he stayed in Vienna.

"Why are you so sad, Aunt Isabella?" Jamie asked. "Do
you miss Uncle Philip?"

"Yes," she said as she picked Jamie up to balance him on
one hip. Everyone said he was too heavy for her to carry
around as if he were an infant, but she did not care. She
needed the assurance of his arms around her neck at that
moment. She smiled and kissed him on the nose, and he
laughed.

"Now," said a familiar voice. "There is a sight that makes
all the discomfort of a crossing in bad weather disappear."

Isabella gasped and spun around quickly. Then she blinked her eyes, for she could not believe them.

Philip stood there with his greatcoat slung over one arm. His hair was windblown and his uniform badly needed pressing, but his dark blue eyes were alight with affection.

"Philip!" she cried, and ran into his arms.

"Here, love," he said. "Give him to me. Jamie is too big for you to carry like that."

"I am not!" Jamie protested, even though he went willingly enough into Philip's arms. "Will you send for your horse now?"

"Yes, lad," Philip said as he put his other arm around Isabella and gave her shoulders an affectionate squeeze. He looked down into her eyes. "I am home for good now."

"But you were to stay until the Congress was over," she said.

"I found I could not stay away from you for another moment," he said. He gave her a wry smile. "Lord Castlereagh received my resignation with good grace, but my father is seriously displeased with me."

"I wonder that you could tear yourself away from Lady Anne's charms," she said archly. Blast! She had not meant to say that!

"I was afraid that business would come to your ears," he said with a sigh. "It is a lowering reflection that she recovered from her infatuation with me soon enough when I introduced her to Barnaby Hughes, and so I was quick to leave Vienna before she could grow bored with him. He is a major in my regiment, and the best horseman in England. It was love at first sight."

"I always thought she had more hair than wit," Isabella said, laughing aloud.

"And so she waved farewell to me quite happily when I took my leave of her. Father is another matter. He accompanied me to England, but I do not believe he will soon forgive me for depriving him of the satisfaction of parading his heir, the war hero, before the crowned heads of Europe to the bitter end of the Congress. Were the gossip columns that mentioned Lady Anne and me so very lurid?"

"Very," she said. "Mother was certain that I was about to be jilted."

"But you were not a bit jealous."

"Never," she said. At his skeptical look she threw her hands up. "All right. I *was* jealous. Dreadfully. But I would not give Mother and Father the satisfaction of admitting it. Will you be staying at your father's town house until the wedding?"

"Yes," Philip said, "and how I am to keep my hands off you until then, I do not know." The look on his face made her blush. "I am only flesh and blood, after all."

Isabella took Jamie from Philip's arms and set him on the path.

"Jamie, love. Go inside to the kitchen and tell cook I said she was to give you a biscuit. I will be in directly. You are not to leave the kitchen, mind."

"Yes, Aunt Isabella," Jamie said as he scampered into the house.

When he was out of sight, Isabella turned back to Philip and smiled at him.

"I have a better idea," she said. "We can marry immediately, and then we will not have to be apart."

He kissed her hands.

"My darling! I could not permit you to sacrifice your May wedding at St. Paul's," he said. "It has always been your dream."

"I was a child, an idiot. I did not know what I wanted then." She looked him straight in the eye. "I do now. If you procure a special license at once, we can be married next week."

"Are you sure?" he asked, but a big smile was spreading over his face. She nodded, and he squeezed her hands.

"Let us tell our parents at once," she said.

She would have led him into the house, but he pulled her back into his arms.

"Not quite yet," he said as he kissed her.

* * *

The general lowered his bushy eyebrows and reminded Philip of nothing so much as a bull about to charge some hapless victim.

Philip straightened and faced him, ready to take him head on.

"Is she increasing?" the general demanded baldly. He turned to his daughter. "*One* child born on the wrong side of the blanket did not teach you not to—"

"That will do," Philip snapped. He stepped protectively before Isabella. "Your father and I had best conclude this business in private, my dear." He squared his shoulders and matched the general sneer for sneer. "Your daughter has been nothing but virtuous—"

"Virtuous! By God, that's rich—"

"If you dare cast aspersions on—"

"What will you do? Call me out? She is *my* daughter and—"

"Stop it," Isabella said as she pushed Philip aside to confront her father herself. "Philip has been in Vienna all this time. How could I be with child by him?"

"That makes no difference. Everyone will *believe* you are pregnant, which is just as bad."

"We are getting married by special license next week, and that is the end of the discussion on the matter. I am *not* with child, and gossips may believe me or not, as they choose. But *if* they retain the wit to count to nine, my innocence will be proven to them soon enough."

"Then why this unseemly haste?" the general asked.

Isabella turned her beautiful dark eyes on Philip and he felt his insides melt.

"Because I find I want to be Philip's wife—at once— more than I want to be married at St. Paul's during the Season."

Philip kissed her hands, which would have to content him as a demonstration of his ardor until they somehow managed to rid themselves of the general's presence.

He would have gone mad if he had been forced to wait for her until May.

"Phaugh!" the general said in disgust. "You will get over *that* soon enough, I wager."

"Try to be happy for me, Papa," Isabella said as she kissed his cheek.

His expression softened, but he must have moved wrong because he gave a sharp cry and held his hand to his back.

Isabella rushed forward at once to steady him as Philip caught his arm from the other side.

"Poor Papa," Isabella crooned. "And you had been so much better of late.

The general pushed them both away.

"There will be talk," he said glumly.

"There is always talk," Isabella said. "But people will find other matters to amuse them soon enough."

The general's shoulders slumped.

"A wedding next week. I shudder to think what your mother will say."

"It will be all right, Papa," Isabella said soothingly, although she and Philip exchanged a rueful look.

Lady Grimsby threw up her hands in dismay.

"I shall have to leave the country. I will never be able to hold my head up in public after this."

The general had offered to break the news of their daughter's rapidly approaching wedding to his wife, and Philip, who freely admitted that a full regiment of charging French hussars did not have the power to intimidate him as much as one sour look from Lady Grimsby, gratefully accepted.

"Well, if she is not with child, I do *not* understand why they must rush into marriage like this," she said.

"They are in *love,*" the general said, rolling his eyes.

"That is all very well," Lady Grimsby said primly, "but I do not see what that has to do with the matter."

"Well, we did not do such a good job of waiting when we were young, did we, Phoebe?" the general said.

His wife's face went crimson.

"You *dare* throw that in my face?"

"Throw it in your face?" He took her in his arms. "It is one of my most cherished memories."

"It ended badly," she said softly, but she laid her head on his shoulder.

"Our son died," he said, "but I did not regret marrying you."

"Until later," she said.

"Not even then," he said as he kissed her temple.

She gave a snort of skepticism, but she did not detach herself from his embrace.

"Silly man. You should know better than to try to bamboozle me with your pretty lies."

"That is all in the past," he murmured. "Let us think of the future."

"The future," she said with a sigh. "A wedding to plan for next week. Or they will elope and cause even more gossip. And so ends my sad career in planning weddings for that ungrateful girl."

The general kissed her, and she gave a reluctant laugh.

"You old satyr! You are only trying to distract me from my grievance," she said as he took her hand and led her to the bed. She could have extricated herself with little effort—he was still not completely steady on his feet, although he rarely needed his cane now—but she chose to pretend otherwise.

"Not at all," he said as he gave her a playful leer and skillfully began undoing the hooks on the back of her gown. "I am distracting myself. And quite effectively, too. After all, we will have many years together now that neither Isabella nor the army require our services."

Lady Grimsby gasped and regarded him with wide eyes.

"Does this mean you are retiring from the army after all these years?"

He grimaced.

"I am healing well enough, but it is time for this old war horse to be put out to pasture. The war is over. My work is done." He grinned. "Do you think you can endure the hardship of having me underfoot for the rest of our lives?"

She took the lapels of this coat and pulled him down to give him a smacking kiss on the lips.

"At the moment," she said coyly as she pushed the coat off his shoulders, "I find the prospect not unpleasant."

CHAPTER 27

Flowers and gifts had been arriving all afternoon, for Philip and Isabella's wedding was to be in three days. It was to be a simple wedding in the chapel of a nearby church, and the number of guests would be fewer than fifty. Since most of the world was still in Vienna for the Congress, the guest list was hardly exclusive, nor were the arrangements nearly impressive enough to please Lady Grimsby. It was the best she could do on such short notice, however.

The elaborate bridal gown that had been ordered for the now canceled May wedding at St. Paul's would not be ready in time, and so Isabella would wear a new white evening gown trimmed in silver and crystal beads by the bride herself and her maid, for Isabella refused to marry Philip in any of the splendid gowns that had been created for her aborted weddings to his brother, and Lady Grimsby quite agreed. To do so would be to invite bad luck.

The house was filled with the scents of baking, for the cook was already preparing food for the wedding breakfast.

"It will be so . . . Spartan," Lady Grimsby said dejectedly to Isabella. "I wanted so much more for you. I tried to give you *everything*."

Isabella smiled at Philip, who was playing with Jamie and

the new rocking horse he had purchased for the child at one side of the parlor.

"And I shall have it," Isabella said as she gave her mother a squeeze on the shoulder.

Lady Grimsby shook her head in disbelief.

"I gave birth to you. I reared you. But I will never understand you."

"But you have done your best," Isabella said. "And for that, I thank you."

Lady Grimsby's mouth opened and closed in sheer astonishment, and Isabella laughed out loud.

"I am a mother myself now, and so find myself in more sympathy with you than ever before," she said. "My son is a sweet-natured creature, and I still find myself at wit's end. I can imagine how it must have been for you, for I was a stubborn child."

"You still are," Lady Grimsby said wryly. "This paltry, hole-and-corner wedding is the most exasperating thing you have inflicted upon me yet."

"I know, Mother," Isabella said, patting her hand. "Try to be happy for me." She caught Philip looking thoughtfully at her and smiled. He smiled back and patted Jamie's head.

They looked up when the butler entered the room. Isabella blinked, for he looked flustered. Lady Grimsby's butler *never* looked flustered.

"My lady," the butler said. "There is a gentleman from the war office to see his lordship—"

"Out of the way, my good man," the gentleman in question said as he rather abruptly pushed the butler aside. Lady Grimsby visibly stiffened at the incivility. "My errand is too urgent to wait upon the niceties."

"General Cathcart," Lady Grimsby said, surprised. "Whatever is the matter?"

"Lady Grimsby," he said. "I must speak with the general at once."

"Of course," she said. "Inform my lord that General Cathcart is here to see him on a matter of some urgency," she said to the butler.

"*Great* urgency," the general added. "Tell him that."

At that, Philip stood and came to Isabella's side. He put his hand on her arm in reassurance.

"What is it?" he asked.

"Ah, Captain Lyonbridge," the general said with a smile that did not meet his worried eyes. "I had read in the newspapers that you are betrothed to Miss Grimsby. My felicitations."

"Thank you, sir," Philip said impatiently. "Has something happened?"

The general hesitated, and then gave a long sigh.

"You will know soon enough. Napoleon Bonaparte has escaped from Elba and returned to France, where he has raised an army to march on Paris. We are mobilizing the troops. We need General Grimsby to report to Whitehall immediately."

"What do you mean?" Lady Grimsby demanded. "My husband has been injured, and he is far from being fully recovered."

"He will have to do. We need his head, my lady," the general said. "Not his back."

"You are sending him to war. Again," she said flatly.

"Yes, Lady Grimsby. At once." He turned to Philip. "Your regiment is being mobilized as well. The messenger probably went to your father's house to inform you that your leave has been canceled, and you are to prepare to sail tomorrow."

"Philip!" cried Isabella. Her fiancé took her hands and murmured soothing words to her, but she turned away.

"Captain Lyonbridge and my daughter are to be married in three days," Lady Grimsby said.

General Cathcart looked uncomfortable, but his expression turned to one of heartfelt relief when Lord Grimsby came into the room. His stride was not brisk, to be sure, but it was steady, and made without the aid of a cane.

"Cathcart," Lord Grimsby said genially as he shook hands

with his visitor. "This is an unexpected pleasure. What brings you here?"

"The war," he said. "I have been sent to fetch you along to Whitehall. Napoleon has escaped and is marching on Paris. We leave at once."

"No!" cried Lady Grimsby. She grabbed the lapels of her husband's coat and glared into his eyes. "You have given enough. They will *not* take you this time. You are not well."

Gently, he removed her clutching fingers and held her hands. "I am well enough, my dear. I must go. It is my duty."

"What about your duty to your daughter, and to me?"

"I must go," he said again. He caressed her cheek. "Coming, Lyonbridge?"

"Philip," Isabella said.

"I will come to you later," Philip said as he took Isabella's shoulders.

General Cathcart gave a short cough. "Yes. Quite," he said as he took Lord Grimsby's arm and ushered him toward the door.

Lady Grimsby's eyes were furious.

"Men," she said in loathing.

"You are not going," Isabella said in disbelief to Philip. When he did not answer, she burst into tears and Jamie came running to put his arms around her legs. She picked him up and wiped her nose with the back of her hand.

"Aunt Isabella," Jamie said. "Do not cry." She buried her face in his soft hair and cried all the louder.

"Isabella, my love," Philip said, but she could see the answer in his beautiful, sad eyes.

With an effort she pulled herself together and even managed to give Jamie a weak smile of reassurance.

"It is all right, sweetheart," she said to the child, who had already started to puddle up in sympathy.

"We must talk," Philip said to Isabella. He glanced over his shoulder at Lady Grimsby, who was still staring in fulminating silence at the door through which her husband had disappeared. "Alone."

"If you are going, there is nothing left to say," she said.

With that, she gathered Jamie to her breast and started to leave the room, only to collide with Lord Revington, who was almost breathless from exertion.

"Philip, we must leave at once and secure your resignation," he cried. "Adam's regiment is already returning from Scotland. I will not risk you. Not again."

"Papa!" cried Jamie happily as Isabella tried to shush him. She handed him off to her maid, who had come to the door, wide-eyed with horror. Apparently the news that Bonaparte was free had already made the rounds of the servants. "But I want to see Papa when he comes home!" Jamie cried mournfully as he was borne away. As the maid passed him, Philip placed a fleeting caress on the top of Jamie's head, but the child thrust out his bottom lip and turned away from him.

"Make haste," Lord Revington said as he took Philip's arm and forcibly pulled him toward the door.

"Father, I cannot resign," Philip said as he dug in his heels and removed his father's hand from his sleeve. "Not now. I should be branded a coward."

He turned to face Isabella.

"I am sorry, my dear," he said.

"If you walk out that door," she said, "do not bother to come back."

He bowed his head. Then he turned to his father.

"Please excuse me, Father," he said. "I must report to my commanding officer at once."

"Then I will go with you," Lord Revington said purposefully. "I am not giving up my heir without a fight."

Lady Grimsby and Isabella were left facing one another.

"Now you see," Lady Grimsby said, "what I have lived with all these years. They go off to war. We sit and wait." She put her arm around Isabella's trembling shoulders. "Come, my love. We will have cook make us a cup of tea and wait for news."

CHAPTER 28

It was late, and Isabella sat alone in the darkened room fragrant with the scent of hothouse roses. She would permit the butler to light only one candle, for she had wept so long that the light hurt her eyes.

There were no more tears.

There were no more words.

Philip was lost to her. Again. She had driven him from her side, and there was nothing she could do to bring him back.

"Captain Lyonbridge to see you, miss," the butler intoned as he appeared in the doorway with a candle lifted in his hand.

She stood up and watched as Philip approached her. The flickering light of the butler's candle turned his scarlet uniform to living fire. He had not resigned his commission, then. If he had, he would be wearing civilian clothes.

"Light some of these candles, if you please," Philip said with a wave of his arm toward the butler. The butler complied. "What are you doing here, sitting in the dark?"

"Thinking that I would never see you again. I told you not to come."

"You did not mean it," he said as those wicked dimples she loved danced in his cheek. He pulled her to him and kissed her. She tried to protest, but she was soon kissing him back with all the pent-up fury in her heart.

"You cannot go off to your war and expect me to be waiting here for you when you get back," she said breathlessly when they had to break off the kiss or turn blue. "Another canceled wedding. Mother is beside herself with vexation."

"I know. I have no right to expect you to wait for me, but I hope you will with all my heart. I love you, Isabella."

"How can you say so when you are leaving me?"

"It is because I love you that I am leaving. I do this to defend you, our son, and our country. Do you not know what will happen to everyone and everything we care about if Bonaparte wins? Have you ever seen what happens to a country he has conquered? To the women? To the children? I have, and I will *die* before I will risk having anything like that happen to you or to Jamie."

He frowned and held her shoulders out at arms' length. "Is this—are you wearing—"

"My wedding dress," Isabella said with a wry smile, "such as it is. The others were much more elaborate. This is the fourth. I thought I may as well wear one of them, even if it would come to nothing."

"You have been sitting here in this dark room wearing your wedding dress?"

"I did not expect you to come," she said as she averted her eyes from him in her embarrassment. "I did not expect you to know—"

"You are beautiful. So beautiful," he said as he kissed her again. "When I return, I want you to wear this dress for me." He gave her that wicked smile again. "I may return to you, may I not?"

"You know you may, you *dreadful* man!" she said as she cuffed him on the shoulder. "You *would* come here and catch me sitting in the dark and mooning for you like some lovesick ninny in a Minerva Press novel."

"Would you have thrown yourself from the battlements?" he asked with one arched brow.

"Hardly," she scoffed.

"That's my Isabella," he said fondly.

He turned toward the door at the sound of knocking from the street. Soon the butler ushered in a pair of dusty travelers.

"Adam!" Philip cried, laughing. "And Marian." He stepped forward to kiss Marian on the cheek and buffet his brother on the shoulder.

"We have just arrived from Scotland," Adam said. "You will forgive us for coming in all our dirt, I hope. Philip, Father is furious with you for not selling out, but I wanted to tell you at once how proud I am of you."

"It is merely my duty," Philip said with a self-deprecating shrug. "How did you know where to find me?"

Adam looked soulfully into his wife's eyes.

"I know where *I* would have been my last night in England." He smiled at Isabella. "All dressed up for the occasion, I see."

She gave him a wry grimace.

"Yes, Adam. It is my wedding dress. One of my *four* wedding dresses, that is."

"It is very beautiful," Marian said as she threw her arms around Isabella. "Darling, I know it is late, but may we see Jamie?"

Isabella bit her lip. She knew very well why Marian and Adam had rushed here straight off the road from Scotland. Jamie might not be their son by blood, but that did not change their love for him.

"Of course, Marian," Isabella said as she forced a smile to her lips. "He would never forgive me if I did not wake him. I will fetch him." She looked up at Philip. "Will you come with me?"

"Certainly," he said as he picked up one of the lighted candlesticks and followed her.

They held hands as they made their way to the nursery.

"It is hard to pretend you are not his father, is it not?" she said as they climbed the stairs to the nursery apartment.

"Yes," he admitted with a start. "How did you know . . . but of course. How stupid of me."

"It does not get easier," she said. "But one becomes accustomed. We cannot tell him yet. To tell him the truth now would only confuse him. It will be hard enough for him to know they must leave him again."

"I understand. It is what we agreed upon, after all," he said.

They reached the child's chamber to find him awake. He went easily into Isabella's arms and curled there like a small, sleepy animal.

"Come, love," Isabella said as she forced cheer into her voice. "Mama and Papa have come to see you." When Jamie let out a hurrah, she added, "Be quiet, sweetheart. The whole household is asleep except for us. We do not want to wake Lady Grimsby."

"Papa?" the boy said as he peered into Philip's shadowed face.

"No, Jamie," he said. "It is Uncle Philip. Papa and Mama are in the parlor, waiting for you." He put his hand on Jamie's back. "May I carry him?" he asked Isabella.

"Of course," she said, but her voice broke on the words. She took the candle as Philip took Jamie.

"Are you crying, Aunt Isabella?" Jamie asked.

"No, darling," she said, forcing a smile.

"Papa! Mama!" Jamie cried as they reached the parlor. His little arms and legs were moving so fast in an attempt to escape that Philip had no choice but to put him down so he could run to his brother and his wife. Adam picked him up with a glad cry and Marian kissed him soundly on both cheeks and took him from Adam's arms.

"Did you bring your horse?" Jamie asked.

"Yes, Jamie," Adam said fondly as he ruffled Jamie's hair. He put his hands on the boy's shoulders so he could look straight into his eyes. "Jamie, Mama and I must leave again tomorrow. You will see us off at our ship, will you not?"

"When will you come home?"

"As soon as we may," Marian said as she hugged the child tightly. She closed her eyes as if to savor the feel and little-boy smell of him.

"We must beat Napoleon Bonaparte again, lad," Adam said, and Isabella marveled at how easily he put the matter in words a child could understand.

"Because you are a hero," Jamie said with shining eyes.

"Well, um, yes," Adam said. He looked at his brother. "And Uncle Philip is going, too."

Jamie cocked his head and looked at Philip, considering.

"Are you taking your horse this time?"

"A cavalry officer needs his horse when he goes to battle," Philip said, smiling. "Otherwise, he could not be a cavalry officer."

"Then you are a hero, too," Jamie said. "Almost as good as Papa."

"Almost," Philip said ruefully.

"Uncle Philip is every bit as good as Papa," Isabella protested indignantly.

"Hush, love," Philip whispered as he put an arm around her, but he looked pleased, just the same. He kissed her temple. "I hope you are going to come to the ship tomorrow and give me a great, noisy, maudlin send-off. I rather missed out on that the first time I went to war."

"I shall wear black," Isabella said tartly. "With a veil. And afterward I shall throw myself from the battlements."

"What is a battlement?" Jamie asked, bright-eyed. "May I do it, too?"

"Aunt Isabella is being silly," Marian said in a tone of reproof. "Now you must go back to bed like a good boy. You must rise very early in the morning if you do not want to miss the chance to see us off."

"I will be awake," Jamie said.

"Come, love," Isabella said as she reached for Jamie. "Back to bed with you."

"Please, Isabella," Marian said. "Let us take him."

Isabella bowed her head and stepped back.

"Of course," she said.

Philip put his hand on her shoulder as Marian and Adam took Jamie away; his cheerful questions and their calm replies receded.

"They need time alone with him," Philip said. He turned her to face him and took her into his arms. "And I need time alone with you."

CHAPTER 29

Lord Revington was puffing with exertion by the time he reached the quay.

"I thought you were not coming," Philip said in surprise. "You said if I left now—"

"I have your discharge papers signed by Lord—"

"What have you *done,* Father?" Philip said as he snatched the papers from his father's hands. "You went behind my back to have me discharged?"

"Is it true?" asked Isabella, who had been standing next to Philip with Jamie in her arms. The hope in her eyes made Philip's heart hurt, for he could not give in to it. "If you have been discharged, then you need not—"

"It is for your own good," Lord Revington said stubbornly. "I do not expect you to thank me for it."

"And I do not, sir," Philip said as he grasped the sheaf of papers and tore it in two pieces.

Isabella gave a strangled gasp.

"Philip! How *could* you?" she cried.

"I am sorry, my love," he said.

She turned her back on him.

Lord Revington put both hands on his stomach, as if he felt a sharp pain there.

"Go, then," he snarled. "I wash my hands of you."

"If only that were true," Philip snarled back.

"And what of me, Philip?" Isabella demanded. "What of my son?"

"Do you have a son, Aunt Isabella? May I play with him?" Jamie asked brightly.

Isabella bit her lip.

"We will talk about it later, love," she said.

"Isabella," Philip said as he held out his arms. She turned her face away from him. "You knew I would go."

"Papa! Mama!" cried Jamie excitedly as Adam and Marian came striding toward them. Marian held her arms out and Jamie leaped from Isabella's arms into hers. Adam patted Jamie on the head and kissed his cheek. Then he turned to his father and held out his hand. Lord Revington took it and his jaws worked, but no sound came out. Instead he threw his arms around Adam and just held on as Adam patted his back.

"What is this, sir?" Adam said in a rallying tone. "Will you miss my ugly face, after all?"

"Can you doubt it?" he said. "Can *either* of you doubt it?"

"Never," said Philip grudgingly as he shook his father's hand.

"Father!" called Isabella as she spotted Lord Grimsby walking slowly but without his cane, and his batman directing the footmen carrying the general's trunks.

Isabella rushed to him and put her arms around his waist. He patted her on the back.

"What is this, my girl?" he asked. "Tears for your old father?"

"Tears for everyone," she said. "End this tiresome war once and for all, will you not, Papa? As a favor to me?"

He grinned at her.

"I will do my best," he said as he moved on to shake hands solemnly with Adam and Philip. "God willing, we will meet again, gentlemen." He looked around him. "Your mother did not come with you, did she, Isabella?" He looked disappointed.

Isabella shook her head.

"Her maid said she was not to be disturbed," she said. "I am sorry, Papa."

"She was angry last night. She said she would not stand on the quay waving her handkerchief as I sailed away again. But, still, she had said so before, and I hoped—"

"There she is," Adam said suddenly. He gave a great laugh. "Oh, General mine. I think you will fight your greatest battle before you take to the ship."

The general turned to see Lady Grimsby, dressed for traveling and bearing down purposefully upon them. Her maid and three footmen loaded with trunks followed her brisk strides.

"What is this, Phoebe?" the general asked with a frown. "Are you going on a journey as well?"

"I am going with *you,* you silly old goat!" she said.

"But . . . you cannot. There have been no provisions made for your passage, and you do not understand the conditions—"

"I understand the conditions perfectly well," she said. "Our daughter is grown and she has proved herself able to care for herself and that child without my help. I am free at last to have an adventure, and I choose to have it with you. Have you any further objections?"

"No," the general said almost meekly.

Lady Grimsby gave a smile that made her look twenty years younger. She hugged Isabella.

"Good-bye, my dear. Take good care of yourself. If this cursed war goes on too long, you may close down the London house and take the boy to the country, if you would be more comfortable there, although why people will persist upon regarding the country as comfortable, I will never understand."

"Mama," Isabella said in utter shock. "You cannot mean to go on campaign with my father."

Lady Grimsby looked her husband right in the eye.

"It is what I should have done twenty years ago," she said. "Now, stop dawdling, my lord. Let us get aboard ship."

"But no passage has been booked for you," he said.

"Well, book it at once," she said impatiently. She gave him a sly smile. "It is not as if we will require an additional stateroom." She took his arm and hurried him away as the footmen with the trunks scurried in their wake.

"A stateroom," Adam repeated. "She expects to occupy a stateroom on a military transport."

Philip gave a low whistle of appreciation.

"And one will be found for her, I have no doubt," he said with a roll of his eyes. He kissed Isabella, then Jamie, then, after a short hesitation, his father.

"Take care, sir," he said to the older gentleman.

"Captain Lyonbridge!" shouted man from his regiment. "We are boarding!"

"I must go," Philip said. He gave Isabella a quick kiss on the lips. "Be well," he whispered.

Then he was gone.

Isabella's vision blurred in a confusion of red from the soldiers' uniforms and the blue of the sky. She had thought she had no tears left, but she was mistaken. She dimly heard Lord Revington give a sort of groan, and turned just in time to see him crumple to the ground.

"Aunt Isabella, what is wrong with Uncle Philip's papa?" Jamie asked as Isabella quickly set him on the ground.

"Do not move from this place," she said sternly to Jamie as she bent over Lord Revington. "My lord, what is the matter?" she asked the white-lipped, fallen gentleman, but he could only stare at her with glassy eyes. The left side of his face began to twitch. She stood up and looked about her.

"Help! Help!" she cried. Men rushed forward and bore the fallen man up. "My carriage is over here," she said as she directed them forward. She gave one wistful look toward the ship. She had come to wave her handkerchief sentimentally at her departing hero, but there was work to be done.

"Carefully," she added as she picked up Jamie and herded the men and the groaning Lord Revington toward the carriage.

* * *

"Where am I?" Lord Revington said. His words were slurred, even to his own ears, and he felt like the very devil. But when he tried to move, he found that one each of his legs and arms would not obey his brain.

"Your lordship! You are awake!" his valet cried joyfully from beside him.

Lord Revington frowned at him.

"Good God, man! You look terrible. When was the last time you shaved?"

"Your pardon, my lord," he said, grinning. "I will call Miss Grimsby."

"Miss Grimsby? What the deuce is *she* doing here?" he said, but the valet was already out the door.

A moment later, she was framed in the doorway with that boy in her arms. She was wearing a white gown and her hair was plainly dressed. She brought the fragrance of roses to his bedside. Aware of his unkempt appearance, Lord Revington tried to move to a more seemly position, but he found he could not.

"I cannot move my leg," he said in astonishment.

"It was your heart," she said wryly. "It seems you have one, after all."

His eyes narrowed as he gazed at her.

"*You* have been taking care of me?"

"Your valet has done most of the actual work. And your housekeeper," Isabella said. "But I have been watching over you in a manner of speaking, yes. Kiss your grandfather, Jamie."

"I am not his grandfather," the old man said.

Jamie kissed Lord Revington's cheek. The child's lips were soft and warm against his unshaven face. The boy put his hand on his other cheek, but Lord Revington could feel no sensation from it at all. Isabella's eyes dared Lord Revington to object, but he did not. He had not the strength.

"Jamie, run along to the kitchen," Isabella said. "Alphonse will give you one of those little cakes you like and a glass of milk."

Lord Revington half raised himself in sheer alarm. All he needed was for the temperamental artist who ruled his kitchen with an iron hand to resign because of the importunities of small boys begging for treats in the middle of the day, but he fell back, exhausted from the effort, and the child scampered away.

"This changes nothing," he said to Isabella. "I do not intend to acknowledge him. You win no advantage for him with this mawkish display of counterfeit affection."

"The advantage is for *you*," Isabella said. "He is a sweet child willing to accept you as his grandfather. He neither knows nor cares about your wealth or your power. He would love you, if you give him half a chance."

"I do not need his love."

"What if you lose both of them? Jamie is all you will have left."

Lord Revington's grizzled jaw hardened.

"I will *not* lose both of them," he said. "I will not lose *either* of them."

"I hope you are right. But until the day they return to us, Jamie and I stay here with you."

"Why? Why are you doing this?"

"Because, like it or not, we are family. We are linked by blood by your son and mine. My parents and my sister have gone to war. Your sons have gone to war. The three of us have no one left except one another."

"I do not need your pity," he said with a grunt of discomfort even as he heard the slur in his words.

"Nor do you have it," she said, standing up. "I have sent orders to the kitchen that we dine at six o'clock. Unfashionably early, I know, but Jamie must go to bed at eight."

"Alphonse will resign for certain," Lord Revington said glumly.

"He will not. He has said it is a pleasure to cook for a young man with a healthy appetite again," she said smugly.

Lord Revington fell back at that.

"I am no longer master in my house," he said.

"At last you understand," she said. She poured a glass of water for him from a pitcher and held his head as he drank it. The scent of roses surrounded him. "I will call your valet now," she said as he finished drinking. She left the room and the valet came in at once.

"My lord?" he asked. He looked anxious.

"Shave me," Lord Revington said with a sigh of resignation. "It appears I am to dine with a lady tonight."

CHAPTER 30

"A soldier!" cried Jamie in delight when Lord Revington handed him the well-worn toy. "Thank you, Grandfather!"

"Here is a horse to go with him," Lord Revington said as he handed the boy the wooden horse. "And I am not your grandfather, you know."

"I know," Jamie said, nodding. "Not my *real* grandfather. Mama told me."

Lord Revington's eyes narrowed.

"She did, did she?"

"Yes. She said that my real father died in the war. Then Mama married Major Lyonbridge. I had no papa and he had no little boy. So he said I could call him Papa to take the place of the papa who died."

He was quoting Marian and not Isabella, Lord Revington realized.

"Watch my soldier take a fence!" Jamie said as he bounced the toy soldier and horse over an imaginary obstacle.

"Careful there, boy! That soldier is very old."

"Like you, Grandfather?"

"Not quite so old as that," Lord Revington said wryly. Oh, why bother to correct the stubborn child? Besides, the title of grandfather sounded unexpectedly sweet to his ear. "But my sons played with it when they were small, and you would not want to break it."

Jamie regarded the toy with real reverence.

"My papa played with this when he was a little boy," Jamie said. He regarded Lord Revington through wide, solemn blue eyes, and at that moment he looked so much like Philip that Lord Revington could feel himself melt inside. Being an invalid, he told himself in some disgust, had made him maudlin. "I will be very, very careful with it."

"I know you will," Lord Revington said softly.

Jamie's lower lip puckered.

"What is the matter?" Lord Revington asked in alarm. "I thought the toy would please you."

"I miss my mama and my papa."

"I miss your papa, too," Lord Revington said softly. He looked up in some annoyance to find that managing female, Isabella Grimsby, watching him from the doorway with a look of satisfaction on her catlike little face. Thanks to her, this small boy had somehow wormed his way into his affections, just as she predicted he would.

"It is hard to wait for the men one loves to come home, is it not?" she said. "I know now why my mother was so angry with Father much of the time."

"They say one becomes accustomed to it, but I never did," Lord Revington said. "It was difficult enough when it was just Adam, but now—" He bit his lower lip hard.

"Surely there must be some news from the war office. If you went to Whitehall in person, they would have to tell *you* something. I know very well that you have access to information that is not in the newspapers."

"I will not have them see me like this," he said. He was much improved, but he still had some paralysis of his facial muscles, and his walk was still halting at best. It was a wonder the boy was not frightened by the sight of him.

"We have been in this house for weeks, going nowhere and receiving no one," Isabella said. "It is not good for any of us."

"*I* did not ask you to come," he said. "You sneaked inside while I was in a weakened state and unable to prevent you."

His words were meant to chasten her, but she merely grinned.

"How could I leave my future father-in-law lying in the dirt of the quay?" she asked. "My father is gone to war, and you are all I have left, heaven help us both. I have made arrangements for us to remove to Derbyshire tomorrow."

"I beg your pardon," Lord Revington said, jaw set and ready for a fight. "*You* have made arrangements for us to remove to *my* house? Without my permission? Who do you think you are, to be giving orders to *my* staff?"

Jamie's eyes widened and he scooted back from the place where he had been playing at Lord Revington's feet, because he had used his "voice of thunder," as his sons had called it when they were small. It always brooked instant obedience from everyone. Until now.

Isabella merely raised one brow.

"I am soon to be the wife of your heir," she said. "Like it or not—and I honestly do not care which it may be—it is my home, too, for the present. Your housekeeper accepts my orders without question, as does the rest of the staff. With some relief, I might add. It is time they had a mistress."

"Opening the country manor is not something that can be done at a moment's notice," he said. "I have had all the furniture put in Holland covers and put the remaining servants at half wages. It would take time to assemble adequate staff."

"True. That is why we are not going to your country house. We are going to Adam's, which is already in a state of readiness because I wrote to Adam's housekeeper as soon as you were stricken ill. You are now well able to travel, and we may as well do so if you will not exert your influence to get news of the war."

Lord Revington opened and closed his mouth.

Outmaneuvered by a mere stubborn chit of a girl.

Adam's house was a poky little place that he did not think

adequate to serve as a hunting box. He would be deucedly uncomfortable there.

And worse, not a single servant would pay a bit of attention to anything he said, because the only permanent staff consisted of an elderly, live-in couple entirely loyal to Isabella, who had been the household's virtual mistress for two years. Several times a week, the place was invaded by a succession of giggling village girls who did the heavy cleaning. And there would be young Jamie's nurse and nursemaids. And Isabella's personal maid and his valet, all crowded together.

It would be absolutely insufferable to him, and Miss Isabella Grimsby bloody well knew it.

He began to think the more stubborn of his sons richly deserved her, by Jove.

"We will stay in London," he said. When she looked a question, he added sourly, "and have my valet lay out my town clothes. I will go to Whitehall this afternoon."

"Excellent," Isabella said, pleased that she had won. "We will take Jamie for a stroll in the park while we are out. He has hardly been outside for weeks. It will do him some good to get some pink in his cheeks, will it not, my precious?"

"A stroll in the park!" Lord Revington huffed. "You go too far, missy."

"It will do *you* good to get some pink in your cheeks, too," she said.

"Aunt Isabella will push you in the chair if you are too tired, Grandfather," Jamie suggested helpfully. "I will carry your cane for you."

Lord Revington stared goggle-eyed at the boy and took a deep breath for control.

"I will *never* be that tired," he choked out. He glared at Isabella. "Well, do not stand there grinning at me, girl. Summon my valet."

"Certainly, my lord," she said demurely.

* * *

Isabella stood when Lord Revington stepped out from the office at Whitehall. Naturally females and young children were not admitted to the inner sanctum, and Isabella had encountered many disapproving stares as she sat waiting on a bench, which she returned with head held high.

Her betrothed husband was risking his life to give these petty bureaucrats a country to rule. Her father was a general. And her son held both their bloodlines in his small, restless body. She had as much right to be there as any man in the kingdom.

Lord Revington's face was pale, which she at first attributed to fatigue. Then she saw that his lips were trembling. Quickly, she grasped his arm and helped him to sit on the bench.

"What is it?" she asked.

Which one of them is it?

"Philip. There has been no news of him since a severe cannonading several weeks ago. Correspondence may have been lost, but this is not good news."

"He could not be dead," she declared, a bit too loudly. She glanced at Jamie, who was mercifully quiet for once. She picked Jamie up and took her father-in-law's arm.

"The stubborn fool *would* tear his discharge papers in two," Lord Revington said glumly.

"Stop it!" she cried. "Philip *will* return. I refuse to believe otherwise. Come. We will go home."

"Aunt Isabella," Jamie said plaintively. "We were to go for a walk in the park."

"I am sorry, my dear," she said. "We must go home so your grandfather can write to everyone of influence he knows." She glared at her future father-in-law. "He is *not* dead, I tell you. I will not let you rest until you locate him."

Major Adam Lyonbridge paused in the process of giving one of his enlisted men a severe dressing-down when he spotted a familiar figure being escorted into the camp.

He rubbed his eyes. It *could not* be his fastidious brother. This man was covered with the dirt of travel, and as he grew closer, Adam could see that his hair was sticking out in tufts— not from carelessness but from having been shaved in spots and bandaged. His eyebrows were missing.

Adam had never seen so beautiful a sight.

The startled enlisted man found himself clasped in Adam's embrace and whirled into a wild dance, then pushed out of his superior officer's way to fall on his behind as Adam set off at a run.

"Philip!" Adam cried as he clasped his brother in his arms. "Lord, where have you been?"

"Wandering about with the rest of my surviving men, trying to keep out of Boney's way, of course," he said. "Then out of the fog comes a whole troop of soldiers who apparently had been looking for us. At Father's orders, of course."

"The privilege of being the heir," Adam said as he thumped Philip on the back. He put an arm around his brother and led him to General Grimsby's tent.

"Captain Lyonbridge?" Lord Grimsby said, standing. "Is that you?"

"Reporting for duty, my lord," Philip said formally. "Apparently my father somehow managed to have me transferred to your command so that my younger brother could keep my precious person safe for the duration of the war."

"The devil you say!" Lord Grimsby exclaimed.

"There were not many of us left, so all of us were absorbed into other regiments, those who were not sent home because of the severity of their injuries. I was one of the fortunate ones in that regard."

"Yes, very handsome," Adam said as he ruffled the tufts of his brother's hair and received a good-natured shove for his pains. "It should impress the ladies."

Philip produced the pertinent papers and handed them with some ceremony to the general.

"Have you received news of Isabella? I have not received

any letters from home in months. I wrote to her both at your house in London and Adam's house in Derbyshire. Not one letter from her in all this time, although that is probably because I have been on the move almost constantly."

Adam's face broke into a grin.

"You did not know? Your delicate bride has been living in London with Father and cracking the whip over him in the process. She has taken over his household, bullied him into a successful convalescence after he suffered a stroke, and managed to insinuate Jamie into his will for an independence when he dies."

"What?" Philip said as his jaw dropped.

"I have cause to give thanks for my escape. Father is firmly under the cat's paw. As will you be, my brother."

Philip got a silly grin on his face.

"Is she not splendid?" he said. With that, he straightened his shoulders and smiled at the general. "Come, gentlemen. Let us get on with this war so I may go home and marry the woman of my dreams."

At that, Lady Grimsby bustled into the room with Marian close on her heels. They had both been at the hospital and wore white smocks over their gowns as they dispensed tea and comfort to the men housed there. Marian had at first resented Lady Grimsby's insinuation into the nursing operations at the hospital but gradually, though grudgingly, came to appreciate her organizational skills. Her powers of intimidation were so strong that a wounded recruit did not *dare* die on Lady Grimsby's watch.

"Philip!" Lady Grimsby cried. "I am delighted to see you in one piece. Perhaps now Isabella will stop badgering her father to drop whatever petty responsibilities he has to his own men and send searching parties out to the front looking for you."

"She has written to you? About me?" he asked, pleased.

Lord Grimsby gave him a look of utter disgust.

"She writes of nothing else," he said. "She is a single-minded chit, and the very image of her mother." He grinned at his wife. "You are a lucky man, Lyonbridge. Take care you do right by her."

"I will. I promise you I will," he vowed. "May I see these letters?"

With a snort of impatience, Lady Grimsby took him by the arm and ushered him out of the tent.

"In good time, young man," she said. "First you must have a good, thorough wash before you set foot in *my* quarters."

CHAPTER 31

Derbyshire, July, 1815

"Uncle Philip is here!" Jamie cried as he went clattering out the door of the house and straight into Captain Lyonbridge's arms.

Philip gave a laugh as he hefted the child up so he could sit on his shoulder. He had appropriated his father's traveling coach as soon as his ship landed in England, for he would not wait a moment longer than necessary to see the woman he loved and this precious boy.

"You did not bring your horse," Jamie said, frowning.

"No, lad. But I brought you a French sword captured in battle," Philip said. "I left it at my father's house in London. For when you are older."

"Did Grandfather come with you?" Jamie asked eagerly.

"In a moment, Jamie," Philip said absently. His eyes were on the doorway.

The door opened, then, and Isabella stepped out, looking like the embodiment of every dream that had given him courage while he was at war.

She was wearing a pretty yellow gown, and her dark hair was done up in a classic chignon.

She looked so beautiful. So perfect.

He could not wait to disarrange her.

Isabella gave a glad cry and came pelting into his arms, nearly unseating Jamie, who gave a squeak of alarm and held onto both of them. Philip lowered the child to the ground, but managed to retain a firm hold on his beloved.

"I thought you would never come home," Isabella said tearfully as she kissed him. He tasted the salt of her tears on his lips. "Can we be married immediately? At the village church?"

"What about St. Paul's?"

"That would take too long," she said, hanging onto him possessively. "I am never going to let you out of my sight again."

"Your mother will be disappointed then, for she has set the wedding for next week. I have come to fetch the two of you to London."

"Next week?" she cried.

"She has directed the whole by letter." He reached into his pocket. "And I have the special license."

"Then we could be married today," she said.

"If I marry you today," he said between frantic kisses, "your father will come after me with a broadsword. And *my* father will be right behind him. I am to do all honor to my bride." He gave Jamie an affectionate squeeze. "And his grandson. Or else."

"Will there be cake?" Jamie asked. It was the thing he remembered best from Marian and Adam's wedding.

"An *enormous* cake," Philip assured him as he led them both to the coach. "The largest cake in London, or Lady Grimsby will start the war all over again. Face it, love. Your mother is *determined* to marry you off in style at last, and *I* would not want to be the one to oppose her."

"But wait," cried Isabella as she dug in her heels and tried to hold him back. She gave a glance at the house. "I cannot go to London *now*. I have nothing packed. And the cook has already started to prepare dinner—"

At that moment, the door to the coach opened and her mother came down the steps, followed by her husband, whose elbow she held possessively as he rather gingerly alighted from the coach, then Marian and Adam, who helped Lord Revington, who was quite remarkably recovered from his stroke, but whose limbs were still not quite as obedient as they once had been.

"Mama! Papa!" shrieked Jamie as he ran straight into Marian's arms and almost knocked her over. After Marian had kissed him soundly, Adam picked the boy up around the middle and swung him about in an arc that caused him to erupt into giggles.

"Take care, boy," Lord Revington snapped. "That is my grandson you have there, and if I find a mark on him from your rough handling, there shall be the devil to pay!"

"Yes, sir," Adam said, laughing, as he put Jamie on the ground so the boy could give Lord Revington a noisy kiss on the cheek.

"In with you, now," Lady Grimsby said to her astonished daughter as she took her elbow and bundled her into the coach when Isabella would have kissed her. "There is time for all that in London."

"I cannot go *now*, Mother. I have no clothes packed," Isabella protested, but she was laughing.

Lady Grimsby wrinkled her nose.

"Whatever you brought into the country will not do, I am quite certain," she said. "I ordered your trousseau by letter before we boarded ship for London, and you must have at least one fitting before the wedding."

"Perhaps I would have liked to choose my own bride clothes," Isabella objected.

"We have been through this process often enough that I think I know your tastes by now," Lady Grimsby said wryly. "You *do* want to marry this man, do you not?"

"Oh, yes!" Isabella said with a glowing look at Philip.

"Then get into the coach, girl!" Lady Grimsby frowned at all the others, who were watching the farcical little drama with grins on their faces. "What are you waiting for?" she demanded with her hands on her hips. "Into the coach, all of you!"

"Will there be enough room?" Isabella asked doubtfully.

"There will be," Lady Grimsby said. She put a hand on Jamie's head. "The boy will have to sit on someone's lap." She smiled down at the lad. "Anyone's but mine."

Philip exchanged a look of commiseration with his future father-in-law.

"We had better do as she says," Lord Grimsby said, beaming with pride. "Being with the army only made her more bossy. It is quite wonderful how she abuses us all, no matter that we number a captain, a major, a general, and a member of the House of Lords among us. " He placed a kiss on his wife's cheek, and her lips twitched at the corners as she batted him away and herded them all into the coach.

The newspapers were to say later that the marriage of Miss Isabella Grimsby, daughter of General Lord Grimsby and Lady Grimsby, to the dashing Captain Philip Lyonbridge, son of the powerful and influential Lord Revington, had been the most stunning and opulent event of the year.

The bride's gown, an exquisite creation of white and silver adorned with countless crystal beads, brought so much custom to Miss Lacey of Conduit Street that the enterprising modiste was compelled to expand her shop and hire more seamstresses to keep up with the demand for her wares.

Lord Revington's Alphonse outdid himself in producing a wedding breakfast that appreciative guests declared cast the Prince Regent's most extravagant state dinners into the shade, praise which that temperamental artiste considered his due.

But all this celebrity was in the future as Philip waited at the church for the bride to arrive. He could not help glancing nervously at his watch.

"She is late," Adam, his best man—and Philip was beginning to consider him an ill-chosen one—said cheerfully. "Do not get your hopes up, lad. She has been this close to being wed before and it came to nothing."

"She will be here," Philip said through gritted teeth.

"Stop teasing him," Lord Revington said sternly to his second son. "Every lady likes to make an entrance. Besides," he added as he touched the top of Jamie's head, "we have the boy as hostage. She will not leave *him* at the altar."

"He's as pale as milk," Adam observed of his brother, unabashed. "I'll wager you twenty guineas that he falls down in a swoon before the vows are spoken."

Philip gave him a clout on the shoulder that caused Adam to give a surprised bleat of pain.

"Stop it, the both of you," Marian scolded. "You are worse than children." She kissed Jamie on the top of his head. "You are being so *good,* darling," she told the boy. "I am so proud of you." She glared at the Lyonbridge brothers. "I wish *somebody* here would follow your example."

"The bride and her parents have arrived," Lord Revington's valet announced.

"Come, my sons," Lord Revington said. "The performance is about to begin."

Isabella left the coach on a cloud of French perfume as her mother fussily settled the veil of imported lace made by Belgian nuns around her shoulders. The sky had never been so perfect a blue. The clouds had never been so fluffy or so white. The morning sun warmed her face and shoulders as she returned absent answers to her bridesmaids' chattering. The diamond necklace that had been Philip's gift was a pleasant weight against her collarbones.

She wanted to remember everything about this day.

Her father escorted her to the vestibule as her mother went on ahead to arrange the bridesmaids in a phalanx before the doorway. Lady Grimsby frowned.

"Where is that girl?" she asked with a huff of impatience. "She was to meet us here."

"There," Isabella said as she saw Marian walk quickly down the side aisle with Jamie to put him in the first pew with

Lord Revington. He looked so adorable in his new suit! She gave a coy little waggle of her fingers at him when he immediately turned in the pew to look at the back of the church. He grinned and waved back enthusiastically.

"It is about time," Lady Grimsby said huffily as she placed Marian into the formation of bridesmaids. There were twelve of them. Twelve! She glanced approvingly at Marian's hands, which were much smoother than they had been when they had worked together at the regimental hospital. "I see you took my advice."

"Yes, thank you. The Holland lotion worked wonders. It was very kind."

"Well, I could not have you snagging the fabric of one of Miss Lacey's most outrageously expensive gowns with your rough hands, could I?" Lady Grimsby said as she made a minute adjustment to the drape of Isabella's veil. "You look lovely, darling," she said mistily. She hugged her daughter quickly and accepted the arm of the groomsman for her walk down the aisle that would signal the beginning of the ceremony. Her husband clasped her free hand for a moment and gave her a smile. Then he offered his arm to his daughter.

"Nervous, my dear?" he asked.

"No. Not at all," Isabella said as she looked down the long aisle and saw her future husband waiting for her. He gave her a brilliant smile.

"Good," the general said, "because *I* am."

Isabella gave him a mischievous grin as the bridesmaids filed up the aisle and toward the altar.

Then she gave a gasp of surprise and pleasure.

"Is that the Prince Regent?" she whispered in disbelief. "And Lord Wellington?"

"Your mother has outdone herself," Lord Grimsby said proudly as the last bridesmaid began her stately walk up the aisle. He caught his daughter's elbow, and she realized that she had begun to set a pace that was less than decorous. "Slowly, my dear. Your mother will have my head on a platter if I permit you to race up the aisle like a hoyden."

She tugged on her father's arm.

"I am afraid you will just have to endure it, Father," she said serenely. "Philip and I have waited long enough for this moment."

BOOK YOUR PLACE ON OUR WEBSITE AND MAKE THE READING CONNECTION!

We've created a customized website just for our very special readers, where you can get the inside scoop on everything that's going on with Zebra, Pinnacle and Kensington books.

When you come online, you'll have the exciting opportunity to:

- View covers of upcoming books
- Read sample chapters
- Learn about our future publishing schedule (listed by publication month *and author*)
- Find out when your favorite authors will be visiting a city near you
- Search for and order backlist books from our online catalog
- Check out author bios and background information
- Send e-mail to your favorite authors
- Meet the Kensington staff online
- Join us in weekly chats with authors, readers and other guests
- Get writing guidelines
- AND MUCH MORE!

**Visit our website at
http://www.kensingtonbooks.com**

More Regency Romance
From Zebra

Embrace the Romance of
Shannon Drake

Discover the Romances of

Hannah Howell